OUR BROKEN
FAIRY TALE

BY CALVIN WADE

Foreword

I remember an old joke that used to be told by comedians in Liverpool, it went something like this :-

An old lady is on her deathbed in hospital with her husband by her side. She has been almost motionless for some time then begins to stir and with much effort, sits up in her bed.

"What's the matter, Hilda?" her anxious husband asks.

"Arthur, when I die, will you marry Ena at number 58?"

"Why, love?"

"Because I hate her!"

A lot of men I know and I would include myself in this, do not have a fear of what their wives will do after their death, if they are outlived by their spouse, but a lot of women I know do fear what their husbands will do. This fear formed the foundations for this book.

I started writing 'Our Broken Fairy Tale' prior to the outbreak of Covid-19. The first draft of the initial third was written whilst on holiday in Majorca in October 2019, so I have subsequently tried to blend the pandemic into the storyline. As the book was finished during lockdown, I have created a 'near future' world where people, on the whole, can interact and socialise without too many restrictions placed upon them. I appreciate that in reality this is unrealistic but this is fiction and I wanted to give the characters some freedom.

With regards to mixing fact and fiction, there are a few things to clear up (you may have to come back to this section after you've read the book)! Back in 2018, Janice Alty, the landlady of 'The Derby Arms', a pub in Aughton, the village where I grew up, ran a Charity Auction and one of the auctioned items was to have a character in my next book named after them. The winner, David Moorcroft, asked if the character could be named after his son, Dominic. I have never met the real

Dominic Moorcroft so any resemblance to him is purely co-incidental. When I communicated via email with Dominic, he could have asked for a bit of input into the character that bears his name but chose not to which I really appreciate. He is older than the character and may have liked a more dynamic, super hero type namesake but at least the fictional Dominic is one of life's good guys. This book release is around two years after David won the Charity Auction so I appreciate Dominic and David's patience.

With regards to the setting, I have lived in Chorley for eighteen years and this is the second time I have used Chorley as the setting in five fictional books (for the record, two have been set primarily in Ormskirk and one primarily in Rochdale – I will move some characters out of the North West of England eventually). The village names, Euxton and Buckshaw Village are real as are the bars and restaurants named. 'Lost' is a bar my eldest son occasionally goes to and is apparently the best place for young people in their late teens and early twenties to frequent in Chorley but the 'Lost' in the book has a fictional layout and fictional staff as I have never been there. 'The Ale Station' is a bit different. I have been in there and asked permission from the landlord, Mick Barker, to namedrop him in the book, which he was fine with. I know Mick pretty well as his son and daughter played junior cricket with my two sons for a number of years at Chorley Cricket Club, so it amused me to give him a little cameo.

As for the main characters, friends and family often assume that certain characters resemble people we know but I have never based a fictional character on anyone I know. I may borrow a phrase, a conversation or a characteristic from real life or real people from time to time and try to embellish it, but 99.9% of every character is just randomly made up.

Music wise, I always like to furnish my books with music I love. I do think it adds to the storyline if you listen to the music referenced but that's your choice. In the same way 'The Slow Show' and Ludovico Einaudi had a huge influence on my last book, 'Living On A Rainbow', Lana Del Rey, in particular, had a huge influence on this one.

Finally, sorry it's been over three years between the last book and this one. It isn't always easy to write when a million other things are happening in your life but a massive thanks to my loved ones for giving me the space to do so, especially Alison, my wife, who has to put up with the light in the bedroom being on late into the night or me wandering off in the early hours of the morning when I get an idea I want to put down on paper. I still hand write the books in the first draft, putting Chapters on to the Laptop as I go along and then subsequent drafts are amended on the computer.

I know I will never be gifted enough to write a classic but hopefully you'll still think I can write a good, character led story. I'll try not to leave it as long next time!

Calvin.

3rd June 2020.

PART ONE

CHAPTER ONE

JAY – January 2020

We were sat on the settee in the lounge when Hunter came in. It was a winter's evening. I can't remember what we were watching perhaps it was the first season of 'Dead To Me' which we did watch that winter. Amy was stretched out across the sofa, legs over my thighs, with a glass of red wine in her hand when, as was so often the case back then, our television programme was interrupted. I pressed pause on the control to hear Hunter's announcement.

"Where's Wuhan?" Hunter asked, "Is it in China?"

"I've no idea," I replied honestly, "why?"

"There's a load of stuff on social media about there being a virus breaking out there which has no cure."

"I wouldn't panic just yet," Amy said reassuringly.

We were used to Hunter barging in with stories he had picked up from the internet. They were often about killer diseases that were going to threaten the human race. It tended to be killer diseases or conspiracy theories. He was insistent no man had ever stepped foot on the moon. It was hard teaching him not to believe everything he read on the internet. Amy and I were the other extreme. We were cynical about everything we read on the internet unless it had a very reliable source.

"I've got a bad feeling about this one," Hunter said.

"Hunter, you have a bad feeling about everything! Now can you shut up and let us watch our programme please," I requested.

"I'm telling you, this one's going to be bad," Hunter stated as he departed back up stairs.

"Jeez, what a panic merchant," I said with a smile as I pressed play on the remote.

CHAPTER TWO

<u>**Twenty One Months Later**</u>

<u>**JAY – September 2021**</u>

I had been desperate for Sunday to last forever. I suppose most office workers feel this way most of the time. With the exception of a few short weeks after the latest Coronavirus lockdown when the novelty of going back to the office was actually appreciated by most, not many people would choose to go to work. I was not one of the fortunate group that were allowed to rejoice in the post-lockdown high this time around though. When everyone else was returning to work, I was still on compassionate leave. My time had now come to return which was why I feared that particular Monday morning more than any other in my forty years of existence. I had been off work for three months but so much had happened in that time that it felt more like half a century. I certainly felt fifty years older than I had ninety days before. Up until then, Coronavirus had just been a major inconvenience, an item on the news and a worrying statistic.

It wasn't as though anyone at work would be giving me a hard time, quite the opposite in fact. I knew the women in the office would be fussing around me like I was Hugh Hefner in the Playboy mansion. The men would tone down the banter they used to enjoy ribbing me with and even Martin, my boss, who had been known to smash Laptops with one swift swish of his squash racket would be adopting diplomacy that Mo Mowlam would have been proud of. Mo Mowlam, another wonderful woman taken from this earth far too soon.

Despite me hoping it never would, Monday morning arrived. I headed down to Buckshaw Parkway train station, with trepidation, whilst Hunter was still sleeping. I had ironed his uniform as best as I could, just before heading to bed, leaving it on the bannister. A note about what time to expect me home, along with his dinner money, was left on the sideboard in the kitchen. With good reason, things had been strained between us recently. For the first post-Amy week we had united in self-pity, but like any fifteen year old, empathy wasn't his greatest strength so when I needed to return to some sort of reality, he had resisted joining in. Hunter had not appreciated my insistence that he return to school as at that stage he felt that he would be happier remaining in his bedroom forever. I totally understood but I had to mask my sympathy. We needed to soldier on whilst our hearts still bled.

I surveyed my surroundings nervously that Monday morning. There was something about Buckshaw Parkway train station that took my mind back to a backpacking trip around the world that Amy and I had been on when we were in our early twenties. It just seemed to belong more in Singapore than on the outskirts of a market town in central Lancashire. It looked fresh and spotlessly clean. It didn't have warnings about enormous fines for selling imported chewing gum or feeding pigeons though, which helped bring me back to my modern day reality, along with the rather apt blanket of grey cloud. Chorley had begun to look considerably darker over the last three months. I felt a sense of belonging in that dismal weather. The Walker Brothers had got it spot on.

Buckshaw Parkway had only existed for a few years, the village it was set in, not much longer. Developers had acquired the land between Chorley and Leyland that had previously been home to the Royal Ordnance Factory. An area that had been occupied by bunkers and rabbits for fifty years now had a Tesco, an Aldi, four thousand people and a Kentucky Fried Chicken. I reflected on how deliriously happy I had been when we had moved into our new build home there, ten years earlier. I had, for the most part, managed to maintain that state of delirium until I had awoken one morning to discover that I had been unknowingly transported to a darker, more miserable world.

I was about to head into Manchester on the 7.30a.m train. I hadn't renewed my monthly pass, due to circumstance, so knew I had to arrive at the station before seven twenty. Despite there being a massive car park beside the station, Buckshaw's residents had grown averse to walking even the shortest of distances, so an early arrival was a necessity. Joanne, the ticket seller, did not assist the stragglers, as she could always be relied upon to engage customers in inane chatter so there was often a queue that stretched out the glass doors, particularly in these new dark days when people queued a distance apart.

Having struggled to sleep, I was there by quarter past. Ticket purchased, I had sat in the waiting room for a few minutes, awkwardly avoiding conversation with half familiar faces before heading outside to wait for the train. Social distancing had encouraged a lack of social interaction which I felt suited me down to the ground. There were thirty or forty of us scattered along the platform. Some with masks over their mouths, most not, I stood, eyes right, awaiting the train from Preston but I knew, like everyone else knew, that there was no need for speed once its double doors slid open, as at this stage of the journey there would be seats aplenty. The acquisition of a vacant seat only became a competitive sport on arrival in Chorley, by the time the train arrived in Bolton, it became an Olympic event. I had always had a chivalrous nature and had previously always been prepared to forgo my seat, I was going to be sat at a desk all day after all, but this unselfishness had won me no friends and fate had seemingly not taken my good deeds into consideration, so as I stood on the platform I debated whether altruism should be sentenced to death along with my sense of happiness and my wife. I reached a compromise in the debate within my head. I would now only vacate my seat for any elderly or pregnant commuters. This was not perhaps as altruistic as it may initially sound. There were very few elderly people or pregnant ladies who were prepared to travel by train these days.

From a distance I could see the train approaching the station. Unlike the station, the train didn't take me back to a Singaporean setting but drew my mind back instead to childhood days of 'Frankie Says' t-shirts and a war of words between Thatcher and Scargill, as like me it was a tired looking fortysomething. When Hunter was at pre-school age, he used to love the Thomas The Tank Engine books and I remember telling him stories of sparkling new trains and untidy looking old ones. This was one of the latter. Once it arrived, I boarded the back carriage of my fellow weary traveller, taking an aisle seat and leaving the window seat spare. No-one would ask for that seat unless there was absolutely no other option.

As we pulled away slowly from the station, leaving a breathless and exasperated businessman behind to curse his misfortune, I lost myself in my thoughts. I was thinking about a Saturday night out four months earlier. We had been to a black tie event at Southport Floral Hall. Amy had looked fantastic. She was tall, toned and elegant. Those from work that had not met her before joked about me 'punching at my actual weight'. Amy was 38, but looked so good on it, that there had been times recently that young shop assistants, leaning on the side of caution, had asked her for ID. Sometimes when I was with her, I would offer up my ID too and would be given a look of dismissive scorn, on each occasion, by the previously pleasant shop assistants. Amy looked like she had been at the crossroads with Robert Johnson and sold her soul to the devil for the secret of eternal youth whilst the devil was tuning Johnson's guitar. I, on the other hand, looked like I had lived every day of my adult life with chocolate, cigarettes and alcohol as my constant companions. I owned a paunch that pressed so tightly on my shirt and trousers that I had long since dispensed with the use of belts. My waistline measurement and age were neighbourhood numbers and my BMI was only just down the road too. Amy was different. She was a Gym bunny. The Gym would draw her in with its magnetic charms, every day, either before work or after or sometimes both. She did weights that made her toned rather than muscly and she did spinning classes and pilates and fucking yoga. It was starting to piss me off how much time Amy had devoted to keeping healthy. Perhaps if she had stuffed her face full of custard doughnuts she would have lasted longer.

"Excuse me, is anyone sitting there?"

I was brought out of my daydream by a softly spoken, female voice. Some young girl was standing over me pointing towards the empty seat by the window. At the time, I didn't look long enough to ascertain whether she was fourteen or twenty one, I just knew she was young. She had long, brown hair enlivened by flecks of blonde. I remember noticing that straight away as it was in contrast to my hair having been dulled by its greyness. She was the type only certain young men would find attractive. She was pretty but not at all sexy. I probably didn't come to that conclusion on that first train journey. It was most probably concluded on a subsequent trip. I think all I concluded at that initial meeting was that she had blonde bits in her brown hair and was softly spoken. I may also have realised she was relatively small. Not small enough for a part in the Wizard of Oz but a long way short of a catwalk career.

"No."

"Would you mind moving in?"

"No, of course not."

I moved along. She sat down next to me. She adjusted those little things you put in your ears, pressed a few buttons on her mobile phone and then escaped into her own little world of music until we reached Bolton. That was 'Day One'. I probably realised she was a regular back carriage traveller a week or two later. For several more weeks, we never spoke again. By the time we did speak, I had created an imaginary life for her. That softly spoken girl was christened Chloe. She was eighteen and had a boyfriend called Ben who played rugby union at University. He captained the side too. Chloe would visit him at weekends. She would head up there on a Friday evening or, if it had been a busy working week, on a Saturday morning. They had been dating for two years and everyone said they were destined to be together. Ben with his boy band, blond, chiselled good looks and Chloe with her natural, girl next door beauty and her big, brown eyes. She did an administrative role in the Bolton office of Simon James, an entrepreneur who was a friend of her Dad's. This was the identity I gave her, but it turned out that, other than her age, I wasn't even remotely close. Her real name was Alice Moorcroft and she was indeed eighteen years old.

CHAPTER THREE

<u>**ALICE**</u>

Sapiosexual. Mark called me a 'sapiosexual' when we were over at Morrison's on lunch break from College. I had laughed at the time but I had no idea what it meant. I hope my laugh didn't sound as false as it was. I ended up Googling it on the train from Bolton to Chorley and I think I gave out a reasonably loud, genuine snort when I realised what it actually meant. I must learn to control my tendency to snort. It is not, I would imagine, a desirable noise, unless you are a drug dealer and the noise is being made by a desperate client. Anyway, give Mark his due, he probably wasn't far off.

During my transition from girl to woman, I imagined, or in some cases knew, that I was being given various sexual labels. For the majority of people at College I would be labelled a 'lesbian', back in school it would have been 'Bi'. I am pretty sure my mother would label me 'straight' and from my father, my label would almost certainly be 'Virgin'. With regards to the accuracy of the definitions handed out to me, bisexual or pansexual are the most accurate but I must admit I really liked 'sapiosexual' too.

A 'sapiosexual', according to the explanation I found on Google, was somebody who found intelligence to be someone's most sexually attractive feature. I had said to Mark in College that I wasn't that interested whether someone had nice tits or a big dick, they just had to have a fit brain and as a lad with a bit of a brain he had called me a 'sapiosexual'. On the basis of the definition, I was surprised I hadn't heard of it before. Surely most people wanted to be classed as a sapiosexual. Nobody goes out searching for a life partner who is an imbecile. They may end up with one but I would think that would be down to poor judgement rather than desire. When Paddy McGuiness presents 'Take Me Out', no-one ever says,

"Tonight Paddy, I want to be heading off to the Isle of Fernandos with someone so stupid they can't even spell their own name with a crayon."

"No Brighty, You Likey," Paddy would have to say in such a scenario. It would never happen.

Thinking about it, I suppose physical attractiveness is generally put before intellectual capacity but I'm guessing most people rate intelligence as the second most desirable quality in a partner. Maybe they don't. Maybe it's only me that wants an intelligent partner. Perhaps these days as long as a partner has a pert bum and the ability to love your Tik Tok and Instagram posts, that's all that's needed.

I have no idea whatsoever what anyone else craves in a relationship but personally I just want to be with someone who makes me happy. I think they would be incapable of doing that if they weren't intelligent. I would say my quest in life was to get through each day making myself and those around me as happy as possible without it negatively impacting on anyone else. It was a simple quest, in principle, but wasn't proving to be in practice. I think a factor in my struggle to spread happiness at that juncture in my life, was that the negative attitude of a small bunch of people had made me collectively wary of almost everyone. Thankfully, I could be easily swayed back in the right direction.

It was a Friday afternoon when I first recall speaking to him. I'd had another good week at College but was aching from a Friday afternoon football training session on the 'All Weather' so was glad to find a seat on the train. I didn't realise I was sitting next to him as I'd never noticed him before. According to him, he had spotted me much earlier. I was flicking through Instagram or Snapchat after Googling 'sapiosexual' and something made me laugh. I don't recall snorting on the second occasion thankfully. It was probably a photo of one of the lads from College, or a group of them, doing something daft or childish.

"You sound like you're in a good mood today," he said, from a seat facing me, "any plans for the weekend?"

  Looking back now, it was just Jay being friendly, but at the time, I thought it was weird. It put me on high alert. Some random man next to me, who looked older than my forty something parents and about as old as my fifty something stepfather, was trying to strike up a conversation with me. Commuters sometimes did this and it didn't disturb me but I think it was the familiar tone Jay used, like he knew me but I didn't know him. I briefly stared at him to gain some intelligence as to what I was dealing with. He had a suit on but still managed to look scruffy. His beard was multi-coloured, predominantly grey though and it needed trimming or preferably shaving off completely, even Tom Hardy doesn't look hot with an unkempt beard. His navy blue jacket and trousers looked old fashioned and a little discoloured. I immediately decided he was a potential rapist or murderer. I couldn't have been more wrong.

"Not particularly," I said, forcing out something which must have looked like a sarcastic smile, before putting my earphones in, putting Spotify on and ignoring him for the rest of my journey.

CHAPTER FOUR

JAY

My new normality tortured my soul. For seventeen years, I had gone to sleep with Amy beside me, woke up next to her, kissed her goodbye each morning, greeted her fondly of an evening, laughed and cried together, shared interests and weekends, yet now, in a manner I was still struggling to comprehend, she had been taken from my life. No-one understands death. It is beyond human comprehension and although the human species have, for centuries, tried to diminish its impact, by creating religions and spirits that promise an afterlife, for me it just seems final. Amy and I had been by each other's sides, enjoying our lives together and now she had gone. She had not walked through a door into another room, her spirit had not risen up to a heavenly place - she had just gone. The grim reality of my own logic regularly upset me. It seemed incomprehensibly unfair that someone so kind and so well meaning had her existence wiped out, if anyone should have been granted eternal life or at the very least a long one, it was Amy.

Hunter, after a month or so, had adjusted better than me. He would take two steps forward and one step back which was much better than me as I just walked around in confused circles. His school friends had rallied around and, for the most part, he seemed contented. I often heard him laughing, speaking via his X-box to his best friend, Dominic, as they played 'Fortnite' or 'FIFA'. Dominic even started calling around a couple of times each week which hadn't happened whilst Amy was still with us.

My son still appeared to resent me though. For reasons only he could explain, Hunter appeared to blame me for his mother's death. I don't know whether it was because he thought I had brought the virus into the home from my office in Manchester or whether he thought I had reacted too late to get medical help or perhaps it was something else entirely but whatever the reason was, at that time, I felt he hated me. One evening, that assumption was confirmed. I had arrived home from work, went to grab myself a glass of water and every glass in the kitchen had gone. Hunter ignored my puzzled shouts, I presumed because he had a headset on playing X-box, so a lengthy search began, culminating in me finding a mass of broken glass in the recycling bin outside. I went up to Hunter's room to ask why and he had kitchen roll wrapped around a crimson coloured right palm.

"What happened?" I asked, probably in an annoyed rather than a sympathetic or concerned tone.

I sensed I already knew the answer.

"Fuck off, Dad!"

Expletives aimed at me weren't uncommon. Generally they were an attempt to generate a reaction so I responded by ignoring them. I concluded, Poirot style, that the glasses had been smashed in a temporary act of rage against life and the resultant cut from the tidying up process.

"Have you had your tea?"

"No."

"Do you want some?"

"Not if you're making it."

"OK, just let me know if you change your mind."

I turned to walk out of his room and with my back turned he

delivered his judgement.

"This is all your fault," I heard Hunter mutter under his breath.

I genuinely don't think this comment was Hunter goading me, trying one last time to trigger a reaction, I think it was purely an observation he had only intended to share with himself but he had inadvertently spoken out loud.

"How exactly?" I responded, turning back to him.

I felt like jumping on top of his bed, grabbing him and just shaking some sense into him.

"What are you on about?" Hunter asked, trying to convince himself that he hadn't spoken.

"How exactly is this all my fault? I take it you mean Mum dying is all my fault?"

"Well, it is."

"How exactly?" I asked again.

"You should have stayed at home and you should have got help when she started coughing"

I truly wished I had.

"Hunter, I had to go to work until the Government advised people not to."

"It had been all over the news that there was a second wave. You should have had the balls to stand up to your boss and tell him you weren't coming in," he said dismissively.

"Did you stop going to school?"

"I'm just a kid, I have to do what I'm told. I would have stopped going if you and Mum had told me to"

I felt a sudden sense of pain and betrayal that my only son could find a way to blame me for his mother's death.

"We have no idea how Mum contracted it, Hunter. You can't

just pin this one on me, son."

"Well, I am. I wish it was you that had died, not Mum."

"Me too, Hunter. Me too."

The following morning, I was feeling particularly out of sorts. I had had a bad night's sleep, which had now become the norm. I had watched 'The Italian Job' between two and half three but even after that I couldn't settle down well enough to fall asleep for a couple more hours. I just drifted off temporarily a few times before I had to drag myself up and prepare for work. Somewhat in a daze, I followed my daily routine, dragged myself down to Buckshaw Parkway and boarded the train.

Once I found a seat, I set the alarm on my mobile phone in case I fell asleep on the journey. I put my head back and was drifting in and out of consciousness, in my more lucid moments pondering about whether I needed to make an appointment to see my GP. I think I began drifting into a heavier sleep but when the train came to a halt at Chorley, I was awake once more.

I spotted the girl I called Chloe boarding. It was a Tuesday. I had briefly tried to engage her in a pleasant chat the previous Friday, on my way home, and she had been dismissive and somewhat rude. If I had noticed her on the train on Monday, I would have probably just let it pass but I hadn't, it was now Tuesday, I was tired and in an irritable mood. There was an empty seat next to me but I felt she deliberately avoided it and found an empty seat amongst a collection of four empty seats further down the carriage. I stood up and walked over to her. I wasn't intending to sit down, I just wanted to say my piece and go back, but when I looked over my shoulder a lady with a young baby had taken my previous seat and all the surrounding seats had been taken leaving only the cluster of three seats around 'Chloe' spare. The lady was bouncing the baby on her knee and he was giving out a high pitched chuckle.

Things like that used to brighten my day. I now just hoped the mother would live long enough to see her son grow up and questioned whether I would be bringing my child on to a train if I was her.

I sat facing her, 'Chloe' that is, not the woman with the bouncing baby.

"You were rude to me on Friday," I began but despite me looking directly into her cold, brown eyes there was barely a flicker of emotion from her. I'm not good with confrontation either and could feel myself shaking a little as I spoke.

Chloe's only response was to tilt her head to look out the window. The other two seats next to us remained vacant. This emboldened me. I was still reluctant to make a scene in front of a watching audience. I noticed once she tilted her head that she had those things in her ears once more. I presume they still call them earphones even though they are miniscule things these days. I briefly recalled that Amy always used to tease me about how out of touch I was with technology and fashion.

"My goodness, Jay," she would say when I became puzzled by the workings of the Sky remote or my mobile phone, "you're forty not seventy!"

I motioned at 'Chloe' to switch her music off. I think I did a twisting volume sign with my hand which she probably didn't understand. It was enough to make her take her earphones out of her ears though.

"Is something the matter?" she asked innocently.

A lot was the matter. My world had been tipped upside down over the previous two months. My wife had died. My thirty eight year old, super fit, beautiful, compassionate, intelligent wife who understood me better than anyone else on earth had died. I felt lost. I felt empty. I felt hated by my only child and I didn't understand why. I temporarily wanted to blame this young girl for the catastrophes I was enduring, solely because she had been temporarily dismissive of me the Friday before. It was ridiculous. I felt a little ashamed. Instead of berating her for her rudeness, which had been my objective, I backtracked and went for a more conciliatory tone.

"I just wanted to say that I'm sorry if I startled you on Friday."

I was going to carry on by explaining that I was from a different era. An era before political correctness when two strangers could exchange a few brief words on a train without anyone thinking there was anything odd about it. I started to feel myself welling up inside though so before I said anything else and before 'Chloe' had an opportunity to respond, I stood up and went looking for another seat elsewhere in the carriage. Realising there wasn't one, I remained standing all the way to Manchester because I knew if I returned to those three spare seats around 'Chloe', I would appear even weirder than I already did.

With hindsight, I'm glad I didn't mention all that crap about political correctness. Levels of sensitivity amongst the younger generation may have reached an all time high but one thing it had done was to remove the justification perverts used to have to be mildly perverted. The wolf whistling, bum pinching, breast fondling types are no longer accepted as just being a bit 'laddish' and that can only be a good thing. I wasn't that type but perhaps an elongated explanation may have given her the impression that I was about to be. She would have been wildly off the mark. I was just a lost soul reaching out for a bit of social interaction to try to make my day slightly more bearable but felt like I was being treated like a fox in a chicken coop. I was overwhelmed by misery and there seemed no end in sight.

CHAPTER FIVE

<u>**ALICE**</u>

I would say the majority of people who know me would consider me to be a nice person. There was a group of kids at school who still wouldn't speak fondly of me, as far as I am aware, purely because of whom I choose to fall in love with, but apart from them and the odd ex-boyfriend and ex-girlfriend, especially the ones I finished with, I think most people who have crossed my path would have seen me as a friendly soul.

When Jay approached me on the train for a second time, I pretended I was listening to music. Truth be told, I had only just sat down and hadn't had time to choose any tunes but once I saw him heading in my direction, I panicked and tried to appear musically distracted. It didn't keep him at bay for long. He started mentioning about how rude I had been but I ensured I showed no emotion and kept up the pretence of being unable to hear. He signalled for me to turn my music off so realising he wasn't going anywhere until I did so I went through the motions of switching my pretend music off. Given I had already given him a sex pest tag I anticipated that it was going to be an angry tirade, some sort of chat up line or a combination of the two. Something along the lines of,

'It upsets me that someone special like you is rude to me. Do you mind if I sit with you for a while so we can put things right?'

Jay hesitated before saying anything further, nervously said something apologetic about startling me on Friday and then just went away again. At first, I still thought it was weird. It was weird for a middle aged man to strike up a conversation with a teenage girl and it was weird for the same man, despite pretty much being ignored, to think about it so much that he was still referencing it a few days later.

I watched him. Between Chorley and Bolton, which is probably about a twenty minute journey, I kept glancing up at him. This was partially for self-preservation purposes. I decided if he came my way again, I was going to stand up quickly and move through to a different carriage. If he kept following me, I decided I would ask the ticket collector for help.

It was whilst I was glancing up at him that something changed. Something he did must have made my heart soften and I started looking at things from a more compassionate perspective. I was trying to think of a word that summed him up but the ones that sprang to mind didn't seem quite right. He seemed anxious, agitated, uncomfortable, sad, lonely, annoyed, emotional, scared and almost tearful. Like any teenager I can be narcissistic but I knew this multitude of emotions he was displaying were not down to his quickly halted conversations with me. There were far deeper rooted problems with him. He looked at breaking point. He was a tall man but moved around in small, unsteady steps. From time to time, he dabbed his eyes with a white handkerchief like he was surrendering to his emotions. He blew his nose more than a happy man would and I presumed it wasn't because he had a cold. There was a sense of sadness in his eyes that I had never seen in a man before.

I thought about the middle aged men I knew best, my Dad and my stepfather, John. They were both friendly, outgoing sorts and I realised if they were on the train with a teenage girl, they would probably both strike up a conversation without any comprehension that they may come across as creepy. My

Dad would have chatted about the weather and John would harp on about his allotment, Test cricket or Bush radios. Bore the poor girl to tears, no doubt. I felt bad for assuming the worst about someone and immediately stopped seeing Jay as a potential rapist or murderer and instead correctly started seeing him as a sad, middle aged man.

As I headed down the carriage to get off at Bolton, before the masses pushed their way impatiently on, I caught the eye of the 'lonely guy'.

"Bye," I said with a genuine friendly smile, "I hope you have a good day."

He seemed taken aback by my brief pleasantness and looked a little choked up.

"Thank you," he said with real gratitude, " but I... ," he stopped himself continuing and started on a separate sentence, "No, it doesn't matter," he said, "thank you very much! I hope you do too."

I headed over to the bus station feeling pleased with myself. I knew I still couldn't altogether dismiss the notion of him being a rapist or a murderer, just to be on the safe side, but if he was on my carriage again, I would definitely make an effort in passing to say hello. Weird thing was, after that, I didn't see him again on the train for quite some time.

CHAPTER SIX

JAY

Hunter was named after Harry Dean Stanton and Nastassja Kinski's son in Paris, Texas. As a teenager, I had loved that film but it was Amy that had chosen the name. I must have seen 'Paris, Texas' half a dozen times before Amy and I started dating, quite simply because I thought Nastassja Kinski was beguiling, but once we started dating, we watched it together too. I don't recall Amy being overly enamoured with the film, Nastassja Kinski reached parts of my body that she couldn't reach with Amy's, but I remember Amy thought the child actor who played their son was incredibly cute.

"If we have a son, we should call him 'Hunter'," Amy had announced as I took the 'Paris,Texas' video out the recorder and she subsequently never wavered. If we had a boy he would be 'Hunter', if we had a girl, we had thousands of names, none of which ever mattered as we never had a girl. We only had one child. The magic of conception just never happened again. We had found it easy to conceive first time around, I think it was either the first or second month of trying, but Amy's body seemed to decide it didn't want to go through that process again. We would have liked more children and we had tests to see if it was possible to rectify any issues we had but the tests didn't reveal any obvious problems. The consultant said, in his rather undiplomatic way, that our bodies were just probably incompatible and if we split up and went our separate ways, we would both probably find ourselves conceiving with other partners without difficulty.

"Not that I am suggesting you do that!" the consultant had commented with a demonic laugh.

Up until our struggle to conceive, life had always been good to us. Amy and I had known each other from an early age, as we had been to the same Primary School, Balshaw Lane, but then ended up going to different Secondary Schools. I went to Parklands, Amy to St Michael's. Your parents had to attend church regularly to get into St Michael's so that was never going to be an option for me. My Dad was an atheist and my Mum had what she described as a 'quiet faith' which meant she avoided going to church to avoid an argument with my father who thought religion was the most stupid invention mankind had ever come up with.

"Religion was only ever intended to be a comfort blanket for people who cannot accept everything has a beginning and an end," he would say, "but now pretty much every religion has been manipulated to exploit the masses."

Amy had caught my eye at primary school largely due to her sporting prowess. I had always enjoyed a variety of sports but I wasn't particularly good at anything. I occasionally played for the school football team and could compete adequately in athletics, particularly in middle distance running and in the high jump but Amy was a proper athlete. She could have represented our school in every athletics event there was both in track and field, because she was miles better than everyone else at everything, but 200 metres was her main event and in the District Sports she was almost at the finishing line by the time others had managed to negotiate the bend. She was just phenomenal. She matched that ability in long jump and high jump but I think, District wise, the throwing events were her poorest. She was tall and slender and wasn't designed for the power events but could still compete reasonably as she could master the technique. Amy was two year's younger than me but once she caught my attention, there was no way I could forget about her. Even now, despite the fact that she is no longer with me, I still can't take my mind off her. I accept I never will be able to.

Sixteen and a half weeks after Amy died, mentally and physically my body just shut down. I thought I had been coping adequately with her sudden passing until one morning, a Wednesday morning, I just couldn't get myself out of bed. My body was unwilling to conform and my brain wouldn't entertain the idea of going to work or even going downstairs. The furthest I could manage was the bathroom.

Even Hunter, who had been trying to verbally joust with me at any given opportunity since Amy had died, showed his compassionate side. He phoned his friend Dominic in a state of panic and Dominic calmly suggested to Hunter that he should ring my work to explain that I would not be in for a while and that he should also phone my GP. Our GP surgery had long since dispensed with home visits, but coincidentally our GP lived at the bottom of our road so was aware of Amy's passing, and he therefore said he would call to ours on his way home after surgery. I barely recall him coming, the next four weeks were pretty much a blank but Hunter said the Doctor explained to him that grief shouldn't be considered to be like stepping stones across a stream where you progressively move away from an ordeal to the safety of the other side. It was more comparable, he said, to a game of 'Snakes & Ladders' whereby you think you are moving along well until all of a sudden something catches you unexpectedly and you take a giant slide backwards. This has stuck with me ever since and I am a little less harsh on myself when I take a step in the wrong direction. Life now is like one endless game of snakes and ladders that will never finish until the day I die but sometimes I congratulate myself for moving quite a distance from my starting point.

I was off work for over a month. The Doctor signed me

off for another two weeks but when you are Head of Under-writing for a major insurance company you have the sort of bosses that only have a certain capacity to sympathise. Once I started to return to some sort of sanity, I began to fret that my deputy might become so proficient in my role that they may not want me back. Returning after a mental setback did not arouse the same level of sympathy as the death of your wife, nor was I expecting it would, but I returned second time around somewhat revitalised. It was as if my batteries had switched off for four weeks to enable them to recharge. The grey clouds that had been hanging over me for several months had partially lifted and I discovered there were times that I could actually see through the haze. I started to care a lit-tle more about my appearance too. I shaved off my beard and stopped opening a fresh bottle of wine or two every night.

Whether it was because I was less stressed, Hunter was or we both were, our relationship changed. He still had his moments of going completely bat shit crazy over the smallest of things, like me not having the correct change for his dinner money or not having his gym kit adequately ironed but most of the time I enjoyed his company. His GCSEs were on the horizon but they didn't seem to worry him at all. Schoolwork was perhaps a welcome distraction from the turbulence of his family life.

When I returned to travelling to work on the train, I started to get on the front carriage rather than the back. There was no real rhyme or reason for this, perhaps it was just a way of see-ing everything as a fresh start. Soon there were new familiar faces on the carriage and I started inventing back stories for them too. I wouldn't say I was happy but for the first time I felt I was coping and that felt like a bigger step forward than you could possibly imagine.

CHAPTER SEVEN

<u>**ALICE**</u>

My Mum and Dad divorced when I was six. I can remember fleeting moments from my childhood when they were together, like when we went to Cala D'Or on a family holiday when I was five. I remember playing in the children's swimming pool with my brother, Dominic, who was about two at the time. I can still close my eyes and picture my Mum putting sun cream on us and my Dad building sandcastles with us or splashing around in the sea.

The split itself is not something I can recall at all. I don't remember any raised voices or things being thrown around the house nor do I remember my Dad packing his bags and moving out. I just remember growing accustomed to the fact that Dad lived elsewhere. Subsequently, I grew accustomed to my Mum having a new boyfriend, John and then John becoming her new husband. I've always liked John, he is about as crazy as my mother but he has a good heart. They are well matched. Dad was different, I grew accustomed to him having female friends at his house when we visited and we had to call them 'Auntie'. There was an Auntie Vicki, an Auntie Claire, an Auntie Jane and then confusingly another Auntie Jane, who was smaller than the first one and wore glasses. There were lots of different Aunties, some I liked some I didn't. Some lasted from one summer holiday to the next whilst others didn't last from October half term to Christmas.

I had grown up in Garstang, a town halfway between Preston

and Lancaster. I went to Primary School there, loved every second of it and then completed my first year of Secondary School there too. In the summer holidays after that first year ended, Mum announced we were going to be moving in with John in Euxton, Chorley. I remember fits of tears, begging my Mum not to put us through it, telling her I hated Euxton and telling my diary I hated her too, but my emotional protests were to no avail and in 2014 we moved. John made every effort to make us feel welcome. He's about fifteen years older than Mum so his own children were already adults so it wasn't like there was any resentment between the kids and the step kids. We just moved in and he spoilt us rotten. Mum was always the disciplinarian. Both Dad and John I could wrap around my little finger.

Throughout my teenage years my own sexuality was a source of confusion. I'm eighteen now and to a certain extent my sexual feelings still confuse me, but I'm fine with that. In my early teens, I came to realise that there were certain people who could make me tingle and it didn't really matter if they were male or female. I could watch 'Friends' and feel attracted to both Joey and Rachel in the same scene. None of the others did it for me in the same way. I struggled to understand how you were expected to believe that Rachel could fall for Ross. As for Chandler and Phoebe, Chandler was just a little too odd for me and Phoebe just seemed too 'cartoon' a character for anyone to find attractive. I wasn't sure about Monica but there were definitely times she worked her magic on me including when she wore the 'fat' costume.

There were many others on TV I found myself attracted to. When David Tennant was Dr Who, I found it impossible to decide who I was most attracted to him or his assistant, Rose Tyler, played by Billie Piper. They both had the charm and the voices to drive me wild. I would regularly lock myself in the bathroom at John's, close my eyes, put my fingers to work and imagine I was in a threesome with the pair of them. In my imagination, Rose Tyler tended to last a lot longer than Dr Who. Others who became my imaginary sex buddies included Eva Longoria when she was Gabrielle Solis in Desperate Housewives, Jennifer Carpenter when she was Dexter's sister, Debra in Dexter, Liam Gallagher, Brandon Flowers from The Killers and Mollie King from The Saturdays. I really don't like facial hair on a man though so a bearded Liam or Brandon was a right turn off. They needed to be cleanly shaved. Same rules actually apply to David Tennant, but he still had the sexy voice so I was a bit more forgiving with him.

Back in reality, my school days from year eight onwards were spent at Parklands. I'd say it took a good twelve months to feel like it was my school and they were my friends. For that first year, I just felt like a visitor. Near enough everyone was lovely and friendly but I had been at school with some of my Garstang friends for seven years and I just didn't have that initial sense of belonging at Parklands.

By Year 9 I had adapted and by Year 10, I was starting to realise there were classmates who could make me 'tingle'. I developed a type, or two types really as my type differed if they were boys or girls. I liked confident, intelligent, slim and full chested girls. I liked quiet, sporty, intelligent and muscular boys. I didn't like confident boys. Confident boys were always cocky and would show off by belittling weaker, less confident classmates which just struck me as mean. As a pretty flat chested girl, I can vividly recall being jealous of and aroused by Pippa Johnson's incredible tits.

I had my first sexual 'thing' with a girl at fifteen and with a boy at sixteen. In the inbetween stage, I was confused in my confessions to my diary about whether this classified me as a virgin or not. If a boy had placed his fingers and tongue inside me but not his dick, I knew this would definitely not count but if a girl did it, where did this leave me?

I wanted my first sexual experience to be with a girl. I was concerned if it was with a boy it may hurt more. I was almost entirely responsible for making it happen. I invited Becky Palmer, who was the only girl in our year who was an 'out' and 'proud' lesbian over to our house on the very first occasion that Mum deemed me old enough to look after Dominic overnight. Within half an hour of Mum and John heading over to Manchester to see Bruce Springsteen, I had raided their drinks cabinet but ensured the measures I passed Becky were far more significant than my own. By ten o'clock we had kissed, by half ten I made sure Dominic's light was out and by eleven we were in bed too. Once it had happened though, I wanted it to be our secret. I was pleased it had happened, I very much enjoyed it happening but as I was fairly popular amongst the boys, I didn't want that popularity to be damaged. I also didn't want girls I was friendly with, but not sexually attracted to, suddenly avoiding me in case I pounced on them.

I learnt a few things from that encounter with Becky Palmer. Firstly, never trust a girl to keep a secret, especially a sexual one. Secondly, I learnt boys, on the whole, are more attracted to you rather than less, if they know you have had a thing with another girl. It only seems to become an issue once they are in a relationship with you and then it seems to make them possessive and paranoid. Thirdly, your good friends are your good friends for a reason and won't fall out with you if you sleep with lots of women, lots of men or lots of both. In fact, they just enjoy hearing about it.

Over the last three years, I wouldn't say I've been particularly wild, I've avoided drugs, had a handful of nights that I've drunk enough alcohol to cause me to vomit and not been sexually promiscuous but have had six regular sexual partners, four male and two female. This doesn't mean I have a slight leaning towards males, it just means my relationships with women have lasted longer. I am currently single. I am not specifically seeking a male or female next, I will just wait to see what fate has in store.

Fate can be more flexible with me now as I can get around more easily. Six months ago, I passed my driving test first time. John has leant me enough money to buy a five year old, white Fiat Uno which is my pride and joy. I have a weekend job in a local pub called 'The Talbot' so have been paying him back about £100 per month. I should really drive to College now rather than getting the train but I'm still a little bit scared of driving on the motorway. There is a route to Leigh College via Adlington and Westhoughton which avoids motorways altogether but it's still rush hour traffic and I just imagine it would be really stressful. I get a free bus pass and discounted train travel, which Mum and John pay for anyway, so I'm going to stick with the train to Bolton and then the bus from there to Leigh for now. Who wouldn't want their nose stuck between loads of sweaty armpits as they try to barge their way through the crowds anyway?

Mum and John aren't bothered about me not driving to College. Mum suggested I should have a trial run one weekend but has said if I don't fancy driving there, that's up to me. They just like the fact that I can ferry Dominic around everywhere now. Mum and John are serious wine fiends and tend to hit the bottle as soon as they are home from work so having to pick Dominic up from his friends or from football training can be a bit of a bind. I'm happy to drive him around. As kid brother's go, he's the best – he's very chilled out, dry witted and makes me laugh. His best mate, Hunter is a funny kid too. I keep taking the mick out of the pair of them saying I will be there for them when they grow a set of balls each and admit to everyone they are in a loving, same-sex relationship. They just laugh it off. Little does Dominic know that I am the gay one in the family, perhaps he does know and just doesn't let on.

One Sunday evening, Mum asked me if I would go to get our Dom from Hunter's house. Hunter lives over on Buckshaw which is less than ten minutes in the car from ours and as I was just lounging around listening to a bit of Catfish and the

Bottlemen, I was happy to help out.

A few months ago, tragically, Hunter's Mum died. She was only in her thirties so a rumour spread around Chorley that she must have topped herself. I am pretty sure she didn't though. I've asked Dom and he said it was the Coronavirus. The second wave wasn't as bad as the first but it still killed significant numbers. Dominic just said she'd been completely happy and well beforehand, started with a cough, a few days later developed breathing problems, was admitted to hospital, went on a ventilator and then she passed away. The way Dominic talks about her, I think he had a little bit of a crush on her. Bless him. I don't really talk to him about her dying because I can see his eyes going all teary. Anyway, it's been a terrible thing for Hunter and his Dad to have to go through.

Hunter's house was in a really posh part of Buckshaw, where all the proper expensive houses are by the astroturf pitch and Buckshaw Bernabeau. Once I pulled up outside, I text Dom to tell him I was there and to come out. I didn't get a reply. I gave it five minutes and then sent another couple of texts through but still the little bugger didn't respond. I was a bit annoyed with him, Mum had told him I was coming to get him so he should have been looking out for my texts.

Ten minutes after I had parked up, there was still no text from Dominic so I decided to push things along. I was fed up of waiting. I got out my car, walked to the front door and rang the bell. Almost immediately the door was pulled open and a man I presumed must be Hunter's Dad stood staring at me. There was an awkward few seconds before either of us spoke. I looked at him and he looked at me, trying to work out where we knew each other from. It's weird when you see someone out of context to where you normally see them, it just completely throws you.

I started the introductions.

"I'm sorry. I'm Alice, Dominic's sister. I've come to pick him up."

"Dominic's sister? OK. I did offer to give him a lift home but he said it was already sorted."

"It's not a problem."

"Sorry, I'm Jay by the way, Hunter's Dad, which I'm sure you must have worked out already."

"Hi!"

"Dom, your sister's here," Jay shouted from the hallway, up the stairs.

"We're in the middle of a game of Fortnite, Dad," Hunter shouted down, "we'll be five minutes."

"Are you OK stepping in for five minutes? I can get you a drink if you'd like one."

"That's fine. I'm OK for a drink though, thank you."

I stepped in thinking Hunter's Dad was a bit soft on him, probably because it hadn't been long since his Mum had died. If that had happened at our house, Mum would have told the lads to finish up straight away and if they hadn't done what they were told, she'd have just gone upstairs and switched it off anyway. It was continuing to bug me where I knew him from. I knew I had seen him fairly recently too. Was he a lecturer at Leigh? Did he work in a shop I'd been in or was he one of the regulars at The Talbot? This was going to drive me potty but I knew in the end the answer would come. It always did.

CHAPTER EIGHT

JAY

Initially, it confused the hell out of me when she arrived at our doorstep. I remember staring at her, bewildered, wondering why 'Chloe' from the train would be coming to our house. I couldn't fictionalise a story in my brain quick enough before the truth was revealed. She was Alice, Dominic's sister.

For some reason, I can't really explain why, I was interested in finding out whether she was more like the rude teenager who dismissively cut my pleasant chit chat down or the friendlier teenager who exchanged pleasantries the following week as she departed the train at Bolton. I was also curious to see how good my guess was that she worked for her Dad's entrepreneurial friend in Bolton and had a University boyfriend called Ben who captained the rugby team. Hunter and Dominic provided the opportunity when they requested five minutes to finish off their game. I would normally have told Hunter not to be so rude and would have told him to get downstairs at once, but their delaying tactics actually pleased me.

Alice turned down the offer of a hot drink but came through to the lounge and sat down on one of the two seater sofas, so I sat on the other one. She had less make-up on than during the week but she was naturally pretty. Her big brown eyes would always be a positive feature, I thought, as they can never age or wrinkle.

"Was it raining outside?" I asked.

It was a stupid question that made me cringe a little after I had said it. I had just opened the door and could see it wasn't raining. With only having a son, chit chatting with a teenage girl was not something I had done for a very long time.

"No, it's stopped now."

"Good. Good."

There was an uncomfortable silence for twenty seconds or so before I tried again.

"He's a cracking lad, your brother."

Alice smiled. You could tell she thought a lot of Dominic.

"Most of the time he is. He goes a bit mental on that X-box from time to time. It's the teenage version of giving a five year old too many sweets. Sends him hyper."

"I know what you mean. We used to limit the amount of time Hunter played on his X-box but he's almost sixteen now so he's a bit beyond those constraints. We still threaten to take it off him now if he misbehaves."

I noticed that I was still referring to 'we'. There was no 'we' any more. Everything was just shit. I could tell Alice wasn't fully listening anyway. Her mind seemed elsewhere which was confirmed by her next sentence.

"Did you not used to have a beard?"

"Briefly, I shaved it off last week."

"I thought so. I know you from somewhere."

The penny didn't drop. Alice still looked puzzled and confused. I was tempted to drag this out as a bit of pay back for the time I felt she was rude to me. I didn't though I put her out of her misery.

"The train," I said, "you get the train from Chorley to Bolton every day. I go from Buckshaw to Manchester."

"That's it!" Alice exclaimed loudly as if her brain had been taken out of a vice.

"Can I just say," she continued, "you look so much better without a beard. I know it's none of my business, but if I were you, I wouldn't let it grow back. You look ten years younger without it, you really do!"

"Thanks. I don't normally have a beard, certainly not one like I've had recently anyway. Just with everything that went on with Hunter's Mum, I just didn't feel like shaving for a while. Didn't really feel like doing anything if truth be known."

"Oh, I'm sure. I was so very sorry to hear about that."

"Thanks."

"How come she died of Corona? I mean I thought it was mainly old people, overweight people and people with underlying health conditions it killed. You don't have to talk about it if it's too upsetting but I just wondered. I mean you'd have thought she would have fought it off pretty easily."

I was surprised by Alice's bluntness. People rarely questioned it. Obviously close friends and family did at first. You face a barrage of questions from them early on as they try to make sense of it.

"What happened?"

"Why did the Doctors not do more?"

"How could this happen?"

The questions only come from people close to you though. Work colleagues, neighbours and social media friends don't tend to ask. Everyone, other than those close to you, is afraid to ask because of some strange sense of political correctness. Alice asked though. Morbid curiosity had got the better of her.

"She was just one of the unlucky ones who got it really badly and her body wasn't able to fight it off. As she was struggling so much to breathe, she asked me if I would arrange for her to be ventilated. I didn't make that decision though, the Doctors did and once she was ventilated, she just never came back around."

"Really, that's awful."

"She was the fittest, healthiest woman I have ever met. We went to bed one night, just like any other night, but the following morning she just complained she was getting a bit of a cold and then everything just went off the rails very quickly."

"Fuck...oh, I'm so sorry for swearing, it's just so awful."

"Obviously it's not something that happens regularly to fit young people but apparently it's not incredibly rare either. It's been very hard for me to get my head around but whether I get my head around it or not, it doesn't change the fact that Amy's no longer here."

"How's Hunter been?"

"Better than me but as you'd expect, he has his ups and downs. Anyway, this must be a miserable conversation for you..."

"No, no it's fine," Alice replied with a sympathetic smile.

To be honest, I think Alice was pretty intrigued by Amy's death and would have quite happily continued to talk about it and its impact but I wanted to stop.

"Where is it you work in Bolton?" I asked.

"Oh, I don't work in Bolton. I just get off there to get on a bus to Leigh College. I do a BTEC in Sport there."

"From what I remember, seeing you on the train, you don't dress like a student."

Alice tended to wear Laura Ashley type dresses and tights rather than tracksuits and trainers.

"I prefer dresses to tracksuits. I tend to change when I'm there on the days we do practical."

"That's a long way to go to College from Chorley. How come you didn't go to Runshaw?"

Runshaw College is a massive college in Leyland about four miles from Chorley. Leigh College must be twenty miles away.

"It's a long story but I just wanted to get away from some of the kids I went to school with. I started working full-time at The Talbot for a few months after the first lockdown finished, just doing odd jobs, collecting glasses and helping out but then I decided I wanted to go back to College. I still work at The Talbot part-time though. I was all set to go to Wigan College but they transferred the course over to Leigh."

I could hear Dominic and Hunter moving around upstairs. Alice and I simultaneously stood up.

"By the way," Alice enquired, "when you started talking to me on the train, did you already know then I was Dom's sister?"

I was tempted to say 'Yes' just to make her feel a little worse for being rude to me when we first spoke.

"No, I was just being friendly," I replied honestly.

"I'm so sorry if I was rude. It was the beard, Jay. I have a thing about beards. Not a good thing. It made you look a bit creepy."

"I'll make a mental note not to grow it back."

"Yes, don't grow it back. You look much warmer and friendlier now. I've not seen you on the train recently though. Is that because of the new look or have you been getting a different train?"

"I still get that same train. I was off ill for a while but I just get on a different carriage now."

Dominic and Hunter were now coming down the stairs.

"Well start getting back on the rear carriage from tomorrow,

Jay," Alice instructed, "It'd be nice having someone to talk to rather than just listening to music for an hour and a half."

"Sorry," Dominic said, "we were doing really well on Fortnite and didn't want to pack in halfway through."

"It's fine," Alice replied, "I've been having a chat with Hunter's Dad. We already sort of know each other from the train."

I almost added, 'I'm the pervert from the back carriage' but thankfully I stopped myself. Often things I say these days are incredibly embarrassing for Hunter and that would certainly have been added to the list.

"Thanks Jay! See you in the morning!"

"Bye, Alice."

It was a brief meeting with a young woman, a woman young enough to be my daughter, someone who I didn't have any romantic interest in but irrespective of all that, it left me feeling temporarily happy. I was a lonely middle aged man and any time spent with good company was precious to me now. That's what I decided Alice was - good company. Without a shadow of a doubt I knew I would be returning to the rear carriage of the train to Manchester every morning from now on.

CHAPTER NINE

<u>ALICE</u>

It was our second week of journeying on the train together. We always took the same train in the morning, the one that left Chorley at 7.35a.m, but unless I stayed to work late in the library or had an afternoon football match, we tended to get different trains home. Jay didn't even have a regular train he went home on. It was dependent on his workload that day. I suppose Hunter was capable of sorting himself some tea out and there was company at work which I don't think Hunter provided much of back home. Once that first week, on the Wednesday, I had spotted Jay in the carriage when I got on at Bolton, but it was rush hour and everyone was crammed on, so there was no way I could have managed to get anywhere near him let alone have a conversation. People don't like you squeezing past them on trains these days. I enjoyed our morning conversations though. Jay was mature and, other than Hunter and Dominic, knew no-one I knew, so I could be myself around him. If I told him anything private, I made sure I firmly stated it was private and that he mustn't mention it to Hunter or Dominic. He would always laugh when I said that and would re-assure me that him and Hunter only ever had conversations that lasted ten seconds and they were almost always about food or money.

"Morning! How was your weekend?" Jay asked brightly, as soon as I sat down next to him.

"Not the greatest Jay, to be honest. How was yours?"

I felt a bit of a fraud grumbling about an indifferent weekend when I was sat with a man who had lost his wife to Corona but I tried not to treat Jay differently just because he had tasted tragedy. I don't think he would have wanted me to.

"I didn't win the Euromillions rollover, Brexit is still giving me headaches and Everton lost but I put about six washes on and ironed everything without burning it so on balance, that's a success. How come yours wasn't so good?"

"Gonorrhea," I said with a straight face pointing between my legs.

"Seriously?" Jay queried but with a dubious tone.

"Obviously not, who am I going to catch an STD from? I'm virtually a nun these days which links in well with the real problem, Jay. I'm getting bored of being single. I think I'm missing the human touch. I've been trying to reach my pansy with my tongue but I'm just not that flexible and I don't have a particularly long tongue."

"They must have cut those bits out of 'The Sound of Music'," Jay countered in his deadpan tones without even a hint of cracking a smile.

  It was probably a bit weird discussing my sexual habits (no pun intended) with a guy older than my Dad but it didn't bother me and it didn't seem to bother Jay one iota either. He never flinched when I discussed anything of a sexual nature. A few people around us, especially older men, would shuffle their newspapers awkwardly or younger folk would stifle a laugh and then pretend they were doing something on their phone or Kindle but Jay was cool about it. I hadn't yet discussed my recurring dream of having my face in between Jennifer Carpenter's legs, but felt it would probably pop up in conversation at some point. I had presumed he considered me to be 100% heterosexual so was interested to see if I could shock him.

"Did you go out?" Jay asked, matter of factly, with no visual signs of blushing or awkwardness after my previous disclosure.

"I was knackered on Friday night because I had worked Wednesday and Thursday nights at The Talbot so I just stayed in and watched half a dozen episodes of Dexter. I love that show. On Saturday, I went to 'Lost' in Chorley with a few friends."

"Any good?"

"It was alright. It was heaving and a few drunken or coked up lads tried their luck with me, but I haven't reached those levels of desperation just yet. Give it another fortnight and it may become a distinct possibility."

"If I can give you one piece of advice, never settle for something or someone less than you deserve. Whilst you're settling, you might miss out on someone fantastic."

"Is that what you did, Jay? Saved yourself for Mrs Right?"

Jay didn't seem to voluntarily bring Amy into our conversations very often but if I introduced her, he seemed happy to talk about her.

"I didn't have to. We started dating when I was sixteen and she was fourteen. We were engaged when I was twenty, married at twenty two and then Hunter came along before I was twenty five. I've never been with anyone else since the day I met her and never intend to be with anyone else."

"Did you only want the one child?"

"No, we wanted more but it just didn't happen. I suppose, whichever way you look at it, Amy wasn't the luckiest of people."

It saddened me when Jay said that. I'm sure it made Jay sad too. I felt the need to lift his spirits by putting a more positive spin on it.

"Jay, you mustn't look at it like that. For whatever reason, Amy was only destined to be on this planet for thirty eight years but for twenty four of those years she was able to spend her time with her one true love. Very few people are that lucky."

Jay smiled. It was a sad smile but it was still a smile.

"Thank you! 'One True Love' is a bit Disney for me though."

"Well, how would you describe it?"

"Love of her life."

"That's hardly a major change, Jay!"

"It's a subtle difference which makes it much less 'cringeful'."

"Whatever! The point is that you were lucky to have each other and over time you'll move on and you might find love again."

"No, I won't," Jay stated this very firmly as though what I was suggesting was ludicrous.

"I'm sorry. I suppose it's too soon to be mentioning anything like that. I'm really sorry."

Jay shook his head which made me feel worse.

"No, Alice, it isn't too soon to mention it. Mention it whenever you like, it won't change anything. I won't replace Amy."

I started backtracking. I could feel my face flushing with embarrassment because I felt like I had put my foot in it.

"I know you won't. I didn't mean that. I meant you might find love again with someone else. She won't be a replacement, just someone new."

"No."

"OK, you won't then."

This was obviously not the reassurance he was looking for. I really regretted bringing it up but I was only trying to be nice.

"I'm not being funny with you, Alice. I'm just stating a fact. I won't date anyone again. I won't kiss anyone again. I won't have sex with anyone again. I won't marry again. It would be wrong."

I couldn't help myself. Sometimes when I get an idea in my head I don't know when to back off.

"It might feel wrong now, Jay, but in twenty years' time it might not."

"It would still feel wrong. My heart has to be in a relationship and my romantic heart died the moment Amy's stopped beating."

"That's lovely, Jay and very noble but..."

"No but's, Alice."

"OK, I'll shut up."

"Let's just talk about something else."

"Have I told you I'm bisexual?"

CHAPTER TEN

JAY

Alice was bisexual. Nothing surprises me about young people these days so it didn't come as a shock. Well, not entirely a shock anyway. It was just a bit unexpected. I think I went quiet for quite some time after she made this revelation. I just knew if I said something I would put my foot in it. As it happens, the delay didn't prevent me doing that anyway.

"How come you aren't saying anything, Jay? You normally have plenty to say. What are you thinking?"

"I just don't…," I let my words trail off.

"You just don't what, Jay?"

"It doesn't matter."

"Go on."

"I just don't think you look like a lesbian."

I shouldn't have said it. I should have come up with something better. Alice and I had been getting on really well but I knew what I said was unacceptable to her. It was written all over her face that she was fuming.

"And what do you think a lesbian looks like?"

I kept digging. I think at one point I hit Australia.

"Fat, cropped hair, dungarees."

"And ugly?"

"Not always, but normally."

"Wow, Jay, just wow!"

"What?"

"I had just never realised before that you were such a bigot."

"It's not about being bigoted, Alice. It's just an observation most lesbians I have ever come across look like that."

Sometimes, once you start saying something stupid, it becomes very difficult to say, 'hang on, I'm talking a load of nonsense here', so instead you continue talking complete crap in the hope that somewhere along the line it'll start making sense. I was being an arse. I'd like to think at the time, I knew I was, but perhaps I didn't. Perhaps I've only realised subsequently.

"That's like saying all heterosexual men are beer bellied, tattooed, Sun readers who buy porno mags, pinch girls arses and have a monthly subscription to the British National Party."

"It was meant as a compliment, Alice! I just meant you're a pretty girl."

"That sounds mildly condescending but even if it didn't, since when has it been a crime for a pretty girl to be attracted to another girl?"

"Not once have I said it was a crime but it used to be."

"But society moved forward, Jay. Well, most of society did anyway. Jeez!"

"I get it, I'm old fashioned. Honestly though, when I was at school, the only girls who were lesbians were the ones who attracted no male attention."

"So what you're saying is that every female is actually straight but when the ugly fat ones realise they aren't attracting any male attention they crop their hair and purchase several pairs of dungarees and give it a go with a same sex relationship."

"Or sometimes they have been treated very badly by a man. They might just feel it's better to have someone than no-one."

"So you don't think anyone is naturally drawn to people of the same sex?"

I could hear the venom in Alice's line of questioning.

"Stop getting so annoyed with me! It's probably all coming out a bit wrong. I'm absolutely fine with you being a lesbian."

"That's very good of you and, for the record, I said I was bisexual."

"I'm sorry I've only ever been aware of 'butch lesbians', although to be fair, thinking about it, I've seen some butch ones with some good looking partners. That always seems weird too! If you are going to choose a woman that looks like a man, why not just choose a man? To be fair though, if I was a woman, I'd be a lesbian."

I think it was at this point Alice completely lost her temper with me. She was seething before but at this point she was full on crazy.

"For fuck's sake, Jay! I don't even know if you are giving me your own opinions any more or whether you are just spouting some old fashioned, right wing dogma. If I had a pound for every time some macho lad said 'I get it, if I was a woman, I'd be a lesbian,' I'd be a millionaire several times over. The thing is though, if you or any of those macho dickheads were born women and were attracted to someone of the same sex, you would hide it because you'd be too concerned about complying with society norms to come out."

"Can we go back to talking about my wife dying, please? It felt less awkward than this."

Alice remained unimpressed.

"Don't make light of this, Jay."

"I'm not."

"You absolutely are. This is a serious subject and you've handled it like a thirteen year old boy."

Alice didn't speak to me again until she got off the train at Bolton. Once she left, I was pretty convinced she was not going to speak to me ever again.

CHAPTER ELEVEN

<u>**ALICE**</u>

I was caught off guard by Jay's reaction to my bisexuality. Up to that point he had been so chilled about the mention of sex toys and sex talk in general so I had naturally anticipated that he would be equally twenty first century about me being attracted to both sexes but it turned out he held some pretty antiquated opinions when it came to lesbianism. I can't remember exactly what he said but it was along the stereotypical middle aged lines of 'women in comfortable shoes' and the 'dungaree brigade'. I was not impressed. The word 'Gammon' sprang to mind but I resisted using it.

When I saw him on the train the following day, I sat down next to him and greeted him with my normal friendly 'hello'.

"I didn't think you'd be speaking to me," he said with what sounded like a slight nervousness to his tone.

"Why would I not be speaking to you?"

"Because I said some stupid things yesterday."

"You're entitled to an opinion, Jay. If I never spoke to you again, you would be unlikely to change that opinion but perhaps if we can continue to speak regularly I can educate you."

"Perhaps."

"Maybe one day we'll have a night out together and I'll take you to Canal Street in Manchester. There's also a chance, if we stay friends long enough, that I may start dating a woman at some point and if I'm true to form, she may not be fat, have cropped hair and wear dungarees - not that I'm ruling that out as an option mind you – just because that would fit in with your dated impression of what every lesbian looks like. All shapes and sizes, Jay. When you think of lesbians from now on just think 'All shapes and sizes'. Fat, thin, tall, small, feminine looking, masculine looking, plastered in make-up, no make-up at all, tattooed, pierced, long haired, short haired, shaven headed, pretty, mediocre, ugly, clever, not so clever, white, black and mixed race.

"I apologise unreservedly. What I said yesterday was pretty stupid."

"I don't need an apology, Jay. I just want you to say, at some point in the future, that you got it wrong."

"I could say that now."

"You could say it but you wouldn't necessarily mean it. Nothing has happened in the last twenty four hours that could have changed your opinion."

"Well, that's not entirely true. I Googled 'Famous Lesbian Women' last night and was surprised who popped up."

I didn't ask who, it was immaterial.

"That's a start, Jay. Anyway, I wanted you to know about my sexual identity but I don't want to spend every train journey discussing it."

Jay smiled. He had an attractive smile. The fact that it temporarily hid his sorrow was obviously a good thing.

"Notes to future self – Point One, don't grow a beard or people will think you're a pervert. Point Two, remember lesbians come in all shapes and sizes."

"Progress! Baby steps, Jay. Right, let's move on. Brexit, what a farce that's becoming, do you think we'll live to see the day that we actually leave?"

CHAPTER TWELVE

<u>May 2021 – JAY</u>

It was Friday night, 10pm and once again I had forgotten to change my Fantasy Football team. The lads at work were taking the piss out of me because there were one hundred and eighteen in our League and I was in 118th place. The previous season had been severely delayed because of the pandemic so this one had started late. I was determined if it was to come to a hasty, early conclusion because of the recent spike in the Coronavirus 'R' rate, I would not be coming last when it did.

"Are you coming to bed, honey?" Amy asked as she found me messing with my phone in the kitchen. She had been going around the rooms unplugging things, switching lights off and making sure the front and back doors were locked. She was now pouring herself a glass of water.

"I'll just be a few minutes. I almost forgot to change my Fantasy Football team. You know how much I hate coming last."

"I thought that's what you were always striving for," Amy joked, but I was barely listening, I was thinking about whether to put Richarlison or Mo Salah as captain. As an Evertonian putting Salah, a Liverpool striker, as captain, felt like a betrayal, which probably went a good way to explaining why I was bottom of the League.

"Sorry, what was that?" I queried after picking my captain, Richarlison and posting my team.

"Doesn't matter, the moment's gone. It was just a joke about coming last."

"Sorry honey, I was concentrating."

"It's fine. Are you coming up now?"

"Yes."

"Are you alright taking Hunter to football in the morning? I've got a parkrun."

"That's fine."

"You need to be at Gregson Lane for 9.15. I'll be done at Cuerden by half past so I'll follow you over."

"OK great…you know, I was reading an article today that said female park runners who have sex with their husbands' the night before the race tend to knock thirty seconds off their personal best."

"Really?" Amy replied in an amused tone.

"Yes, really, it was something to do with the female hormones released during sex stimulating the whole body for the following twelve hours. What time is it now? Ten o'clock. Perfect!"

Amy came across and kissed me on the forehead.

"Not tonight, love. I've had a frantic day at work and I'm shattered. I'll schedule you in for a much needed spot of fornication tomorrow at ten thirty though. Hunter's around at Dominic's tomorrow night so there'll be no interruptions."

"So I'm on a promise?"

"Indeed you are."

"I love you, Mrs Cassidy!"

"I love you too, Mr Cassidy!"

Amy switched the kitchen light off and we both went up to bed.

CHAPTER THIRTEEN

<u>**ALICE**</u>

Leigh College Girls football team are strong, really strong. When I started there, I wasn't sure whether I would break into the team but after a couple of brief cameo appearances as a substitute in pre-season friendlies, I was given a starting position as a central defensive midfielder and I have done everything possible to keep my place. Technically, I know I am not the greatest but I never stop running, tackle hard, link defence and attack well and for a relatively small girl, I'm decent in the air too.

"You make everything look easy," is how my coach describes my game.

Last Wednesday, we beat Runshaw College 6-1. This was a particularly pleasing victory for me as I knew most of the girls on the Runshaw team. When I was in Year Eleven, there were about a dozen kids in our school year, both boys and girls, who had started to make fun of me for being bisexual. It started off as just being the odd joke but it felt by Christmas that it had become relentless. It was stupid childish humour like one of them would hold up a chocolate muffin at lunchtime and say, "Want a bite, Alice? I know you like the taste of a bit of muff!" which tended to be followed by a lot of false laughter and mock hilarity. Although my friends did what they could to stick up for me, it started to affect my moods and early in the New Year I decided I had just about had enough and I had to get away from these people. I told my Mum and John that I didn't want to go to College and wanted to look for a job instead. They protested a little but ended up reaching a compromise whereby if I didn't have a decent job after a few months then I would make plans to return to further education. This was fine by me. I just wanted to escape the verbal, mental and sometimes mildly physical abuse. I knew if I did go back to College, it certainly would not be Runshaw, as that would be where all those dozen kids would be heading.

Two of that gang of twelve bullies played for the Runshaw football team against me, Ceri Littlewood and Katie Kelper. When the final whistle blew, I was happy to shake the other girls hands but there was no way in the world I was going to shake Katie's or Ceri's. That would have been accepting their abuse. They had never apologised or acknowledged they had done anything wrong. Katie headed over to me with a smirk on her face offering her hand. She could piss right off.

"Well played, Alice."

"I'm not shaking your hand, Katie, you two faced bitch!"

Katie just stood still with her hands on her hips a few metres away from me. That smirk still hadn't disappeared from her face.

"Good, your hand probably stinks of fanny anyway, you stupid dyke!"

My adrenalin was already pumping and those comments were enough to tip me over the edge. I completely lost my temper, ran as quickly as I could after ninety minutes of football, straight at Katie Kelper and rugby tackled her to the ground. For a girl who had never played rugby it was a fine tackle. I grabbed her wrists whilst I had her pinned down and used her own hands to slap the cheeks of her face a few times. Ceri raced over and pushed me off Katie and onto the floor, I quickly stood back up and pushed her away with two hands and before we had the opportunity to square up, it had become a twenty two woman brawl with people from both teams grabbing, pushing and exchanging verbals. The two coaches from each side and the three match officials tried to come between the twenty two women but as there were only seven of them and twenty two of us, it took several minutes before peace was restored. Once everything had calmed down, the referee took me to one side.

"What's your name?" she asked.

"Alice."

"Alice what?"

"Alice Moorcroft."

"Well, Alice Moorcroft, this is going to be a first for me. I've never sent a player off after the final whistle before. Which one were you fighting with?"

I felt a little sorry for the referee. She only looked in her early twenties, probably hadn't been refereeing too long and she looked extremely flustered that after a relatively straightforward ninety minutes, she was now having to deal with a full scale brawl. Nevertheless, despite hating Katie Kelper, I wasn't a grass.

"I was fighting with all of them."

"I know that, smart arse. I meant initially, if it's any consolation she'll be getting sent off too."

"I can't remember."

"Of course you can, you had her pinned down on the floor two minutes ago!"

"Well, I've forgotten."

"Suit yourself. Just you for the three match ban then," the referee took out her red card and brandished it above my head, "I'll also be writing in my report that you refused to co-operate with the match official."

"I'm not bothered," I said dismissively but feeling a little worried inside, "do what you like."

The truth of the matter was that I was bothered, really bothered. As the adrenalin levels started to dip, I felt more and more ashamed for losing my cool but, more importantly, I knew I would be facing at least a three match ban for violent conduct. I had let myself and my team mates down.

Once we arrived back at the dressing room, I just sat silently under my peg for a long time. One or two of the girls came across and said some sympathetic words. Both of our coaches were understandably angry with me and reminded me I was representing Leigh College and that this sort of behaviour was unacceptable. I didn't bother explaining the mitigating circumstances, it would have made no difference and their point would have still been valid.

I gradually took my kit off and went for a shower. Sometimes College showers can be weak and warm, rather than powerful and hot but these ones were the latter so I didn't want to drag myself out from their comforting jets. By the time I eventually did leave the shower, dried off and started getting dressed, there was only myself and one other player, Erika Magnusson, in the changing room. Erika was our centre forward. She was a tall, slim girl with lightning pace. She had scored four goals against Runshaw. I felt bad that my post-match antics had taken the gloss off her match winning performance. She had long, white blonde hair that took an age to dry, the reason, I concluded, that she was still around.

"I'm really sorry about that," I said shamefully.

"Don't be daft."

"I feel terrible, you scored four today and we should all have been celebrating that instead of getting a lecture off Alison about the brawl. The brawl I started."

"I wouldn't exactly call it a brawl, Alice. It was mainly just a bit of pushing and shoving. Anyway, are you OK? I've never seen you lose it like that before."

Erika was a second year student. Despite being a year above me in College, we were actually the same school year as I had had that year out. She was doing the same course as me but I hadn't really spoken to her all that much because she was a year ahead so we didn't have the same lessons. She was very popular amongst the boys, which was no surprise as she was stunning.

"I'm absolutely fine. I just used to go to school with a few of them. A couple of them were amongst a bunch of kids who used to give me a hard time in Year 11."

"Because you're gay?"

I had decided not to mention anything about my sexuality when I started at Leigh. That seemed like a good plan after the name calling I had endured at Secondary school. It wasn't that I was denying my sexuality just temporarily denying my-self some potential aggravation until I had settled in. The secret didn't last long. During the build up to Christmas, I had been on a few drunken College nights out and had a couple of cheeky snogs, one with a boy called Mark and one with a girl called Helen. The plan was in shreds and the word was out.

"Bi. Most people were fine with it but some people are just looking for an excuse to give you a hard time. If I had had ginger hair, been skinny, been fat, short sighted, whatever, I am sure the same people would still have given me a hard time. You were either in their little gang or you were 'the opposition' and I was 'the opposition'."

"Well good on you for fighting back. I was bullied at school too but I just let them get away with it. I never let them see it bothered me but I used to go home every night and cry my eyes out."

I was really surprised because she was so beautiful I would

have imagined everyone would have loved her. I know this sort of contradicted my own statement about bullies always finding an excuse to bully but I just imagined that Erika would have been protected by a mass of other 'cool kids'. I imagined that the boys would have been drooling over her and the girls would have wanted to be her best friend.

"That's really shit, Erika. Was it physical or verbal bullying?"

"Mainly verbal but a couple of the girls used to hit me too. I don't mean punching me just things like dead arms and Chinese burns. It stopped eventually. They just moved on to giving someone else a hard time instead of me but it was a horrible time."

"Was it just because you were pretty?"

"Partially, because I stood tall when I walked that apparently meant I was 'up myself' but it was mainly triggered off after a so called friend stayed at our house for the weekend. I was going to play football on the Sunday morning and she didn't want to come and watch so stayed in my room. She must have been snooping around and found my diary. It was in a locked top drawer too but if you put your hand around the back you could pull anything out. A lot of stuff in it was just 14 year old girl's stuff but I went through a twelve month phase of having a massive crush on one of our teachers and that was in there, in all its glory. By lunchtime on the Monday, the whole school year knew about it. I was mortified."

"Did the teacher get to know?"

"Yes."

"Was he OK about it?"

"She. Miss Poolan. She was a PE teacher. She took us for football too. Fantastic teacher, fantastic football coach and a very proud lesbian. Give her, her due, she was lovely about it. She said she had been through something very similar at school

61

and had endured all the same taunts I had. I still found it incredibly embarrassing."

"Did it pass?"

"The crush? Sort of. I'm not sure if the feelings from a crush ever completely go away or if you just learn to smother them. If I ran into her now and she was single and I was single, part of me would still be interested in finding out how much of the fantasy would be true in reality. Having said that, I tend to just date girls my own age these days."

It was the way that she said the last sentence that was the giveaway. There was a coyness mixed with a smile and a blush. I knew then what was happening. Erika hadn't just been last in the changing room to dry her hair. She was making a very tactful move on me. On little me! I had enough confidence in myself to know I was reasonably attractive but Erika was properly gorgeous. She had really bright, pale blue eyes, proper white blonde hair that dropped down to the curve of her slender bottom and the best pair of legs I had ever seen wearing a pair of football shorts. She looked like a Scandinavian supermodel and I was pretty sure she was interested in me. I resisted the temptation of doing a little celebratory dance.

"Are you seeing anyone at the moment?" I asked. There was no way I was going to hide my interest.

"No, I was talking with someone until recently but it just didn't work out. What about yourself?"

"100% single," I stated categorically. I couldn't have been more obvious unless I had grabbed her and kissed her.

"Do you fancy coming out for a drink with me sometime or the cinema or anything, oh I don't know. I'm sorry I'm getting flustered. I find asking someone out really awkward."

"I love the fact you feel awkward asking me out," I said reassuringly followed with the flash of a full smile.

"You sure it doesn't make me look like an idiot?"

"It makes you look like you care. A drink, the cinema, something to eat, whatever you want to do and wherever you want to go, the answer is most certainly 'YES'."

I wasn't exactly playing it cool but she was the hottest girl I'd ever seen. It would have been impossible. I was incredibly excited about the direction this was going but also had my reservations, if we managed to get it together it would never last, she was so far out of my league it was untrue. If it even lasted a few weeks, I was going to make damned sure Jay got to see her. Fat, ugly, cropped hair with dungarees, Jay? I don't think so.

CHAPTER FOURTEEN

JAY

Loneliness is the hardest thing to adapt to when you lose a loved one. For eighteen years we had spent every night sleeping together in the same bed, spent every breakfast together, most evenings together and then one day Amy just slips away and I'm on my own. It's not like she has gone away for the weekend with a bunch of girlfriends or is on a physiotherapy course for a week with work – she's just gone, completely gone.

Whisper this in front of 'believers' but the fact that I was brought up without religion in my life has probably made Amy's death more difficult. I don't have the comfort of thinking Amy is in a better place now and making up for lost time with dearly departed relatives. She went from being totally healthy on a Friday night, to complaining that a mild cough had impacted on her parkrun time on the Saturday, to having a 'bit of a cold' on the Sunday and then being pronounced dead eleven days later. The wonderful memories of our life together which we both cherished so dearly now solely belong to me.

I have stopped watching television altogether. Amy and I had the whole Sky package and Netflix so we would always meet up on the sofa at some point in the evening to watch something together. Pretty often, because of Amy's strict fitness regime, it could be after nine before the television went on, but every night, even if it was only for an hour, we would watch something together. There were some pro-grammes that would tempt Hunter out from the confines of his bedroom, like Breaking Bad and The Good Place, but most evenings it was just the two of us. Since she died, each time I put the television on, I keep expecting Amy to come out of the kitchen with two cups of tea or two glasses of red wine so it just became too upsetting to watch. At the moment, I stick to listening to the radio.

Hunter and I have stopped falling out with each other now. This is more down to a mutual policy of avoiding each other rather than a bonding of any sort. I tend to cook him his tea, wash and iron his clothes, sort his finances out and drive him everywhere he needs to go (other than school which he has to walk up to) but we have very few proper conversations. As well as avoiding each other, we have also avoided talking about Amy. I really hope he talks to Dominic about her but it's just too painful a conversation for us to have. Once I feel our wounds have a scab, I may start talking to Hunter about her once more.

Dominic's sister, Alice, has helped me ensure the dark clouds of death are not ever present. I look forward to our train jour-neys together each morning as it just feels comforting to have some sort of female company in my life. She's very young so I can't talk to her about stuff that would only interest my gen-eration and I try to show some interest when she talks about modern day teenage stuff but despite us sometimes being on completely different wavelengths we tend to find a lot of common ground. Having said that, I have to pretend not to look shocked when she talks about her nipple piercings, her bisexuality and the little heart shaped tattoo she wants on her left groin. I try my best but I know that sometimes I make my-self look like a ridiculous old buffoon.

I dealt with the knowledge of her bisexuality particularly badly. Alice accused me of reacting like a teenage boy and I am ashamed to admit that she was correct. I am not trying to justify my reaction but I am a pretty sheltered middle aged man, I have never had any gay friends of either sex and anyone at work who turned out to be homosexual has only ever been a fairly distant colleague or passing acquaintance. When Alice revealed she was gay, I became flustered and just spouted some crappy generalisations I subsequently felt pretty ashamed about. For about a week, I returned to having nights of disjointed sleep as I felt I had destroyed a fledgling friendship that was becoming increasingly important to my mental health. Alice insisted the damage wasn't that severe but I had my doubts that our friendship would properly recover. Luckily, I underestimated Alice. She is the forgiving sort and we were able to move on without her constantly reminding me of my mistakes. When she had half-terms, study days or end of term breaks, I found the train journeys to work to be a painful process. I realised Alice had become the medicine I needed to get through the day.

One Thursday morning in December, Alice literally bounced on to the train with a spring in her step that would have made Tigger envious.

"Good Morning!" I said with a smile, "Someone looks happy with themselves this morning!"

"Ecstatic, Mr Cassidy, ECS-TAT-IC!"

My smile spread across my face. Alice was a bubbly, happy individual anyway but it was great to see her on a real high. I was intrigued to know why.

"Pray tell, young Alice! Why are you blessed with these feelings of ecstasy?"

"Potentially, and it is only potential at this stage so I hope I'm not cursing it, but potentially there's a chance my days of celibacy may be over!"

"And who could your potential companion be?"

"Her name is Erika Magnusson. I play football with her."

"Does she have a grandfather called Magnus?"

"I have no idea. I doubt it. No-one called Magnusson would call their child Magnus."

A gag from the eighties and nineties was wasted on Alice but that's what amused me most.

"Magnus Magnusson presented Mastermind about thirty years ago," I explained.

"Oh, of course he did, I should have known that," Alice replied sarcastically.

"Sorry, I was just being daft. Tell me more about Erika."

"She's a stunner, Jay. I'm not as shallow as you so I try not to judge people just on looks alone but Erika is breathtakingly pretty. She's like a tall, blonde, Scandinavian goddess. We were 'Whats Apping' each other last night for hours and we're going to go the cinema on Saturday."

I ignored the dig about judging people solely on their looks. I was aware I had brought such comments upon myself.

"What are you going to see?"

"I'm not sure yet. I don't really care to be honest. I'm just really giddy about going which isn't like me."

"That's great. Eighteen year olds should be giddy about relationships."

I wasn't sure if that sounded patronising, it wasn't meant to be. Alice didn't appear to take offence. I think she was too excited. She was speaking very quickly and taking very few breaths between sentences.

"She's the best player in our football team. She scored four yesterday. You should see her move, Jay, she's lightning quick. I play in midfield and I know if I can thread the ball through for her to run onto, more often than not she'll get there before the centre back. She's really composed in front of goal too. Oh, I haven't told you, I got sent off yesterday."

"Alice! What for?"

"Violent conduct."

"You did not!"

"I pinned down a girl I used to go to school with, Katie Kelper and made her slap herself in the face a few times."

"I wasn't aware you had such aggressive tendencies."

"She had it coming, Jay. She used to pick on me at school."

"Still, you should have left your revenge until after the game."

"I did leave it until after the game! I wouldn't shake her hand, we called each other names, I pounced on her, there was a twenty two woman brawl and then I got sent off. I don't regret doing it, I just regret the timing – it should have been two years ago."

"Can't turn back time now," I said, despite desperately wishing during every second of every day that we could.

CHAPTER FIFTEEN

<u>**ALICE**</u>

Erika and I went to see a special one-off showing of 'A Star Is Born' at the Vue cinema at Middlebrook. It's a top quality film, Bradley Cooper was excellent as the ageing rock star and Lady Gaga was amazing as the emerging new star. Halfway through, I felt Erika's hand reaching over to interlink her fingers into mine. We kept them clasped like that for the remainder of the film.

Once the film had finished, we went for a drink at a bar called Missoula. It's just over the road from Bolton Wanderers ground. At that stage, I still hadn't spoken to her all that much other than after the Runshaw College footy match and via several hundred WhatsApp messages. I was still a little nervous that she might not like me once she got to know me. I wasn't nervous at all that I might not like her. I can't help but be candid, I have that design flaw built into my DNA (I take after my mother) so after a couple of drinks I couldn't help blurting out about my recurring Jennifer Carpenter dream.

"I'm going to have to watch Dexter now to see what I'm up against!" Erika said with a giggle.

I noticed that there was something particularly attractive about Erika's teeth, I can't really explain what. I suppose it's because they're quite small and delicate. They soften her features somehow.

 "She's not all that pretty," I said attempting to explain my feelings of lust for Jennifer Carpenter, "but there's just something about her that does strange things to me and sends me a little bit wild. Does that make sense or does it just make me sound really weird?"

We smiled at each other. It was a 'I'm so happy to be here' excited exchange of smiles.

"No, I get it. I first knew I was a lesbian when I used to feel all flush watching Jessica Ennis do the pentathlon, or is it the heptathlon, doesn't matter, anyway she just made me wet and I sort of felt ashamed about it at first and then eventually I learnt to own it. It's Holly Willoughby these days."

"Wow, you and Holly would make a gorgeous couple! I don't think I could compete with her."

"Don't be daft, Alice, you could compete with anyone. You genuinely don't know how stunning you are, do you?"

We were sitting at stools at a high table and I felt Erika's hand come across to grab mine under the table. I could feel myself flushing with excitement and nervous anticipation. She was so lovely. I started to wonder how long it would be before I kissed her and realistically what sort of timeframe it would be before we slept together. I didn't want to rush things but none of my previous partners had been as sexy as her and just imagining me getting it on with her was sending my heart racing. I was desperate not to screw this up.

"Can I be honest with you about something?" Erika asked, her face looking more serious than it had done all evening. She pulled her stool closer to the table as she said this so I could feel her breath on my lips.

"Of course you can," I replied, being careful not to drool out the sides of my mouth because she was that bloody gorgeous.

"It scares me a little that you're bi."

"In what way?"

"OK, on a simple level, there's the dual threat thing. If I go over to the bar and you see me getting chatted up by a man, you could dismiss it because you know men aren't my thing. With you, potentially you could feel an attraction."

"Potentially I could but that's just not me. I may be attracted to both sexes but I believe in mahogany."

"Mahogany? Do you mean monogamy?"

I could see Erika was trying to stifle a laugh.

"Don't laugh at me!"

"I'm sorry. It was funny!"

"It was stupid. I'm embarrassed now."

Erika squeezed my hand tighter.

"Go on. Look, I'm deadly serious. You believe in monogamy."

"And mahogany! It's an underrated wood. Seriously though, I've been out with half a dozen people and every time, whether it's been a boy or a girl, I've been faithful. I can't see outside that relationship when I'm in a relationship."

"I just think though, over time, from my limited knowledge, bi girls end up playing it straight. I don't necessarily mean forever, often it doesn't work out and they end up later in life going back to females but when it comes to the whole marriage and kids thing, it's a lot less complex being with a man."

I was trying to be cool about this but the very fact that Erika was thinking long-term on our first date was pretty epic.

"Erika, we're eighteen, we're on our first date and I've never been out with anyone longer than six months before so I have no idea where this is going or how long it will last but I have never, and I mean never, been so excited to be on a date before, nor have I ever been so turned on by the person I'm sat with. If you are asking me now, on our first date, if I want this to work out, I can tell you, hand on heart, I desperately do. Will that do for now?"

Erika smiled broadly. I could see there was love in her eyes.

"Do you think there's a quiet corner we can go right now so I can kiss you?" she said softly.

"I'm sure we can find one," I said without hesitation.

I stood up, took her hand and led her in search of that quiet corner.

CHAPTER SIXEEN

JAY – Puerto Pollensa - 2013

I was on the hotel balcony with a glass of red wine in my hand watching the boats bobbing in the water and admiring the stars in the cloudless, early evening sky. We had been away from home for four days and as a consequence my face and body were looking decidedly tomato coloured.

The sliding doors were pulled open and Amy emerged with a glass of red wine. She was wearing a white summer's dress. She was brown, toned and healthy.

"He's flat out," Amy revealed, more in a whisper than a voice.

"You don't need to speak quietly, hun, the poor lad's shattered. He's been in and out of that pool more times than a sea lion at Marineland!"

Amy beamed a broad white smile at me as she sat down next to me at the balcony table.

"He's loving it here though, Jay. He's made a couple of little friends and he's running around everywhere having the time of his life. I wish we were staying for two weeks."

"So do I, honey, maybe next year."

"Oh, two weeks would just be magical. It takes a couple of days to unwind so by the time you're settling into it, you're starting to think about going home. Two weeks would be so different."

"OK, well if we're going to do it, we need to start saving as soon as we get back. We both need to put away a bit of money each month as soon as we get paid. You can't just rely on me like this year. You'll need to cut down on the fancy lunches out with the girls and maybe even drop one or two of the Spa days."

Amy didn't look over enamoured with that suggestion but she was prepared to run with it.

"If it means coming away for two weeks, Jay, I'm prepared to make sacrifices. Hunter will grow up so quickly and in no time at all he won't want to come away with us anymore."

I polished off what was left of the red wine in my glass and filled it up again from the bottle on the table.

"But we'll have forty years or so of it just being the two of us going away together which will be wonderful too."

"Oh I know that, but these are special times and we need to create memories, both for Hunter and for us, that will last forever."

"Yeh, I know. Anyway, you never know, there's still a chance Hunter may have a little brother or sister in the next few years."

Amy scrunched up her face so her bronzed nose wrinkled.

"Realistically that's not looking likely, Jay. Unfortunately nothing seems to be happening on that score."

"We could always go and see someone, Amy. See if a bit of scientific assistance might do the trick."

Amy shook her head.

"No, I really don't want to go down that route. I don't want to feel under pressure to produce a child. If it's meant to be it will happen. If it's not meant to be then it won't."

"No-one would be putting you under any pressure. It would just be bringing in the help of experts to identify the problem and to see if there is a way of working around it."

"I know but I'd rather just leave it and see what happens. There's such a gap now anyway. Even if we conceived this week, Hunter would be eight by the time the baby was born. They would never be best pals."

"Not initially but they might become best pals by the time they are adults. Anyway, if your indirect message is that we just need to have lots of sex and see what fate has in store for us then I'm completely on board with that!"

"Thought you might be. I'm sure it won't be too much of a hardship for you."

"It'll be a struggle but I'm willing to make that sacrifice because I love you so much."

I reached across to kiss her.

"I can't believe Hunter's seven already," Amy said reflectively, "it only seems like a couple of years ago that we were bringing him home from Preston, when he was two days old. We were both crapping ourselves about whether we were capable of caring for such a tiny little thing. Do you remember?"

"Of course, we didn't have a proper night's sleep for two years!"

"But we were so proud of the little bundle we'd created. We were so knackered all the time but we were just overflowing with pride. It was a special time."

"Every time is a special time. It's a special time now watching him running around with his little Scottish and Irish pals."

"I know. It just scares me how quickly time goes. It doesn't seem long ago that we were at school going to discos and drinking Hooch and White Lightning down at the park. Now, in the blink of an eye, we are in our thirties. Proper adults, Jay! You and I are proper adults!"

"You hate being thirty, don't you?" I said playfully.

"I am enjoying this time in my life. I just don't like the sound of the word 'thirty'. It sounds so old."

"We'll be pensioners before we know it!"

"Don't say that! It scares me enough being thirty."

Holidays seem to make you reflect on things that perhaps you wouldn't normally discuss. The conversation we had on the balcony that night has always stayed with me and always will.

"Amy, I know this is a really selfish thing to say but when we are old, I hope I die first. I don't think there would be any joy in a life without you."

"Don't talk about dying, Jay. That's such a miserable thing to talk about when we're on holiday."

"No, it isn't. It's going to happen one day. As I say, I just hope you outlive me. I adore that little lad asleep in there but as he grows up he'll become independent and eventually he won't need us anymore. He won't be asking us to watch him jump into the pool when he's twenty five. We'll always need each other though. I'm thirty two now and for the last half of my life we've been together. My main purpose during that time has been to make you happy and for the rest of my life that will continue to be my main objective. If I outlive you, and God I hope I don't, there would be no purpose to my life. What fun would there be in my life if our fairy tale was broken?"

"That's so sweet, a bit sad but still really sweet."

Amy came across to me and gave me a big hug and then kissed me.

"It's 100% true."

"Do you think if I died first you'd marry someone else?"

"I doubt it very much. I really don't think I'd be capable of loving anyone else."

"You love Hunter."

"That's different, as well you know! Romantically you're the one for me. You've always been the one for me and will always be the one. I'd want you to be happy though, Amy, so if I did die first, then do not mope around after me. I'd be dead, I don't believe for a second that I'll be looking down at you from a fluffy cloud so just crack on and get together with some caring old bloke who makes you smile."

"You're my soul mate, Jay. I wouldn't look for another one. I'm not as generous as you though, I couldn't bear the thought of you being with anyone else if I died first."

"I can't see that happening. Firstly, look at you and look at me. You work very hard to keep in shape and I'm like an ant stuck in the middle of a marshmallow. Secondly, you have longevity in your genes. Your Grandma is still going and she's in her nineties and you had two grandfathers who lived well into their eighties. Seventy five is a good knock in our family."

"That doesn't necessarily mean I'll outlive you though."

"The odds are stacked in your favour."

"Anyway, all I'm saying is that I'm not as convinced as you that when we die, that's it, 'finito'. I'm not saying there's a heaven and a hell or even a Christian God, I'm just saying there just might be something. We might live on in spirit."

"We won't."

"Jay, that's your opinion. Shut up and listen."

"OK."

"I'm just saying if there's a slight chance we might live on in spirit and I die first, it would completely destroy me to see you with someone else. Please don't do that to me."

"I never would."

"Promise me. Promise me that if I die first, you will never get together with anyone else."

"I promise."

"Cross your heart and hope to die?"

I laughed.

"Amy, an atheist crossing his heart and hoping to die doesn't mean much!"

"It means something to me. Do it!"

"I cross my heart and hope to die."

"Thank you! I promise I won't haunt you as long as you stick to your promise."

CHAPTER
SEVENTEEN

<u>**ALICE**</u>

"Did he win?"

"Lost 4-3. Injury time winner too. Lucky it was a good game because it was bloody freezing!"

"Bugger. Did he play well?"

"He's no Lionel Messi but he gets stuck in and he still looks like he loves every minute of it."

"Well, that's the most important thing."

"It feels strange seeing you somewhere the scenery doesn't change outside the window."

It was a Saturday afternoon. A couple of weeks back I had asked Jay if we could exchange phone numbers. I made some excuse but the main reason was that Christmas was coming and it was going to be his first one without Amy. I just wanted to text him from time to time to make sure he was coping. Most of the time he seemed OK, but there were mornings on the train that he appeared distant and struggling to adjust to life as a widower.

I hadn't arranged to meet him that Saturday afternoon for purely unselfish reasons though. I had a different agenda. I was after relationship advice. College had broken up so I hadn't seen him on the train for a week and wouldn't be seeing him for several more. I texted him on the Thursday asking if we could meet for a coffee on Saturday morning but Hunter had a football match so Jay suggested early afternoon. We agreed a two o'clock meet.

I loved Costa in Buckshaw. It felt a very grown up place to meet. I ordered a Latte, Jay ordered an Americano with milk.

"So have you been missing me on your journey to work?" I asked, genuinely hoping he had.

"Very much so," Jay responded without a tone to his voice, but I took his response to be genuine rather than sarcastic.

"Good. I don't want you to be making any new friends in my absence," I said, teasing a little but he didn't smile, his face just looked sad.

"That sounds like something that Amy would have said."

"Oh, I'm sorry. I was only kidding."

"It's fine, I know you were. I think it's the time of year. Everything seems to be reminding me of Amy at the moment. She was a big fan of Christmas, unlike me. I always thought it was an expensive way of celebrating the birth of an imaginary saviour."

"Happy Christmas to you too. I see now why you didn't order the Festive Latte!"

Jay took a sip from his Americano.

"Fuck me! That's hot!" he said before adding more milk and blowing it.

"Right young lady," he continued, "you were being very mysterious in your text. To what do I owe this honour? I'm presuming, given you have a hot, blonde eighteen year old lover that it's not for the pleasure of seeing my puffy, wrinkled middle aged face."

I reached out and put my hand on top of his.

"I do miss that craggy old face."

"Thank you! You've made an old man very happy."

"That's obviously not the reason I wanted to meet up with you though."

"You've won the lottery and you want to go halves?"

"No, not that either."

"Shame."

"I needed some words of wisdom and I thought you would be the perfect person to provide them."

"Really? Have you forgotten my dungaree speech?"

"That was just a blip, Jay."

"I'm glad to know you see it that way. Words of wisdom, on what subject?"

"Love matters."

"OK, but don't forget I've never been an eighteen year old lesbian."

"You've been in love though."

"I have indeed."

It had been three weeks since I had started dating Erika. Things had been going well. No, that would be underplaying it, things had been going perfectly. Erika was perfect. As a friend, as a lover, looks wise and in every way imaginable she was perfect. The problem was that I was starting to worry that I was in too deep too early. I wanted to spend every second of every day with her but I didn't want to seem needy nor did I want to suffocate her.

"Just to be clear everything is going brilliantly with Erika."

"OK. What's the issue that's led you to buy me a coffee then?"

"I'm just worried I might love her too much."

"Is there such a thing?"

There was an element of inadvertent irony in Jay asking that question as sometimes I felt his problem was that he had loved Amy too much.

"I think so. I've read all that stuff about the one who cares the least having all the power."

"So do you think you care the most?"

"I don't know, probably. I can't imagine Erika, being Erika, could possibly be as head over heels about me as I am about her."

"Have a bit of confidence in yourself, Alice, you're a catch."

"You haven't met Erika yet."

"I've seen photos of her on your phone. She's beautiful, Alice, but that doesn't mean you're less beautiful."

"Thank you!"

"Do you feel she exploits the fact that you care so much?"

"Not at all."

"So the problem is?"

"I try not to show it but there are times when I find myself being totally unreasonable. Tonight, for example, I'm working at 'The Talbot' but Erika is going out with some friends in Bolton. I'm panicking that she might get drunk and end up kissing someone else. I'm trying not to be moody and sulky when she mentions going out, but sometimes I can't help myself."

"So you don't trust her?"

I had picked up on the fact that Jay was starting a lot of his sentences with 'so' like he was some sort of psychologist but I let it pass without mention.

"I just think she might meet someone more on her level."

"STOP THAT RIGHT NOW!"

Jay shouted this or at least spoke it firmly and loudly enough for other coffee drinkers to turn around.

"What?"
"Putting yourself down. You'll get to my age and you'll look back at photos of yourself at eighteen and appreciate how gorgeous you were. You'll think 'Why didn't I appreciate how pretty I was, when I was eighteen?'"

"I don't think I'm ugly, I just think my whole package, looks, personality, boobage, doesn't quite cut it relative to Erika."

"Boobage!"

"I have no tits, Jay. It's pissing me off a bit at the moment. When I get naked I'd like to have something there to be admired but I'm just straight down."

"Amy had no tits. It didn't stop me thinking she was the most wonderful person to have ever walked this earth."

"OK, that's good to know."

"And don't forget I was properly punching above my weight. Look at me, I'm a bit of a chubster, I have a reasonable job but I'm not exactly Richard Branson, women's heads definitely don't turn when I walk into a room but Amy never stopped loving me for twenty four years."

"So what was your secret?"
"There is no secret. You just do all you can to make each other happy. If Erika likes going out with her friends from time to time, let her go without kicking up a fuss. If someone starts chatting her up, let them chat her up, things are more likely to last if you let her fly rather than try to clip her wings."

"OK, thanks Jay. I'll take that on board. There's something else I'm stressing about though."

"As well as your flat chest and your possessiveness?"

"Yep, as well as them."

"Go on then, spit it out."

"I want to tell Mum, Dad and John about Erika but I'm scared it'll break their hearts."

I grimaced a little as I said this. It was a scenario I had been fretting about for a long time.

"OK. They may know more than they're letting on."

"Believe me, Jay, they know nothing."

"So what makes you think it would break their hearts?"

"Every time I see Dad these days he mentions how proud he'll be when he walks me down the aisle and when he becomes a grandfather."

"And?"

"He means when I marry a man and when I conceive in the old fashioned 'sperm and ovum' manner."

"Has he actually said this?"

"Why would he? It's just presumed that I'm straight so he wouldn't need to."

"If I was your father, I would want you to marry someone you love, who I know will make you happy. I wouldn't be specifying that person must be in possession of a penis."

"You've changed since your 'dungaree days', Jay Cassidy!"

"I actually haven't. I've always thought that finding things or people in life that make you happy is the key to everything. You just have to hope if you meet the right person they feel the same and that they stay alive."

"So you're now saying sexuality doesn't matter? So if Hunter came home tonight and said he wanted to marry Dominic, you'd be fine with that?"

"Not now because they are fifteen and sixteen years old but if they were twenty five and twenty six that would totally be their decision."

"And you'd be cool with it?"

"Coolish."

"Which means what?"

"That I probably wouldn't be all that cool but I'd accept it."

"So why not cool?"

"You know this already, Alice. I'm old fashioned. I would worry about how society or at least people of my generation, the generation above me and the bigoted few from your generation would treat him."

"Not how it would reflect on you?"

"What do you mean?"

"Not how it would reflect on you having a gay son?"

"Absolutely not. The only person I have ever wanted to be popular with was Amy."

"Not Hunter?"

"I'm his father. It's not my job to be popular with him. There are some things I need to do which make me very unpopular with Hunter but primarily I am here to teach him right from wrong, despite how unpopular that may make me."

"Fair enough, there's probably too many parents who want to be popular with their kids these days, want to be their mates so let them get their own way all the time and end up wondering why their kids are complete brats."

"My point exactly."

"If you were me, who would you speak to first then, my Mum or Dad?"

"I don't know your Mum or Dad, Alice, so I can't make that decision for you."

"Oh, I don't know what to do. What if things don't work out with Erika, we split up in three months' time and every other partner I have from then on is a guy? I wouldn't need to upset them then."

"Run with that then as long as you don't mind keeping things from them now."

"I'm on cloud nine at the moment though, Jay. I don't want Erika to be treated like my dirty little secret. Erika's Mum knows she's gay and has no problem with me stopping over at their house."

"From what you've told me about your Mum, I wouldn't think she would be quite so liberal, certainly not at first anyway."

"No. John and Dad will probably be upset, Mum will probably be angry."

"Surely she wouldn't be angry."

"She gets very angry about everything. It's her 'go to' emotion. I don't really think you are helping here, Jay."

"I don't really think I can help. I can offer relationship advice because I was in a relationship for over twenty years but I can't offer advice on when it's the right time to tell your parents you have a girlfriend. I have no experience in that at all and as I don't know any of the people involved, I would just be guessing. You wouldn't go to Paris to learn how to speak Spanish."

"I might just hold fire until after Christmas."

"Completely up to you, at some point though, just be honest with them. If you're honest and you've done nothing wrong, if there's a problem, then it's not yours."

"OK, but if Mum kicks me out, don't be angry with me if I come knocking on your door."

"You don't know where I live!"

"Of course I do! I've picked Dominic up from there."

"Oh shit, yeh! I'll have to move!"

CHAPTER EIGHTEEN

<u>JAY</u>

The week before Christmas, the weather turned particularly cold. I had been dreading Christmas anyway as I was scared about how many memories that I had tried to leave in deep water which would now rise back to the surface. I woke up one night, about three in the morning and it was frosty. It really upset me and I found myself crying. It was random and illogical but Amy had been buried rather than cremated, a favour by the Vicar to her Christian mother and I just imagined that she must be very cold. I couldn't shake off that feeling of guilt that she must be laying there, six feet under, feeling desperately cold.

CHAPTER NINETEEN

<u>JAY</u>

Christmas Day was tough. It probably wasn't as tough as I had imagined it was going to be but it was still a day that I was glad to see the back of. Both my parents and Amy's parents invited Hunter and me over for our Christmas dinner, but not wanting to upset either couple, I turned down each invitation. As a compromise, we went over to Coppull to see my parents late on Christmas morning and then went to Amy's parents early in the evening. We didn't stay long at Amy's Mum and Dad's as Hunter wanted me to drop him off at Dominic's.

For Christmas dinner, I just said to Hunter he could have whatever he wanted. I half thought he'd opt for a pepperoni pizza with chips but he said that Mum would have wanted us to have a traditional Christmas dinner so he felt that's what we should have. It was the first time we had talked about Amy together for quite some time but, having done so it opened the door for us to discuss her regularly over the festive period.

I would be lying if I said my Roast Turkey dinner was as top quality as Amy's had been but I felt I made a decent stab at it and Hunter seemed both a little shocked and impressed. We had Christmas pudding too and after having crackers and cheese followed by Christmas cake at George and Jackie's (Amy's parents), I apparently fell asleep on the sofa and, to Hunter's great embarrassment, started snoring. He nudged me back to my senses and whispered, 'Dad, you're making a fool of yourself.' Suitably chastised, I made sure I stayed awake for the rest of our visit.

I probably went over the top in my apologies to George and Jackie but did feel awful about falling asleep at their house. They had three children, but having lost Amy, they only had Tom who had emigrated to Adelaide with work about twelve years previously and Sophie who lived in Kent. Sophie and her husband, Robert, had a four year old son, Jamie and a two year old daughter, Jess so were staying at home over the festive period. George and Jackie were travelling down to see them on the 28th and were staying until the New Year. We had been their only Christmas Day visitors and I had only gone and fallen asleep. I am sure if I had been able to snatch more than three or four hours every night it would never have happened but it was poor form all the same.

I arrived home just after nine. I dropped Hunter around at Dominic's and half thought about getting out the car myself to see if Alice was in but talked myself out of it. It would have looked strange. I had left my phone on charge in the kitchen, I had deliberately not taken it out with me and noticed a WhatsApp message from Alice,

'Merry Christmas, Jay! Hope you got through today OK.'

I noticed she was on-line so text back.

'Merry Christmas to you too! Hope you've had a brilliant one. Hunter seems like he's had a reasonable one which is the main thing.'

'He's laughing away with Dominic here over some crap on YouTube but at least they're happy.'

'He wasn't quite so happy when I fell asleep at his grandparents earlier! He was a little bit ashamed especially when I apparently started snoring.'

'Oh dear. I'm not surprised you fell asleep though. You seem to look constantly knackered. Probably did you good.'

'Not sure Amy's Mum and Dad will have seen it that way. They're very nice though so maybe they did. Certainly more sympathetic than Hunter.'

'Been a few dramas here too.'

'Really? How come?'

'The secret's out.'

'Your secret?'

'Yup.'

'Wow! Major development. Who knows? Mum and John or your Dad?'

'Mum and John.'

'How did she take it?'

'Angrily.'

'She'll calm down.'

'She was angry that I hadn't told her four years ago! Apparently Dominic told her.'

'The grass! Had he found out at school?'

'No, he had apparently walked into my room the morning when Mum and John were away to find me naked alongside Becky Palmer. He had apparently blabbed about it to Mum and John as soon as they arrived home. So Mum wasn't properly angry today, it was like a pretend angry mixed in with a little bit of pissed off. Apparently John and Dad have both known for ages too, they were just leaving it until I brought it up.'

'How did it come to a head today then?'

'Dominic, who had a few cans of Stella, started giggling when John asked me if I had received any presents from my boyfriend? Apparently the lot of them have been taking the piss out of me behind my back for ages. Sort of relieved I don't have to stress about it anymore though.'

'See, I told you they might already know.'

'I forgot you know everything!'

'Don't forget again.'

'I'll be sure not too. Love you, Jay. xx'

Alice quickly followed this with another message.

'Not in a weird Sugar Daddy type way but in a loving Uncle type way.'

'I know. No need for explanations. I love you too, sweetheart.'

I felt awkward about putting 'sweetheart' so quickly sent a follow up message too.

'Do I need to say I meant that in a non-Sugar Daddy type way?'

'No. x'

'Good. x'

'Think Hunter is going to phone you in a minute and ask if he can stay overnight.'

'That's fine. It'll allow me to have a drink if I don't have to come and get him. Enjoy the rest of your evening.'

I was slightly disappointed though. It would have given me a lift to briefly see Alice. It had been a tough day and I felt I needed the hug that I knew she would have given me if I had popped in to collect Hunter. I told myself to grow a pair and went off to get a can of Indian Pale Ale from the beer fridge.

CHAPTER TWENTY

<u>**ALICE**</u>

My relationship with Erika went from being fresh and exciting to being wonderful, loving and comfortable (only in a good way) over the course of the next few months. As the grey mornings and late dark afternoons of winter were replaced by Spring's new dawn, I remained infatuated by my lover but with the self-awareness to show some discretion. From the start, I appreciated her beauty but I grew to value her intelligence too. She had an obsessional interest in music and films so I grew to love some of the things she loved. Film wise, I became aware of stuff like the Tarantino movies, plus the likes of 'Easy Rider', 'Apocalypse Now' and 'Shawshank Redemption', which everyone at school had always mentioned as a classic but I had never seen. Erika also loved old American classic comedy too like 'The Three Stooges', 'Abbott & Costello' (especially the 'Who's On First' sketch which made her cry laughing) and 'Laurel & Hardy'. I had always dismissed this type of comedy as something old people watched but it turns out it's hilarious. Musically, Erika was a Spotify addict but she had eclectic taste and liked the fact that Spotify suggested other artists for you to try out. She particularly loved a lot of singer songwriter stuff like Fiona Apple, Julia Stone (who she had a bit of a thing for which I managed to joke about rather than get jealous), Ani DiFranco, Damien Rice, Tanya Donnelly and Tori Amos. She was also into some dark eighties and nineties music like 'The Smiths' and 'Depeche Mode' and one of their songs, a passionate, moody track called 'One Caress' became our anthem.

As my relationship with Erika intensified, my platonic relationship with Jay went to new levels too. I guess it's weird having a forty year old man as your closest platonic friend but weirdly we just seemed to relate to each other. Over time, rather than just meeting up for a twenty minute train journey, Monday to Friday, we started having the occasional weekend coffee together or once a month or so, we would meet for lunch in the café at Cuerden Valley.

The thing about Jay that I couldn't relate to, however, was his stubbornness. He was understandably lonely and unhappy after Amy's death but he would do very little socially and every time I suggested anything, he would turn the idea down flat. I suggested he join a local 'Couch to 5k' running group which would not only have been a benefit for him socially but it would also have been useful in burning off some of those extra pounds he was always complaining about. His excuse was that he didn't have any shorts he could squeeze into so I told him to order some but he then just said 'wobbling around Chorley with a group of fellow fatties is not my idea of fun'. The thing was, nothing was his idea of fun. He didn't want to have fun. He just wanted to catch up with me from time to time to hear about my fun and then wallow in his own devastating loss. I don't mean to sound harsh or unsympathetic, an absolutely awful thing happened to him but at some point you have to try to move on as best as you can but Jay either would not or could not.

I think the main issue was a promise Jay had made to Amy years and years before she died. Amy apparently once got Jay to promise that if she died first that he would never get together with anyone else. I tried to talk him around over a post-lunch coffee at Cuerden Valley once but it was hard going.

"So you're going to be alone for the rest of your life because of some crazy promise you made to Amy?"

"Well, not just because of that. I'm happy to stay single but I'm just explaining to you that I know it was what Amy wanted too."

"Was it though?"

"What do you mean?"

"Well, it might have been what she wanted when she was a thirty year old who had had a few glasses of sangria too many on holiday in Majorca but it might not have been what she wanted when she died."

Jay shook his head.

"No, if she had changed her mind she would have told me."

"She might have forgotten that she said it."

"Alice, I can remember the evening clearly, Amy had had a couple of glasses of wine, she wasn't falling over drunk. Anyway, all this is immaterial, I can honestly say I don't want to meet anyone else."

"Not yet."

"Not ever."

"Jay, I just think if Amy had known she was going to die at thirty eight and that you would have been a widower at 40, she would never have said that. If she loved you as much as you say she did, she would have wanted you to be happy."

"Happiness isn't all about being in a relationship. I know it is for you at the moment because everything is all hearts and flowers but I can be happy on my own."

"But there might come a time that by having someone else in your life, it will make you happier."

"No, there won't."

"How do you know?"

"I just do. Drop this now, Alice. I know you think you are doing me a favour by trying to give me hope for the future but it's not the sort of hope I want so let's not discuss it."

CHAPTER TWENTY ONE

<u>JAY</u>

Hunter was in a talkative mood one Friday evening. We were sat at our dining room table having steak, chips and peas, discussing a number of things both serious and trivial. These included GCSEs (not confident), whether he wanted to go to College (probably not), football (Everton's continued lack of success) and his plans for the weekend.

"What have you got planned for tomorrow?" I asked.

I liked the fact that for Hunter and Dominic the weekend was still the most exciting rather than the most lonely time of the week.

"Dominic and I are going to get our bikes out. We're going to ride up to Adlington and then stop at Fredericks for an ice cream on the way back."

"Good stuff. Is it not still a bit cold for ice cream?"

Hunter gave me that look he gave me when he thought I was the world's dumbest father.

"I don't get it when people say that. Ice cream is always cold whether you have it in January or July. We often have ice cream for dessert in the winter."

"True."

"What about you, Dad, what are you doing?"

"Tomorrow?"

"Yes."

"Well I'm going to do some washing and ironing in the morning, I need to wash the bed sheets too at some point and then maybe in the afternoon I'll get some rubber gloves on and see if I can clean our disgusting toilets."

"The British Tourist Board should film you in action. I reckon it'd put a few of these immigrants off jumping into the back of lorries."

"Probably not the most politically correct thing you've ever said that, Hunter."

Hunter just shrugged.

"I don't care."

"Oh, before I clean the toilets I'm meeting Alice for a coffee."

"What is it with the pair of you? You're not trying to get into her knickers are you?"

"She's eighteen, Hunter."

"That's legal, isn't it or is it when you're as old as you? Doesn't matter it's paedo-esque. Anyway, if that's your plan, I'd scrap it and move on to Plan B because she's a lezzer so she's not into cock."

"'She's a lezzer, so she's not into cock," I repeated, "You have such a charming way of saying things, Hunter!"

"It's true though. Bet you a tenner she's a lezzer."

"I'm not betting and you're only half right, she's bisexual."

"Being bi is weirder than being lez – not as weird as being gender neutral but a solid second place."

"Hang on! Do they not teach you about political correctness at school?"

"All the time. Sometimes if you hear too much of something you stop listening."

"Well you shouldn't."

"Well I do. Anyway, Alice is weird. You should keep your distance from bunny boilers like her."

"She's a friend, Hunter, nothing more. I will never and I repeat never be interested in Alice Moorcroft in any capacity other than a friendly one."

"Good. Having Dominic's lesbian teenage sister as my stepmother would be like something that used to be on Jeremy Kyle."

"It will never happen."

"It's starting to worry me that you're protesting a little too much, Dad."

"I'm not protesting at all, Hunter, I'm just telling you how it is."

"OK, I believe you, don't go on about it! Can you give me ten quid for an ice cream?"

"No, I'll give you three quid."

"Pov. That won't be enough. Fredericks' ice creams are a rip off."

"Why are you buying one then?"

"Because I'm not paying."

"I wasn't born yesterday, Hunter, they aren't a tenner."

"I need to buy one for Dominic too."

"Why?"

"His Mum and John won't give him the money."

"Too sensible."

"Too tight. Come on, Dad, cough up."

"No, I'll give you three quid and if you need any more you can use the money you get from your grandparents."

"I'm not breaking into that! I'll need that for driving lessons!"

"I thought you said you wanted me to pay for driving lessons?"

"A car then."

"I thought you said you wanted me to pay for a car?"

"Oh fuck off, Dad! Just give me the three fucking quid and I'll just get a povvy ice cream!"

CHAPTER TWENTY TWO

JAY

It was April. It was a Friday night and it was pouring down. I had my Digital Radio switched on to BBC Radio Two listening to a one hour special about Woking's finest band, The Jam. I had never really been into The Jam as a kid, they were a bit before my time but I was surprised how many of their songs I knew. I decided I was going to start listening to them more. The programme had just finished and the ten o'clock news headlines had just begun when the doorbell rang. Apparently a lot of younger people don't have doorbells these days their visitors just phone them on their mobiles when they arrive. The only person who ever came to our door at ten o'clock at night was Dominic and I think he normally just rang Hunter to announce his arrival. I was puzzled.

"Is this Dom?" I shouted up the stairs.

Hunter didn't reply.

"Hunter, is this Dom?" I asked again but louder.

Still no reply, I ran halfway up the stairs as the doorbell rang a second time.

"Hunter!"

"What?"

"Is this Dom at the door?"

"No, he's on Fortnite with me."

"Could it be one of your other mates?"

"Just answer it and find out."

"It could be an axe murderer."

"Dad, you'd be happy if it was an axe murderer."

I made my way down the stairs. Both Hunter and Alice were now suggesting I was miserable. It felt a harsh judgement. I don't really know what they expected from me. Amy had died less than twelve months ago, I wasn't going to be walking around the place with a grin like a Cheshire cat as if I'd come up on the lottery. Hunter was miserable himself most of the time but he tended to ignore that fact.

I pulled the door open and Alice was standing there. She was drenched. Her hair was dripping wet, rain was running down the sides of her face and her clothes were soaked. She didn't say a word. She just looked at me forlornly.

"Bloody hell, Alice! Come in and don't move. I'll grab you a towel."

I ran upstairs to the airing cupboard. I deliberated for a little while over which towel to choose. Some were too small, others too hard and others had Disney characters on them from when Hunter was a kid. I eventually found a big, soft pink towel that Amy used to take to the Gym so ran down with that one. Alice was standing one step into the hallway, a big pool of water had gathered around her feet. She still didn't say anything. She looked as if she was in shock. I wondered whether she had taken something. Drugs were apparently rife these days. I then thought about drying her but thought I best not, if Hunter came out of his room and saw me drying Alice I'd never hear the last of it I passed Alice the towel and she started drying her legs.

"Dry you hair first! Has no-one ever taught you to dry from the top down?"

"No!" she said sullenly.

"Where have you walked from?"

"Buckshaw Parkway."

"It's lashing down, Alice!"

"I hadn't realised," she replied sarcastically but still maintaining that sulky tone.

"You should have phoned me. I would have come to pick you up."

"I knew you'd have had a bottle of wine."

I had had a bottle of wine. A bottle and a half, in fact – I definitely wouldn't have gone to pick her up.

"Well, I'd have paid for your taxi."

"I needed to clear my head, Jay."

"Why?"

"Me and Erika have had a row."

It probably wasn't the time to be correcting her Grammar. As I was telling myself to keep my mouth shut, the anticipated tears arrived.

"Alice, don't cry," I felt like I should give her a hug but I wasn't sure if it was my place to. I held back whilst I deliberated.

"We've had a row, Jay and now she's going to finish with me."

Before I had the opportunity to contemplate further, Alice grabbed me in a tight hug. I reciprocated with an awkward, half-hearted return hug with a little pat on her back thrown in for good measure. I let her hold me for about half a minute, counting the seconds as I did so, before I thought it was acceptable to pull away from her hug.

"Come on Alice," I said in a soft tone, "come through to the kitchen and you can have a hot drink or a glass of wine. Once you catch your breath you can tell me all about it."

Alice sort of shuffled slowly through to our kitchen with me behind her resisting a new urge to give her a push.

"Sit down, Alice. Now I know I don't yet know what's gone on but whatever it is, I'm sure it'll blow over. Every couple has the odd row from time to time. It's perfectly natural."

"This was a massive row though, Jay."

"It happens. Sometimes it's a good way to clear the air. What silly thing were you arguing about anyway?"

"You, Jay."

"What?"

"We were arguing about you."

CHAPTER TWENTY THREE

<u>ALICE</u>

I had heeded the advice Jay had given me about not being jealous or possessive. Just heeding some advice doesn't stop you getting the feelings but it does make you compartmentalise those feelings and I did my utmost not to let them show. It's a pity Erika hadn't received similar advice from someone dear to her.

I spent a lot of my non-lesson time at College with Erika. Once our relationship started, everyone at College became aware pretty quickly that we were an item and most people were fine with it. We occasionally had to deal with a group of lads trying to 'out macho' each other and they would start asking us to do stupid things or would ask stupid questions, like asking us to have a snog at the click of their fingers or asking us which one wears the 'strap-on' – all that sort of crap but to be fair the majority of it was good natured and sexually inquisitive rather than vindictive. I had my group of friends on my course and Erika had her mates in her year, but we were both welcomed into each other's groups. Erika never felt threatened by any of my College mates, male or female, so I genuinely thought she was joking when she started becoming all weird about Jay.

We saw each other after College one Friday and I was always intending to get the last train home from Erika's in Bolton back to Chorley. We had been lying on her bed listening to music for most of the evening. We had been affectionate, kissing and hugging and stuff but we didn't usually have full-on sex unless it was after her Mum and younger sister had gone to bed or they were both out. Probably because she was feeling horny, Erika was trying to persuade me to stay the night. Normally, I don't need asking twice, I'd say I was the more physically needy but for a combination of factors I wanted to go home.

"Please stay," Erika begged, kissing me hungrily and biting my bottom lip gently as she did so.

"I haven't got any of my stuff with me."

"The way I'm feeling we won't be needing pyjamas," Erika said moving her hand up my thigh before rubbing firmly up and down the middle of my jeans.

"Erika!" I said taking her hand off my jeans before I felt the urge to do it right there and then, "You know I love you but I need to go home tonight."

"But why Alice, why?" Erika asked, half-joking but half-exasperated too.

"For starters, I feel like I'm coming on and I've got no emergency tampons."

"I have."

"Yes, but you have those light flow ones because you barely trickle and I have super heavy flow ones because I gush like my whole insides are being dragged out. It's not very pretty and I don't want to bleed all over your sheets."

"I don't care."

"I know you don't but I do."

"I'll put them in the wash."

"You just want a shag before the red 'No Entry' signs go up."

"No, it's not just about the sex, Alice. It's a love thing. I just want to be with you."

"I want to be with you too, Erika, but tonight it makes sense to go home. Anyway, I've already arranged to meet Jay for lunch at Cuerden Valley Café tomorrow."

Erika's whole demeanour changed from sexual, affectionate and romantic to angry and annoyed.

"And there it is….," Erika said moving herself away from me on the bed.

"There's what? I don't understand."

"There's the real reason. JAY!"

"What about, Jay?"

"He's coming between us again."

"What do you mean Jay's coming between us again? Jay has never come between us. He's a forty year old man who has lost his wife."

"And he has you earmarked as her replacement."

I had never seen Erika like this before. I was expecting her to burst out laughing and then say she was only joking but it didn't happen.

"You obviously don't know how preposterous that is, Erika. He's not a middle aged man that looks like Brad Pitt. He's a middle aged man that looks like Johnny Vegas. You need to meet him, Erika. Once you do you'll see things very differently."

"I don't want to meet him. I already know I don't like him."

"That's just crazy! He's a lovely, lovely man."

"You told me that he was a miserable man."

"He is miserable. He has every right to be miserable. His wife died of Covid-19."

I moved towards Erika to give her a consoling hug but she moved away from me once more.

"Erika, come on, this is crazy!"

"I knew you being 'bi' would be a problem."

"Erika," I grabbed both her hands and held them in mine and looked right at her, "me being 'bi' has nothing to do with anything here. You need to stop this. I love you more than I've ever loved anyone but I need you to believe me when I say Jay is just a friend."

"That's the problem, Alice, I don't believe you. I've thought a lot about this. Eighteen year old girls don't have platonic friendships with forty year old men. Even if you don't want to shag him, which subconsciously I think you do, but even if you don't, I am pretty damn sure he will be wanting to shag you. You've seen how desperate the lads at College are for a shag. Jay will be no different, especially if he's gone twelve months without any action."

Erika had everything so wrong.

"You're making my friendship with Jay sound sordid and it's anything but."

"If you loved me, Alice, really loved me, you would stop seeing him."

I started gathering my things together.

"What are you doing?" Erika asked.

"I'm going. If you really loved me, Erika, you wouldn't start handing out ultimatums about who I can and who I can't be friends with."

"If you leave now, Alice, I'm telling you we're done."

"Don't try and blackmail me into staying."

"Just go then. Run into Jay's arms and tell him what a bitch I am."

"This is a ridiculous argument, Erika. I'm going to go. I love you but I need you to see sense and apologise."

"I won't be doing that."

"Then I guess we're done."

CHAPTER TWENTY FOUR

JAY

Over a coffee, Alice told me the whole story, in the finest of detail, about her argument with Erika. It all sounded very petty to me but they were young, insecure and emotionally immature so arguments like this were inevitable. Amy and I didn't row often when we were young but I can recall the odd major bust up. Looking back they were generally about something and nothing.

"So what's made you come around here then, in the pouring rain? You haven't just come to stick two fingers up at Erika, have you?"

"Partly, to be honest but also because I can't talk to Mum or John about an argument. Mum would just say,

'Don't be letting anyone boss you around. Dump her and move on!'

I came here because I knew you'd be more rational."

"Not necessarily. How do you know I'm not just going to say exactly the same thing as your Mum?"

I inadvertently made eye contact with Alice just as she was about to speak and noticed she had welled up a little again.

"Because you know the value of a good relationship."

She made a fair point. I still felt the need to add a touch of devilment to the conversation.

"That's true but you've just told me that Erika isn't exactly my 'Number One fan' so it might suit me to persuade you to dump her."

"You wouldn't do that."

Sometimes people with a nasty streak seem to get through life better because they don't care for anyone else as much as they care for themselves but sadly for my coping mechanisms I can't make myself that selfish. Not that it would have been fair to be unkind to Alice but I had to resist the temptation to make a retaliatory strike on Erika.

"You're right, I wouldn't."

"She's just built up this image of you as this good looking, charming man who is going to steal me away from her."

"As opposed to the funny looking, charmless man that I actually am?"

I raised my eyebrows and smiled at Alice.

"Exactly!"

Alice laughed through her tears.

"You know what I mean," she said after she stopped laughing, "it wouldn't matter if you looked like James Bond or Worzel Gummidge, neither of us is looking for a relationship from this friendship that would be weird."

"It would be weird, but even weirder is that you're a teenager who has heard of Worzel Gummidge! How come you know who Worzel is? Are you secretly fifty?"

"My Dad read all the 'Worzel Gummidge' books when he was a kid and kept them and then passed them down a generation to me."

"I didn't know there was such a thing as Worzel Gummidge

books. It was a TV programme when I was a kid," I informed her.

"Well obviously I haven't seen that but the point is Worzel was a friendly scarecrow. James Bond killed people for a living and shagged loads of women. You're definitely more of a Worzel."

"Not how I see myself but thanks for clarifying. Anyway, I'm happy for you to wheel me out in front of Erika if you need to, so she can see the sort of goon I am, if you think that would help."

"Thank you, Jay but that's not the point. If you were twenty one and looked like a model for Armani, Erika should still trust me. I would never cheat on her, never, not with anybody."

"Maybe just re-iterate that to her tomorrow then, when you're both feeling a bit less emotional about things."

"I might text her now and tell her."

I couldn't see what went on, but Alice spent the next five minutes typing on her phone's keyboard without saying a word. I presumed from the changes in her expression every few seconds that she was getting some sort of response. After those five minutes elapsed, Alice put her phone down.

"Sorry about that, Jay. I realise it was really rude of me."

"No problem. Is everything sorted?"

"No, nothing has changed. She won't apologise for demanding I end my friendship with you and I'm still saying we're finished unless she does."

I felt uncomfortable with this whole business. I didn't want to come in between Alice and her girlfriend, especially because I knew how crazy she was about her, but at the same time I admired Alice for sticking to her guns. If Alice's account of their argument was truthful, which I had no reason to doubt, then it appeared that it was Erika that was in the wrong. A lover's tiff between two teenage lesbians was not something I ever anticipated being in the middle of.

"I'm sorry to hear that, Alice. As I say, things may look very different in the morning. I'll phone Cooper's taxis for you and give you a tenner for the fare."

"Don't be daft, Jay, I'll pay myself."

Just as I was about to pick up my mobile phone, Hunter walked in wearing just a t-shirt and a pair of boxer shorts. His t-shirt was tight on his body and although he had yet to fill out, you could tell there wasn't an ounce of fat on him. His legs were skinny but hairy and he had muscular calves. I was a little bit jealous as I knew I would never have a body like that again.

"Oh, hi Alice, I thought I heard your voice. What are you doing here?"

Alice didn't reply, but looked over at me instead, hoping I would provide an acceptable answer. I wasn't prepared to lie to my son on her behalf but I was diplomatic enough not to tell the whole story.

"She's had a bit of an argument with her partner, Hunter. I'm just about to phone a taxi for her."

"Can't you give her a lift?"

"I've had a few drinks, Hunter."

"Oh right. Shame that. See you soon, Alice. Your partner must be mad to argue with you."

CHAPTER
TWENTY FIVE

JAY

Hunter gave me his best incredulous look.

"Why are you asking me if I fancy Alice?" he asked defensively, "it wasn't me she was calling to see at ten o'clock last night. It's not me that's going to lunch with her today either."

There was definitely a hint of jealousy in his tone.

"We've been through this before, Hunter, she's just a friend."

"It's the authorities you'll have to persuade, not me."

"What?"

"It's against the law for someone over eighteen in a position of authority to have sex with someone under eighteen. I checked on the internet."

"Well, I don't think insurance underwriting is the type of 'position of authority' they're referring to Hunter! Also, Alice isn't under eighteen and I'm not having sex with her, so all in all, I don't think I have a lot to worry about."

"Ok, so what you're saying is that she's just a friend."

"She is just a friend."

"Well, to me she's just my best mate's nutty sister. I hope no-one I know sees you having lunch with her. That would be so embarrassing. They would think you were a right fucking perv!"

"Mind the language. I'll wear a disguise if that makes you feel better."

"It would."

"Well, tough shit, I was being sarcastic."

"Language father!"

"Sorry. Anyway, you're deflecting. I was asking you why you were going all 'gooey' over her last night."

"I wasn't."

"Yes, you were. Telling her that her partner must be mad to argue with her."

"Dad, I was being nice! If I'm nice, you go mad. If I'm not nice, you go mad. I can't win. You get 'stressy' about everything!"

"You do realise, don't you, that her partner is a girl?"

"Dad, I told you that!"

"OK. I just got the impression last night that you liked her. I didn't want you to get your hopes up that she may like you back."

"I do like her, not in the way you mean though. She's Dom's nutty sister, she's almost family to me."

I realised I shouldn't have started quizzing him on how he felt about Alice. It was none of my business. He was sixteen now and sixteen year old boys often have the 'hots' for eighteen year old girls and if Hunter wanted to take a shine to one, he could pick someone far worse than Alice. I was just hoping he might open up to me but the reality of the situation was that we didn't have the sort of relationship whereby he would confide his innermost secrets and feelings to me. He would probably have been more open with his mother.

Overnight, I had been wondering if my friendship with Alice

was worth all the problems it seemed to be causing. Hunter thought I was odd having a friendship with a teenage girl and obviously Erika was now thinking along similar lines. I enjoyed having a female friend to talk to but perhaps we should just limit our friendship to train journeys. I was going to suggest it to Alice over lunch and see how she reacted.

CHAPTER TWENTY SIX

<u>ALICE</u>

Cuerden View Café is gorgeous. It's at the top of a hill within Cuerden Valley Park so you have terrific views across the park and, as an added bonus, the food is amazing too. Under normal circumstances, I used to get excited about going but that Saturday the only emotion I felt was apprehension.

Once Cooper's taxi driver dropped me off at home that Friday evening, further text messages were exchanged between Erika and me for about an hour. She was desperate to meet up the following morning but, out of principle, I said I couldn't as I did not want to cancel my lunch with Jay. I suggested we meet up late in the afternoon and try to thrash things out. The tone of Erika's texts became more appeasing, as did mine and I went to sleep feeling slightly more confident that the damage that this argument had done to our relationship could be repaired.

I slept soundly. I was thinking I would struggle to settle and my mind would be replaying our argument over and over but none of that happened. I must have just been emotionally drained as I fell asleep as soon as I finished texting and didn't stir until the morning other than one very sleepy trip to the bathroom I vaguely remembered making.

I sensed someone was in my room as soon as I awoke. I presumed it must be Dominic, he often barged his way into my room before I woke up looking for a charger or to rob my spot cover-up. Within a matter of seconds, I realised the sense of calmness didn't tally with it being Dom. I opened my eyes and Erika was there, sat at the end of my bed, watching over me like I was her dying spouse.

"Good Morning, my Eponine!" she said softly and with a gentle smile.

It takes me a while to come around after I've been sleeping. The first thing I thought about was being due on but a slight squeeze together of my legs revealed that my night time wander to the bathroom must have subconsciously addressed that predicament. Secondly, I thought it was odd that Erika was at my house. I had been very specific about us meeting late in the afternoon. It all felt a bit 'Single White Female' which was ironically one of the many films that Erika and I had watched together.

"How long have you been here?"

"Just a few minutes."

Erika leaned over the bed and kissed me delicately on the lips. I instinctively kissed a little back.

"Does my breath not smell?" I asked with concern.

"Only of heaven."

"I'm still half asleep, Erika, but are we not fighting?"

"We were."

Erika placed her hands on my cheeks and kissed me more passionately a second time. It was still a gentle caress but the tips of our tongues collided.

"Does this mean you're sorry?" I asked. The competitive, argumentative side of me still wanted to come out of this situation with a win.

Erika leaned forwards and backwards to kiss me three times

and after each kiss she said 'Sorry'. After the third kiss she hugged me tightly.

"Does this mean I can still be friends with Jay without it being an issue?"

"On one condition."

"Which is?"

"I get to meet him too."

CHAPTER TWENTY SEVEN

ERIKA

It was never my decision to be a lesbian. I didn't wake up one morning, aged fourteen, and strategically decide that for the rest of my life I would purely only seek out relationships with girls and would ignore the relationships I wanted to have with boys, on the basis that same sex relationships were somehow cooler or more fashionable. There was no decision process. I am exclusively attracted to people of the same sex in exactly the same way heterosexual people are only attracted to people of the opposite sex.

I have had several arguments about this but I don't particularly like the word 'Pride'. I don't feel proud to be gay, I just am. I totally understand why it is used and given society has often tried to shame and persecute people who loved someone of the same sex, I understand the grouping together of homosexual people as a force against injustice was necessary and that a step change is still needed so gays and lesbians do not have to defend their sexual orientation. 'Heterosexuals' don't have 'Hetero pride' celebrations as it is just deemed normal so I would love it if society moved on far enough to deem homosexual couples as equally normal. If 'Pride' became representative of one person's love for another I would be happy with that rather than it representing a protective shield for non-heterosexual people. Over the last twenty years Western society has probably made more of a stride forward in a small space of time than ever before towards equality in sexual orientation but it still feels like the finishing line is some way in the distance. In the same way black people should not have to say 'Black Lives Matter' because it should be a given, gay men and lesbians should not need to be 'proud' of their sexual orientation because it should just be accepted.

I spotted Alice the first day she started at College. I saw her walking through the car park from Morrison's supermarket to the College entrance and just couldn't take my eyes off her. She has this mesmerising charm about her which is hard to explain but it seems to draw both males and females towards her like moths to light. She is super feminine, the way she dresses, the way she acts and the way she moves.

From that moment on, every moment of every day when Alice was around I felt different. I felt nervous and self-aware in her presence even at times when there were fifty people in the room. Everyone talks about how certain people have the capacity to 'light up a room' and Alice definitely has that quality. She took residence in my brain and I could barely develop any train of thought without it ultimately leading on to me thinking about her.

Fate seemed to decree that we belonged together. Everything started to fit neatly into place. Alice started coming to football training. I was desperate to impress her. I seemed to find an extra yard of pace and be more clinical in front of goal when Alice was there.

Soon enough I picked up from College gossip that Alice was bisexual. I would be lying if I told you I saw this as purely good news but it was better than her being heterosexual. By the way, I hate the words 'straight' and 'bent' much more than the word 'pride' – it is like branding heterosexual people as the normal ones and the rest of us as 'abnormal'. Primitive biology may have picked a side but scientific technology is bringing us back into the generational game.

The day we played Runshaw College was the day I decided I couldn't wait any longer before making a move. Alice had some history with some of the Runshaw players and when a fight broke out after the final whistle, I was the first person there pushing their players away from her. When I realised Alice was taking her time to get changed after her sending off, I made damn sure I was the last one in the changing room with her.

Dating Alice has been indescribably wonderful – the highlight of my life so far. She is funny, affectionate, clever, sporty and kind hearted. Our relationship is the sort of relationship that I have always dreamt of having. All my previous relationships have always seemed to have been missing that vital spark. As a result of finding the woman I think is perfect for me, I realise I have, at times, become a little clingy. We have spoken about it and Alice says she sometimes feels the same but I seem to be the one who lets her possessiveness get the better of her.

I suspect everyone, as they mature, goes through periods of uncertainty about themselves and their relationships but there just seem to be a number of things that scare me. Alice's bisexuality is one of them. Despite Alice's reassurance, I just think if she decides at some stage that she prefers men then I would be powerless to stop her. I've seen Bohemian Rhapsody and couldn't help feel there were similarities between Mary Austin and me. Mary may have been the love of Freddie's life but he still ended up preferring men. I am scared, even though she loves me that one day Alice will do that to me.

Alice has a much older male friend call Jay who she talks about a hell of a lot. I always felt uneasy when he became the topic of our conversation and I also felt there was an element of hero worship in the way that she spoke about him. His wife died of the Coronavirus and although this is a terrible thing that I wouldn't wish upon my fiercest enemy, I just sometimes felt he was using his terrible loss as an emotional tool to entice Alice towards him. The thought that Alice may leave me for a man had been in the back of my mind since 'Day One' but the thought that she may leave me for Jay began to edge to the forefront of my mind. The concept became like a raging bull in my brain that I could not control.

The morning after our first proper, full scale row, I woke up feeling that the raging bull that had been charging around my head the night before had now found a peaceful strip of grass. The possessiveness and anger had gone and I was now more concerned about repairing the damage it had left in its wake. Assessing the situation logically rather than emotively, I knew I had to see Alice and clear things up but subsequently I knew I needed to meet Jay too. Without meeting him, I couldn't make a proper judgement on whether he was doing some sort of weird grooming thing or whether he was just a friendly man who was reaching out to Alice in his hour of need after an immense personal tragedy.

I drove up to Alice's from Bolton at about eight and I was there before half past. She lives in a three bedroom semi detached house on a quiet road off the main road that runs through Euxton village. When I was driving along the main road looking for the turn off, I went past the pub where Alice works, 'The Talbot'. It looks more like a young person's pub than an old man's one. I can imagine it is buzzing in there on a Friday and Saturday night.

I knew Alice's address but had never been there before so could feel my heart racing as I walked along the front path to the door. A bloke who looked in his late fifties answered the door. He had thinning grey hair and a leathery face that hinted that he had spent most of his life outdoors or on a sunbed. I initially thought it was safe to assume that this was Alice's stepfather, John, but then paranoia started to kick in and I began to panic for a few brief moments that Alice's Mum and Stepdad were away and this could, in fact, be Jay, coming to the door to gloat about the fact that he had been shagging my girlfriend. I took a proper look at the man again. He was definitely aged around fifty five to sixty so unless he had had a very difficult life there was no way this could be Jay. I told myself to get a grip.

"Hi, I'm Erika, is Alice in?"

The man had a dressing gown on that looked like it was the nightwear of Joseph when he took his 'Technicolor Dreamcoat' off. He was a shabby looking man with untidy grey hair above his ears and very hairy nostrils that dangled down almost as far as his top lip. He also wore navy blue crocs. Gok Wan would have had a field day with him.

The man I assumed to be John looked me up and down.

"So you're the famous Erika," he said cryptically.

"Is that a good or a bad thing?"

"Seems to be a very good thing for Alice."

I can't read men at all. I can never decipher whether they are being pervy or pleasant and this instance was no exception. He either meant Alice was really happy and that was down to me or he meant that I was good looking and Alice was lucky to be sleeping with me. I decided to reserve judgement until I knew him better.

"Is she in?" I asked again.

"She's asleep, love. I've never met anyone who can sleep like Alice. I reckon she's a reincarnation of Little Briar Rose. Step in. I'll introduce you to her mother. You've come at the right time as she's in her annual good mood today."

"Take no notice of him, love," said a gravelled voiced woman from inside, "I'm happy twice a year."

I was escorted through to the lounge and Alice's Mum was sat on her settee, with the window open, smoking a cigarette.

"John won't let me smoke in here without the window open and he calls me a grumpy sod! Do you smoke, love?"

Alice's Mum picked up her half-full cigarette packet and waved it at me.

"No, I vaped for a few months a while back but I've packed that in now."

"Good for you. Expensive, drawn out suicide, is what this is. I'll probably die a painful death."

I had had cheerier introductions.

"Hi, I'm Erika."

"I'd worked that out, hun. You've probably worked out that I'm Alice's Mum because she obviously got her wit and sparkling good looks from my side of the family. Her father's an ugly bore."

Alice's Mum was, if truth be known, less attractive in the flesh than she was on the photos I had seen of her. Those photos hid a few extra lines on her face but you could still tell with her best clobber on and some decent make-up that she would still be attractive. Twenty five years ago she was probably a stunner. Her hair was the same colour as mine, a light blond, other than the roots which were dark. She too was sporting a dressing gown but whilst John had a pair of bald, skinny legs below his, Alice's Mum wore pink pyjamas with teddy bears on.

"She's got it bad for you, you know," Alice's Mum said, flicking ash from her cigarette out the window.

"I've got it bad for her too," I confessed.

"Young lesbian love, isn't it sweet?" John said, making me lean further towards the conclusion that he was a creep.

"You and I still have 'the hots' for each other too, don't we, John?"

"Yeh, we're like rabbits. Not sexually though, I just mean we eat lots of carrots and shit little circular pellets."

They looked at each other and laughed raucously. They both seemed to have a very dry sense of humour. They reminded me of the Innkeepers in Les Miserables. Alice's Mum laughed so hard she started crying, then coughing, then almost choking. They were very odd.

"Sorry love," John said once they had both managed to calm themselves down, "I don't know what's come over us this morning."

"I think he's put some maroo-jus-arner in my fags! Anyway, up you go, love. Alice's room is the second on the right at the top of the stairs. If she wants a brew, tell her to come down and make us all one."

"Thank you!" I said as I made a sharp exit.

I started calling Alice 'Eponine' from time to time after that. Alice had never seen or read Les Miserables so didn't have the foggiest idea what I was on about which made it more amusing for me, so I didn't explain. The next thing I had to do that day though was to make sure Jay was not her Marius.

CHAPTER TWENTY EIGHT

JAY

I wasn't warned that Alice was bringing Erika with her to Cuerden Valley so when the two of them came over to greet me at the table it felt like a bit of an ambush. I had a sense of guilt too, for no justifiable reason. I was obviously aware that they had been arguing about Alice's friendship with me so knew Erika would be scrutinising every little thing I did.

Erika was ridiculously beautiful. I regretted my 'dungaree' speech every time I saw Alice, knowing how shallow it had been, but Erika's striking looks re-enforced the absurdity of my statement. She was tall, fair skinned, slim, wore very little make up, had full lips that looked real rather than cosmetically enhanced and had smooth, unblemished skin.

"Jay, this is Erika and Erika this is Jay."

"Hi!"

Standing up, I didn't know whether to shake hands or go in for a hug and a peck on the check so instinctively went with what felt right which was the latter. Erika defensively tucked her chin into her chest as I moved to kiss her so I ended up kissing the hair on the side of her head rather than her cheek. After this awkward moment she surveyed me with her piercing blue eyes.

"You don't look anything like Johnny Vegas," Erika said, which was an unusual opening sentence. Presumably it related to some sort of 'in joke' I knew nothing about.

"Neither do you," I replied, "except for the chin hair."

Erika laughed in a bit of a confused fashion. We all sat down.

"Does everyone around here have a really mad sense of humour, like they've been dropping acid or something?" Erika asked.

"Pretty much," Alice and I simultaneously replied.

We sat and chatted for about twenty minutes with a brief gap whilst I went to order the food and drinks. Dogs are welcome at the café and I took it as a positive that Erika tried to befriend every canine that passed by. Dog people are normally kind hearted softies whilst cat people are less affectionate and a little crazier (this is probably as much of a sweeping generalisation as my 'dungaree' one). I thought the three of us were getting on brilliantly but when Alice excused herself 'to go and powder her nose' I thought Erika might suddenly show her true colours.

"Was your food good?" I asked in a friendly chit chat sort of way.

"It was lovely. Listen up Jay, whilst Alice isn't here there's something I need to say to you."

'Here it comes', I thought to myself, she's going to threaten to strangle me with her super long legs if I ever as much as talk to her girlfriend ever again.

"Go on," I said, slumping a little in my chair as I feared the worst.

"Since the first time Alice brought you up in conversation, I have to be honest and say I hated you. In no time at all, she has become so, so important to me and I have always treated you like competition...."

Not a great start.

"But I'm not competition," I began to explain.

"Let me finish, I treated you like competition because every day at College, Alice would be like 'Jay said this today' or 'Jay did that' and I was jealous of how influential you seemed to be on her emotions. If you were sad, Alice would be sad too. If you were happier then Alice would be too. She loves you, Jay, she really loves you…"

"Not like she loves you though, Erika," I interjected again.

"I know that now. She loves you, Jay, because she's a lovely person and you're a lovely person and sometimes when two lovely people meet they just get on. I now feel like a wicked, horrible person for trying to stop my girlfriend from having a lovely friend. Right now, I just feel like the worst girlfriend ever. Alice has never given me a single reason not to trust her and yet I still didn't. I don't deserve her, I really don't. I could have lost the most incredible girlfriend ever over this."

  Erika's voice was wavering and I was concerned the water-works were about to start flowing.

"Look Erika, I used to hate it when I was your age and older people used to give me advice but sod it, the boot's on the other foot now so I'm going to enjoy dishing some out to you. Stop beating yourself up. You made a tiny mistake of being a little bit too protective and caring a little bit too much. You're very young, you'll make other, bigger, more significant mistakes than this but as long as you learn from them, apologise when you can then most of the time things will work out just fine.

On the night before my wife got ill, we went up to bed with her stating that she was too tired for sex but, selfish prick that I am, I still thought I'd stroke her leg a little to see if I could interest her. When she repeated the message about being tired, I made a big song and dance about turning away from her and letting out a deep, sexually frustrated sigh. I don't know if Amy went to sleep that night thinking I was a prick or whether I made her feel guilty for not reciprocating, all I do know is that my pathetic sulk was my final goodbye to my amazing wife. I don't really know why I'm telling you this story, I suppose what I'm trying to say is that people, no matter how nice they normally try to be, will still sometimes make stupid decisions but life is too short to constantly dwell on them and we need to learn to forgive ourselves and move on. Something like that anyway!"

"Heavy shit that, Jay!"

"I know. I surprise myself sometimes. 99% of the time though I just talk bollocks!"

CHAPTER
TWENTY NINE

<u>ALICE</u>

After one lunchtime meeting at Cuerden View café, Erika went from treating Jay as a threat to talking about him as though he was her second favourite person on earth (behind me obviously). I was really pleased about it but sometimes I wondered whether it was genuine or just an act to avoid any further arguments. The more time passed though, the more I felt it must be genuine.

We spent most of our spare time at Erika's house. Life's little luxuries were some of the key reasons for this as they were much more freely available at Erika's Mum's house than they were at ours. For starters, Erika had a double bed in her bedroom with a wall mounted TV, her own Sky Q box, Netflix and Amazon Prime. These weren't the only factors, there were many others including logistical reasons as Erika's house was much nearer to College than mine and, although I love them to death, John and Mum are a bit eccentric. I could only tolerate them in small doses myself so didn't want to inflict them too regularly on Erika.

One evening, we were sprawled out on her bed, tucking into a couple of Starbuck's Caramel Frappuccino's that we would regularly treat ourselves to. We had just finished watching an episode of 'The Good Place' (Erika had a thing for Tahani whilst I preferred Eleanor but, if truth be known, I also had a mild crush on Chidi but kept that to myself as I knew it wouldn't go down well with Erika), when Erika pecked me quickly on the lips before announcing,

"We need to find Jay a girlfriend."

I didn't concur.

"There's no chance, Erika. As far as Jay's concerned, romantically it's just him and his memories until the day he dies."

"I don't get that. His wife has died so it's not as though he's betraying her. If he manages to find someone else to love again then surely that's a good thing."

"Jay thinks it would be betraying her memory."

"No it isn't. Think about it, Alice, there are so many men out there who are complete knobheads! Straight women could do with an extra good one."

Erika often stated how much she hated the word 'straight' but she used it quite often. I loved her too much to point it out.

"I agree but it's not me that you have to persuade."

Erika's beautiful blue eyes seemed to brighten more than ever.

"Maybe we don't have to persuade him!" she said excitedly.

"What do you mean?"

"Maybe we could just set him up."

"How?"

"I don't know, I haven't thought it through yet. Maybe put a photo of him on to Tinder and then we could manage his account and find him someone decent."

"It wouldn't work. He'd not turn up to anything that seemed a bit fishy."

"I'm just thinking aloud. Maybe you could arrange to meet him at Cuerden View and then send her in your place."

"The woman would have to be in on the deception though and that'd get everything off to a bad start."

"Not necessarily, if she knew what he looked like, she'd just find him."

"I can't see it working. Jay is the type of person who would have to grow to love someone over a long period of time."

"How can we grow him a partner then?"

"I think it's impossible."

Erika kissed me again.

"Nothing is impossible, Alice."

"Well, this is as close to impossible as you can get. Unless he gets a message from heaven, which is pretty unlikely seeing he's an atheist, then I can't see us ever fixing him up with anyone."

CHAPTER THIRTY

<u>**ALICE**</u>

The following morning, after our discussions about hatching a plan to find Jay a love interest, we both fell in love with the cutest hatchlings you had ever seen. Halfway up Erika's road there is a large pond, just off the roadside, where apparently the same duck comes to lay its eggs then rear its ducklings each year. There are road signs up warning people to drive carefully as the ducklings could be waddling along behind their mother. As Erika was driving us to College, we spotted the proud mother duck followed by a procession of about ten tiny ducklings.

"Oh my goodness! Look at them! How cute are they?" I said almost whooping with delight as these little tiny creatures scuttled along merrily after their mother.

We had to stop the car as they crossed the road in front of us, the ducklings moving their legs like cyclists in a Tour De France sprint to keep up with their mother.

"They're mallards. We think it's the same female that comes back year after year. She has a celebrity status around here. Deirdre Duck we call her."

"I'm not surprised she's a celebrity. How many of them are there?" I asked, starting to count.

"Nine ducklings," Erika confirmed.

"How long do they follow their Mum around for?"

"A couple of months or so. They have to make sure they avoid the local cats though. Some years there are only three or four that make it, other years the whole lot do."

"Oh, I hope they make it. I've just added duck on to my list of animals I won't eat."

"Along with…"

"Sheeps, cows and pigs."

"Sheep," Erika corrected me.

"Sheep, cows and pigs," I repeated, slightly irked that I was corrected. We loved each other why did Erika have to point out my silly mistakes?

"So that's why you only eat chicken and turkey?"

"Well, I eat fish too and I used to eat duck until just now."

I almost said 'fishes' just to spite her.

"So how do you choose which ones to save?"

"I save the cute ones!"

I would have liked to have come up with a more compelling reason but that was the real one.

"Alice!" Erika laughed, "that's so funny. You will only eat ugly animals! It's a bit shallow though, isn't it?"

"No," I said defensively, "it's the opposite of shallow…"

"Deep?" Erika asked whilst interrupting.

"Well, OK, maybe not deep, but thoughtful. Not like you who just eats anything no matter what it looks like without a single consideration at all."

It was a retaliatory barbed comment. I noticed when we spent a lot of time together we could end up bickering a bit. There was no harm to it though and I thought it was healthier than keeping everything in and then all of a sudden having a massive row.

"No, I don't eat fish," Erika pointed out.

"Not for moral reasons, just because you can't be arsed picking out the bones!"

"Not just that! They're all rubbery too. It would be like eating a man in a wetsuit."

By this time the mother duck had moved from the road and the ducklings were all leaping, one by one, into the pond which was only a few metres from the side of the road.

"By the way," I announced, " I'm going to start swimming a couple of times a week after College."

"How come?"

"To keep this heavenly body," I said in a very tongue in cheek manner. Erika was aware of my dissatisfaction with my body. I was too small where I wanted to be large and too large where I wanted to be small.

"Well if it's to maintain your extraordinarily sexy body in tip top condition that sounds like a wonderful idea," Erika replied, trying to eradicate my uncertainties with compliments.

"Fancy coming with me?"

"Nah, I'm just happy reaping the benefits."

CHAPTER THIRTY ONE

<u>JAY</u>

It was a wet, grey Wednesday morning. I watched as commuters weaved past puddles on the platform at Chorley to board the train. Alice didn't seem to be moving as freely through the rain as some of her fellow Lancastrians. She looked in pain. After boarding our train, I watched her pulling various pain induced faces as she headed along the carriageway towards the empty seat next to me. She sat down with a groan like a man over forty.

"Morning! What's the matter with you?"

"I've taken up swimming, Jay. Not a good move, I'm aching in muscles I didn't even know I had."

"Oh dear."

"…And then there was the Jennifer Clarke-Taylor incident."

"Sounds like the name of a film that – 'The Jennifer Clarke-Taylor' incident!"

"God, I hope they don't make a film about this one. Not my finest moment, Jeremy."

Alice had discovered my full Christian name was Jeremy. I had to take my passport into Manchester one day as I was opening a new savings account. I was trying to manage the life cover money from Amy's death as carefully as possible so would research where the best savings rates where and would swop and change accounts regularly. Anyway, Alice asked to see my passport photo and although she avoided laughing hysterically at my stern passport face from nine years ago, when for some reason I forget I was sporting a military moustache, the revelation of my full name, for some reason, was a massive source of amusement. She had taken to using it on a semi-regular basis.

"Hit me with it," I said, I knew she was dying to.

"Hit you with what?"

"The 'Jennifer Clarke-Taylor incident'."

"Gotya! OK, remember me telling you about being given a tough time at Parklands by a small gang of idiots?"

"Yes."

"Well, Jennifer Clarke-Taylor was the ringleader of that gang of idiots. As you well know, Parklands isn't a religious school like St Michael's but Jennifer proclaimed to be a God-fearing individual and decided the fact that I had had a same sex relationship was an ungodly act. You would have thought that if God was in charge of the whole of the universe for the whole of eternity that he would have more important things to concern himself with, like war, famine and climate change, than Megan Williams and me sharing a bed, but according to Jennifer apparently not."

"Was she just looking for someone to give a hard time to and you just gave her a convenient excuse?"

"Pretty much. Megan Williams had long since left Parklands, she was a couple of years older than me and had moved on to Runshaw College. Her sister, Karen, who was in our year, was struggling to come to terms with the fact that her big sister was a lesbian so reported back to Jennifer that I had somehow exploited Megan. Remember we are talking about a girl who was two years older than me yet I had somehow exploited her. This was seemingly forgotten as was the fact that Megan had been the one who had done all the chasing. Anyway, I then endured nine difficult months with Jennifer, Karen and all their cronies doing their best to make me miserable."

"By doing what?"

"Pushing into me, spitting at me, writing things on my locker, posting things on social media about me, calling me a 'lesbian slut' and generally just ganging up on me. Jennifer orchestrated the whole process of intimidation – she's just not a very nice person."

"Not very pious of her, was it?"

"Pious?"

"Devoutly religious."

"Oh right. Well, she thought it was. She was very good at quoting from Leviticus which is not a part of the bible I have ever heard of. Apparently same-sex relationships are classified as 'an abomination' in there."

"So what's all this got to do with you taking up swimming? Presumably Jennifer was at the baths."

"Yes, but 'All Seasons' is a busy place so although I saw her swimming, it was easy enough for me to avoid her, I just swam in a lane some distance away from her with a load of kids jumping and splashing in between us."

"I sense a 'but' coming."

"A 'butt' with two 't's, Jeremy."

Alice lifted her eyebrows as she said this.

"Sounds interesting," I said genuinely intrigued as to the direction our conversation was going in.

"Have you ever been to 'All Seasons'?" Alice asked.

"Many times."

"Well, you'll know then that when it's busy the changing rooms can be quite cramped."

"Yes."

"OK so within the cramped changing areas there was a cute little girl running around. She must have been about five or six. Old enough to have a little bit of independence but not too much. Her Mum had three little girls in total, she was the eldest, the others were probably two and four, so Mum was drying them one by one. Nature dictates you tend to the youngest first so the cute six year old one was getting a bit giddy and was running around a bit but within watching distance of her Mum. As you know, I'm a bit of a worrier at times and I was becoming increasingly concerned that the little girl might slip. I'd been watching her for a little while, whilst getting myself dry, as she whizzed past me back and forth.

Admittedly over time my concern lessened and my concentration waned. I began thinking about Erika's birthday coming up and what presents I was going to buy her. We've also been invited to a gay wedding and what I am going to wear for that is almost constantly making me anxious. Anyway, I just half caught this little girl coming past again so I put my left hand out to sort of cup the back of her head just to stop her from moving across the wet floor too quickly. She seemed to stay still for a few brief seconds next to me, with me still cupping her head, so I turned to give her a polite 'grown up' warning....but I wasn't cupping a little girl's head, was I? Oh no, I was cupping Jennifer Clarke-Taylor's naked bottom!"

"Her naked bottom?"

"Yes, you know how 95% of people at the baths creep around awkwardly trying to ensure no-one clocks them naked whilst 5% don't give a toss and just think 'Sod it, I'm flaunting my nudity in the faces of everyone' – well, unfortunately for me,

Jennifer Clarke-Taylor is one of the five percent."

"So what did you say?"

"What could I say? I just told her the truth that I thought I was cupping a little girl's head."

"And she believed you and everything was fine?"

"Obviously not! This is not a normal human being we are talking about. A full scale row broke out. When I say full-scale, I mean a force eight row…"

"Force eight?"

"Lots of screaming and shouting but just short of hair pulling which is force nine and then eye gauging would be force ten."

"When they have those signs up in the baths saying 'No running, no diving, no petting'…I don't think they include no eye gauging, perhaps I'll put that in the suggestion box next time I go. Also, I guess 'no cupping other ladies bottoms' might be useful!"

"Very funny. Anyway, there was no eye gauging. She just accused me of cupping her bottom because I was lusting after her, as I am, obviously, a weird sexual deviant."

"Obviously."

"I explained that just because I am attracted to women doesn't mean I am attracted to every woman, irrespective of how physically and mentally ugly they are."

"And of course you said this calmly."

"I did say that bit calmly but she sort of sneered at me like she didn't believe a word of it so I screamed at her that if me and her were the only two people left alive on the entire planet and I had gone without sex for thirty years, I would still not wilfully touch her fat, ugly backside. I think I said I would rather pleasure myself with a cactus than go near her."

"Was she convinced?"

"No. She reported me to the manager, the bitch. The manager believed me though….eventually."

"And this was your first trip to the baths?"

"First trip since I decided to take swimming up again."

"Great start!"

"Eventful. It won't stop me going though. I just need to be extra vigilant for ugly, naked bottoms posing as little girl's heads from now on."

"I have to say I'm not sure I'm buying that excuse."

"Don't you even start, Jay!"

"I was just going to say it's a 'bum' excuse!"

"Arsehole."

I smiled at her. Alice smiled back.

"There are so many places I could take this conversation right now but I'm a gentleman so I won't."

"Thank you! It was an accident."

"I believe you."

"Jay, it was!"

"I said I believe you."

CHAPTER THIRTY TWO

ALICE

Another night spent at Erika's, another morning watching Deirdre Duck and her family of ducklings waddle off to the water as we went to College in the car.

"They're getting bigger, aren't they?" I observed like a proud mother.

"They are. Only a few more weeks and they'll be left to their own devices."

"She's done a grand job."

"She has. Isn't it funny how in the bird world females are dull and unattractive whilst with humans we are the attractive ones."

"Spoken like a true lesbian!"

"No, I'm sure most men would acknowledge that it's the women who are the most beautiful ones."

"True."

"How's Jay doing?"

"He's OK. I don't see as much of him now I'm stopping at yours so often but he seems OK when I see him. He has the odd bad day but I think he's coped as well as could be expected given what he's been through."

"Send him my love next time you see him."

"I will."

"Still not been able to think of a love match for him?"

"I'm not even trying."

"Well, I think you should."

This wasn't the first time Erika had mentioned this.

"I know you do."

"Have you asked him yet if he can pick us up from Andy and Steve's wedding?"

"Not yet, but I will."

"We'll have to stay over if he can't."

"He'll be fine. It's not as if Jay has a wild social life."

Andy and Steve had been friends of Erika's for years. Andy was the older brother of one of Erika's school friends and was the first boy Erika spoke to about her own sexual identity. He is very much a proud gay man and apparently vehemently disagrees with her reluctance to use the word 'Pride'. They have never fallen out over it – they just enjoy debating the point.

I think Andy and Steve have been together about four years. Steve proposed at the top of the Eiffel Tower a couple of summers ago and they have been planning their wedding day since.

"Where better for a gay man to propose than at the top of a gigantic phallic symbol?" Steve commented on his return home.

I was nervous about the wedding for a variety of reasons, the primary one being that Erika knew a lot of the people attending whilst I only knew a handful. Secondly, I had never been to a same-sex wedding before so didn't really know what to expect and thirdly, I knew Erika's ex-girlfriend Michelle was going to be there and once again, I didn't really know what to expect.

On the weekend of the wedding, Erika's Mum was due to have family visiting her from Sweden. I actually think Erika has Swedish family on both her Mum and Dad's side. Anyway, Erika's maternal grandfather was Swedish and his sister, Erika's Great Aunt, her husband plus their daughter and her husband were coming to stay at Erika's. As a consequence, Erika's Mum had asked if we could stay over at mine that weekend, as beds at her house would be in short supply. Erika felt the more likely reason she had been asked to stay away was because her Mum couldn't be bothered explaining to elderly foreign relatives that one of her daughters was a lesbian but perhaps this was just Erika being paranoid.

That same weekend, John and Mum were heading off to Rhos-on-Sea which would, under normal circumstances, have been ideal but it gave us a logistical headache about how we were going to get to and from the wedding in Manchester. Getting the train in at lunchtime would be fine as the wedding was not until two, but getting back to Euxton at midnight was more problematic. Trains don't run that late, we didn't want to leave early, taxis would be a fortune and neither of us wanted to drive (parking in Manchester isn't cheap either). Erika suggested I ask Jay which seemed like a good idea and I couldn't see it being an issue but I just hadn't got around to asking him.

"Do you think my Mum would be a good potential partner for Jay?" Erika asked out of nowhere but with a line across her forehead that suggested it was asked without a hint of humour.

"Your Mum?" I asked with surprise.

"Yeh, she's a fine looking lady for her age."

Erika was right. Her Mum, Britt, was a fine looking lady for her age but at fifty one she was quite a lot older than Jay. I am not saying Jay is superficial, because he isn't, very much the opposite, but based on the whole looks, age and personality package, I just couldn't see her being the one that would tempt him away from his commitment to a life of celibacy.

"I could see them getting along," I said falteringly.

"But…" Erika prompted.

"But I couldn't see a romantic connection," I confessed reluctantly, "I don't think either of them would 'fancy' the other one."

"How do you know though?" Erika persisted.

"I don't know. I'm just stating my opinion."

"What if we tried it?"

"I think he might hate us so much that he wouldn't give us a lift to Andy & Steve's wedding!"

"What if we tried it after the wedding then?"

"How?"

"I'm not sure. We could just find an excuse to bring them together, leave them to get acquainted and see where things go from there."

"We could try, I suppose."

"Fantastic!" Erika said clapping like an excited sealion.

For some reason, all I could picture was Craig Revel-Horwood looking aghast, shaking his head and muttering the immortal word 'Disaster'!

CHAPTER THIRTY THREE

<u>JAY</u>

"Where the hell are you?" said a female voice that seemed to be battling to be heard over the noise of drunken revellers and passing cars.

I didn't need to look at my phone to know it was Alice calling me. No-one else would be phoning me at ten past midnight as Saturday night ushered in Sunday morning. She had already phoned me several times previously that evening too.

"What do you mean, where am I? I'm at home!"

"He's still at bloody home," I heard Alice say drunkenly, presumably to Erika, "Bloody hell, Jeremy! You said you'd pick us up at midnight on Deansgate, by the Hilton, I can't believe you've forgotten!"

"No," I said calmly, "but it seems that you've forgotten that you rang me an hour ago saying you were having a lovely time and would there be any way I could pick you up at one."

"Hang on....Erika, he says we rang him to ask if he'd come and get us at one."

"Oh shit, yeah!"

"See you later then, Jeremy. We're going back in. Thank you!"

"Thank you, Jay! We love you!" I heard Erika shouting in the background.

An hour later, I had managed to find them on the streets of a bustling Manchester city centre with its hoards of wobbly young people seemingly more concerned about phones and kebabs than avoiding the oncoming vehicles. Alice and Erika, looking equally dishevelled, managed to somehow help each other into the back of my car. As I anticipated they would be, they both smelt and acted very drunk.

"Had a good time?" I asked, looking in my rear view mirror, partially to make sure I could pull away safely and partially to establish whether either Erika or Alice looked ill enough to throw up in my car. Erika looked a possibility. She was already lying down with one cheek pressed against Alice's thigh.

"It was lovely, Jay. Steve and Andy are such an amazing couple. We love them so much, don't we Erika?"

Alice gave Erika a gentle prod. She didn't move but did respond.

"Love them," she mumbled.

"And I got to meet the mysterious Michelle."

"Michelle?" I queried. I knew I had probably been told but a lot of what Alice told me went in one ear and out the other. She said I was deaf but it was more to do with being disinterested. Teenage drama can only hold my attention for so long. I was also distracted at that point by a black 'A' class Mercedes that was being driven right up my arse. My theory the richer the driver, the poorer his manners was, at that point, appearing to be proven.

"Jeremy Cassidy, do you not listen to a word I say?" Alice admonished me in her inebriated tones.

"I'm old, I forget things. Who are you again?"

"Piss off...I'm unforgettable."

"I'll give you that."

"Anyway, Jeremy, I was about to say, Michelle is Erika's former lover. I must confess to being a little worried that she could turn out to be far more glamorous than me."

"There's only one girl for me," Erika mumbled once more whilst still with her cheek glued to Alice's thigh. Alice patted her sympathetically then ran her hands soothingly through Erika's hair.

"Is she going to be OK?"

"She's fine, Jeremy, you old fusspot! She's not even been drinking. She's just tired."

"You little fibber," I teased. They were sharing the remnants of a bottle of Prosecco as my car pulled up alongside them.

"Well, just one or two. What was I talking about?"

"Michelle," I reminded her.

"Oh God! Yes, Michelle. What a stunner, Jay! What a stunner! The silly old man who said something about all lesbians being dungaree wearing 'munters' has obviously never seen Michelle."

"Not quite what I said," I responded defensively.

"That was exactly what you said. Word for fucking word!"

I wasn't sure I was too fond of the drunken ladette version of Alice. She was a cockier, more self assured version of the sober one.

"I beg to differ."

"You'd beg to dick who?" Alice asked confused.

"Doesn't matter! Tell me about Michelle."

"She's a stunner, Jay."

"We'd got that far."

"I know! Anyway, Michelle is lovely. She was so lovely, so sexy,

I was going to suggest to her that maybe Erika, me and her could have a sexy threesome some time but Erika dragged me away before I could ask. She knew what I was about to say. She told me I was being naughty. I was only being silly, Jeremy. Erika's so lovely. I love her more than anything in this world but Michelle was lovely. Have I told you she was lovely? Beautiful inside and out."

"I don't think you mentioned it," I replied, feeling relieved to see the 'A' class heading straight on as I turned right.

"Gorgeous," Alice stated to banish any possible doubt.

"I heard she was a 'munter'," I said playfully.

"Well whoever told you that was talking bollocks!"

"Language."

"Sorry!" Alice hiccupped as she apologised.

"Do you know who else is gorgeous, Jeremy Cassidy?"

Alice leaned forward to rest on the back of my chair. I noticed Erika's head dropped off Alice's thigh and on to the car seat.

"Steve and Andrew," I guessed, based on previous clues.

"Well, yes they are but that wasn't who I was going to say."

"Go on, the suspense is killing me."

"You, Jeremy Cassidy. You little chubby chops!"

"Thank you!" I said, a little touched.

"Well, you are. It makes me feel very sad that Amy died. You are too good a man to be on your own. If I was twenty years older and didn't prefer women, which I think I now do, I would marry you."

"Out of sympathy."

"Exactly. Out of sympathy."

"Well, that's good to know! Thank you!"

"My pleasure, Jeremy Cassidy, my pleasure. I love you! You're a sweetheart!"

"And so are you."

Erika started groaning and making strange gurgling noises.

"Could you pull over, please Jay? I think Erika needs to be sick....oh, too late!"

CHAPTER THIRTY FOUR

JAY

Britt was insistent.

"No, no, Jay, honestly you must stay for a coffee. You've come all the way down from Chorley to help me out. The least I can do is make you a drink before you head home. I made some fruit scones yesterday too, if you'd like one?"

Chorley wasn't a million miles from Bolton. It was literally a twenty minute drive. I felt uncomfortable about turning her down though given she had been so friendly and welcoming.

"Go on then! That's very kind of you. Thank you very much, Britt!"

"Don't be daft! It's the least I could do after you fixed my oven. I was starting to worry that I may have to buy a new one."

"I wouldn't go as far as to say I 'fixed your oven', Britt. It had just tripped. I still have no idea how that's happened."

This was a white lie. I did have an idea, in fact, I was almost sure what had happened but I wasn't sharing my idea with Britt, just in case I happened to be completely wrong. I had a strong suspicion that we had been set up by Britt's scheming daughter and her girlfriend.

Britt turned her cold water tap on and collected water for her coffee machine.

"Did you happen to see the ducks when you came down the road this morning?"

"The ducks?"

"Yes, the mother duck and her little ducklings. Well, they aren't actually that little now. They're almost fully grown. They still follow their mother everywhere. Quite the local celebrities they are."

"No, I didn't. I'll keep an eye out for them on my way home."

"Erika and Alice are besotted with them," Britt explained as she went through the procedure of making my coffee.

"Where was it you said they'd gone to?"

"The girls? I'm not sure. I don't think they said where they were going. They just said they had to nip out for a couple of hours."

Of course they did.

"Was it the girls that told you that your oven wasn't working, Britt?"

"Yes, but they told me not to panic as they'd arranged for you to come around to fix it."

"Pity they had to pop out. It would have been good to have a word with them."

The bloody meddlers!

"Did you say Americano or Cappuccino, Jay?"

"I'll have a Cappuccino, please."

Britt was undoubtedly an attractive lady. She was tall, slim, dressed in clothes in the house that looked more expensive than my 'going out clobber' but whether she was twenty or sixty (and she was nearer the latter), I would not have been interested in a romantic sense. I knew Erika and Alice had meant well but if they had been thinking that Britt could mend my broken heart then they were very much mistaken. Nevertheless, I enjoy female company so the opportunity to have a coffee with a friendly female was welcomed irrespective of the circumstances.

"My husband bought me the coffee machine. He was a big coffee drinker – the stronger the better. He used to love Espresso's. I tend to stick to tea or instant coffee unless I have a visitor, which is a bit of a rarity these days."

  I felt sorry for Britt. My loss was forced upon me by death whilst Britt's single life had been inflicted on her through the choice of another. I imagine that was even harder to take. Alice had told me previously that Erika's father had left her mother but it somehow seemed inappropriate to acknowledge the fact that I knew this. I played dumb.

"Does your husband no longer live here then, Britt?"

"No, no. He moved out a couple of years ago. I'm afraid it's a long story."

"I've plenty of time but don't feel obliged to tell me if you'd rather not talk about it."

Britt brought my coffee over and sat don't next to me.

"Thank you!" I said as I took the cappuccino off her and looked around for a table mat.

"It can go on the table, don't worry.....I don't mind telling you about Bernard. It's history now. His lies caught up with him. The thing about lies is that once you start telling them, you need to remember the lies you've told otherwise you just tie yourself up in knots. That's what Bernard did. I started to realise he wasn't being consistent so I made diary notes of the places he said he'd been and then weeks later would quiz him about it. After a few months of investigation, I confronted him. It all came out then."

"I'm presuming he had a mistress."

"A mistress! It turned out over our twenty years of marriage he had cheated on me with at least seventy five women. Isn't that disgusting?"

"That's horrible."

"I don't understand it, Jay. You would have thought the man would have felt guilty for betraying his wife and family but he obviously had no conscience whatsoever."

"I can't condone it at all, it's just a wicked thing to do but maybe he thought he wasn't hurting anyone if nobody ever knew about it."

It felt that Britt's warmth suddenly evaporated and she was now viewing me from a much less appreciative perspective. I suppose my statement was a bit insensitive but I have a habit of sometimes saying what I am thinking without rationalising whether it may be upsetting.

"To me, that sounds like the voice of experience, Jay."

"It absolutely isn't," I reassured her, "I could never have lived with the guilt of having sex with one other woman let alone seventy five. It was never an issue though. I couldn't find something that I wasn't looking for. I was always in love. There wasn't one second when that wasn't the case."

I wasn't deliberately trying to extract sympathy from Britt and ensure her feeling of warmth towards me returned, I was just being candid, but that seemed to do the trick.

"Erika has told me about your wife, Jay. I'm so sorry."

"Thank you."

"Such a terrible shame."

"I don't really have the right words when I talk about it. I can't say 'it's just one of those things' or 'I'm coping' or 'I was lucky to have her for the time that I did' because none of those statements feel true. It doesn't feel right, I'm not coping and

I should have had Amy for much, much longer than I actually did. I feel cheated to be honest. As an atheist, I just can't work out who it is that's cheated me though. Losing Amy is the worst thing that has ever happened to me and no matter what else happens between now and my dying day, I will never get over it. I know it's not what I should be saying as it's not what you want to hear but…"

"But it's the truth."

"Exactly, it's the truth."

Britt was long enough in the tooth to know that my loss was still very raw and it wasn't a conversation piece that either of us was comfortable dwelling on. She moved on.

"You seem to have struck up a good friendship with the girls, especially Alice."

"Is that a genuine statement or do you think it's a bit weird?"

Britt smiled.

"How could a forty year old man being friends with two pretty teenage lesbian girls be construed as being weird?"

"Well, when you put it like that!"

"I'm teasing you, Jay! I don't think it's weird."

"I do. I think it's weird that other than my son the biggest comfort to me since Amy's death has been two young women I had never met whilst Amy was alive. It is strange that we have become friends, I agree with that, but if anyone thinks it's weird in a creepy old man sort of way, they'd be wrong."

"They're smart kids, if there was anything not right with your friendship they would know."

"I agree. Talking about them being smart kids, I suspect they've just tripped the switch on your oven."

Britt looked confused.

"Why would they do that?"

"I'm only surmising but I suspect to get me here."

"Matchmaking?"

"Absolutely!"

"The little scallywags!"

"I know. Britt, you seem like a lovely lady, so it's nothing personal, but if the girls had tried to fix me up with Michelle Keegan, if she ever became single, which incidentally I hope she doesn't, then I still wouldn't be interested. Not that I am saying you would be interested either."

I felt I was rambling a bit just because it was awkward trying to tell someone why you didn't find them attractive. Britt put me back at ease.

"Jay, you don't have to explain yourself. I am very happy with my life as it is. I'm not saying it didn't take a bit of a re-adjustment but I'm not looking for a partner right now either. I would be very happy to meet up for the occasional coffee though as there are times I do feel a little short of male company."

"That would be great," I said with a smile.

"We shouldn't let the girls get away with this though, Jay. Let's get our heads together and see if we can come up with a plan."

CHAPTER
THIRTY FIVE

<u>ALICE</u>

Erika called out as we came through the front door.

"Hi Mum, we're back!"

There was no reply. We knew Erika's sister, Klara, was away at her friend's but we fully expected Britt and Jay to be there. We went through the hallway into the kitchen. Erika's kitchen is lovely with a breakfast table in the middle of the room and four high bar stools around it. There were two half empty cups of coffee on the table but no sign of Britt or Jay. I touched one of the cups, it wasn't stone cold but it was beyond the luke-warm stage. The cups had been there for quite a while.

"Where are they?" Erika asked me, looking a little concerned.

"I don't know. They can't have gone far though as Jay's car is still outside."

Erika took a seat on one of the stools and I quickly followed suit.

"Weird," she said, "do you think they might have gone for a walk…unless Mum's showing Jay the garden, she's very proud of the garden."

No sooner had she sat down, Erika was back on her feet again, striding over to the window to look out into the back garden.

"Are they there?"

"No..."

As Erika answered there was another sound. It was a moaning sound coming from upstairs. It was a female moaning sound which immediately sounded to me like a sexual sound - takes one to know one and all that.

"Did you hear that?" I asked Erika.

"What?" she asked, returning to the table, "they're definitely not outside," she stated as she sat back down. As she did so, there was another moan, deeper and more sustained second time around.

"You must have heard it that time!" I said, suppressing a laugh, but smiling awkwardly and blushing slightly like a school-child being given a sex education lesson.

"Was that what I think it was?" Erika queried.

"There is no way they're shagging," I stated with more conviction than I actually had.

"It doesn't sound like they are playing scrabble, Alice, unless my Mum has just come up with an incredibly long word."

"I can't imagine they're having sex. Jay's still hurting so much from Amy's death. It would be more logical for Jay to have gone home and maybe your Mum is just using some alone time to have a bit of a flick on her bean!"

"Alice!"

"What?"

"My Mum does not 'flick her bean' as you so delightfully put it."

"Double click the mouse then!"

"Shut up! She doesn't do anything to do with touching herself."

"She's a woman."

"She's also my mother and in my world her spare time is spent reading newspapers, listening to 'The Archers' and completing crossword puzzles so don't presume because we have sexual needs that my mother also has them."

The noise came a third time, more breathless this time but sharper and higher pitched then a fourth time. I couldn't help myself laughing.

"Shut up, Alice, it's not funny!"

"Yes, it is. You've obviously got a female burglar upstairs who is trying out your bedroom goodies."

"Do you think maybe they are just winding us up?"

"Who?"

"Jay and my Mum – pretending they are up to something."

"They aren't that inventive."

"True. It has to be Jay then, Alice, his car is outside."

"Perhaps. It just seems totally out of character for him but I suppose I don't really know him all that well and it's not like they're kids."

"They only met an hour ago."

There was a further noise.

"Did your Mum used to make sex noises with your Dad?" I enquired.

"No idea. Don't think they ever had sex, that's why they're divorced. Dad didn't just have a mistress in every port. He had a mistress in every village, every town and every city."

The moan came once more. It was followed by Britt's voice offering some sort of firm instruction which wasn't decipherable from the kitchen.

"Told you," said Erika knowingly, "she's not barking instructions to herself, is she? She's with Jay."

"I still find this hard to believe. He's just spent months telling me that he will never be in a relationship with anyone else until his dying day."

"He may not want a relationship, Alice, but he's a man, they all want a shag...I can't believe I am referring to my mother as a shag. This is all so wrong. I still reckon they might just be winding us up."

"You need to go up then!"

"No, I don't! What if I go up and it's the real thing. Just imagine if the door is open. I might catch a glimpse of something that would haunt me forever."

Just as Erika finished speaking there was a male groan. Loud, deep, prolonged and almost anguished. Erika and I looked at each other aghast.

"This is making me feel nauseous," I said, pulling a face.

"Me too," Erika agreed, "why can't he just shoot his load and put us out of our misery?"

I put my hand to my mouth.

"I can't believe you just said that!"

"It's the truth. I just want it to stop."

Unfortunately, the couple upstairs, who were presumably Britt and Jay had no intention of stopping any time soon. The male then said something that was clear and audible.

"Do you want it deeper?" he asked.

I grimaced once more at Erika. She held her head in her hands then began banging her head on the breakfast table. It then got worse. Britt responded to the question.

"Let me change positions, Jay, you can take me from behind."

"Ewww!" Erika and I said in unison pulling faces like we'd smelt something rotten.

"Quicker now, Jay, quicker!" Britt shouted.

"And you really wanted me to go up and watch that?" Erika spat out as her neck started to come out in pink, flustered blotches.

"If he's going quicker he'll be finished soon," I responded. I knew it wasn't overly comforting but it was the best I could come up with given the circumstances.

"Lovely. I will never be able to look at my mother again now without picturing her carrying Jay's juices around in her faff. We did this, Alice, I can't believe we did this."

"I tried to talk you out of it!"

"Only because you thought it was a complete non-starter not because you thought he'd whip her knickers off before we could say horny old bastards."

"They sound happy."

"Well, isn't that good to know!"

We then had the rather unpleasant experience of what we could only presume to be flesh slapping into flesh. Their interactions gathered pace and the vocalisation of their pleasures alternated until an eventual loud moan from Jay signalled their naked dance was over.

"I honestly think I might throw up," Erika confessed looking disgusted, "I already have a little bit of sick in my mouth. I'm just in shock that my Mum is such a tart. I hadn't even suspected it. I just have this horrible mental image of Jay walking around up there right now with his hairy chest, hairy arse, a big fat belly and a tiddly limp todger smelling of ejaculate. I just don't understand how any woman can find hairy men with their purple veiny things and droopy testes attractive. They're just vile!"

"Stop looking at it from your perspective, Erika. Your Mum and Jay have both had a tough time, just be thankful that something has happened that makes them both happy. We did this because we wanted them both to be happy."

"Well, it has spectacularly backfired! I didn't want them to be this happy, this quickly."

"No, neither did I," I admitted.

We sat in a shell shocked silence for several minutes. We heard a toilet flush and then the creaking of the stairs as someone came down them.

"Shit!" I said, "they might be mortified when they realise we've been here."

"I don't care," Erika replied, really sounding like she didn't, "I hope they are mortified. Might make them think before they next scream the house down."

Jay walked brazenly into the kitchen wearing one of Britt's dressing gowns. It was a pink, above the knee number. He didn't appear to be wearing anything else. His leg and chest hair were on full display.

"Oh hi girls! I didn't realise you were here. Erika, I've had a good poke around in your mother's thingie and I am happy to report it appears to be in full working order. It doesn't look like it's going to be that big but it's like a cavern when you open it up. Probably could do with a bit of a clean though now I've been messing with it. If you could do that for your Mum, Erika, I'm sure she'd be very grateful. Anyway, just to be sure all is working fine, I popped a bun in the oven a few minutes ago. I'm not good on timings but ask your Mum when she thinks it'll be ready to come out!"

CHAPTER THIRTY SIX

JAY

All four of us were sat around Britt's kitchen table. I was still wearing Britt's pink dressing gown that I had put on for comic effect.

"You absolute pair of bar stools!" Alice grumbled sounding more aggrieved than amused.

"Hang on! You pair of muppets were trying to set us up with your 'broken oven' capers."

"It was broken!" Erika protested.

"Only when you deliberately tripped the switch!"

They both looked a little sheepish when I said that.

"Well," Alice confessed, "you are both lovely people but you're also both very stubborn so we both felt you needed a little nudge in the right direction. We knew you wouldn't agree to meet up so we invented a reason to bring the two of you together just to see if you hit it off."

"We did hit it off, didn't we, Jay?"

"We did, very much so, just not romantically. I think Britt is a lovely, intelligent lady but, and sorry to repeat myself on this, I will always be married to Amy."

Alice ran her hands through her hair. She seemed a little cross. I wasn't sure if she was cross with me for not moving on from Amy or cross with me for playing a trick on her. It turned out to be primarily the former but the latter probably contributed too.

"Jay, look, I get you may be grieving, I totally get that, Amy died less than twelve months ago and it's not for anyone else but you to say when you are ready to move on with your life but…"

"Just to clarify," I said interrupting, "I will move on with my life but not with a romantic life."

"It doesn't make sense though, Jay," Alice continued, "I mean it's not like you're religious and you think Amy is somewhere waiting for you. You think, as you often tell me, that she's gone forever as you think you will be too, so why not seize these moments when you're a living, breathing, healthy human being and live life to the full?"

"I intend to live life to the full, Alice."

Alice seemed to be getting angrier. She shook her head.

"No, you don't Jay, you definitely don't. You just want to wallow in your loss."

I found this offensive and a little upsetting.

"I do not wallow in my loss. That's harsh to say that."

"He does, doesn't he, Erika?"

Erika paused for a few seconds whilst she weighed things up.

"Depends what you mean by wallowing. Jay, I just think you're broken hearted and you want to stay broken hearted. If a shop opened in Bolton that could mend broken hearts, you wouldn't take yours in."

She was right, I wouldn't.

"Sometimes things break for good, Erika."

"Jay, sometimes you have to try fixing things first before you throw them away," Alice said before Erika had an opportunity to continue.

"Look, even if I did want to find love again, it wouldn't be fair on the person I met. If you were a millionaire and stayed in all the best hotels in the world and then lost all your money, you wouldn't get any pleasure out of staying in a B&B."

It was a pretty lousy analogy but I was trying to think of something similar to Paul Newman's steak analogy and that was the best I could come up with off the top of my head.

"So using that analogy, what are you saying? You'd rather be homeless?" Erika asked.

"Just let me make my own decisions about where I go. That's all I'm asking."

"Fair enough," Erika said. Alice didn't say a word which to me meant that she hadn't given up on interfering.

I stood up.

"Britt, it's been a pleasure. I am going to go back upstairs now to slip out of this very smooth but very uncomfortable dressing gown and then I am going to head home. If your oven ever does genuinely need fixing or if you need any help in the house, let me know and if I can help then I will."

"Thank you, Jay, I appreciate that."

I gave Britt a kiss on the cheek. I don't like kisses like that, they always feel awkward and uncomfortable but I would have felt even more uncomfortable if I hadn't given Britt a platonic kiss. Having kissed Britt, I needed to speak to the girls. I knew their meddling had been well intentioned.

"Erika, thank you for thinking I'm a nice enough bloke to date your mother. I might not show it, but I appreciate the sentiment."

Erika stood up and gave me a hug. Alice then stood too and waited behind her. Once I had hugged Erika, I hugged Alice too. I prefer a hug to a kiss.

"I'll see you on the train on Monday. Enjoy the rest of your weekend. You don't need a lift home, do you?"

Alice looked at Erika.

"I was going to give her a lift up, Jay, but if you don't mind, that'd be great. I've got a bit of College work to catch up on this afternoon then Alice and I are going to a concert tonight so that'll be a big help."

"Sorry for being a burden," Alice said to Erika, she was definitely in a bit of a mood, the fact she could drive but regularly chose not to was perhaps a sore point.

"Don't be daft," Erika said, "I'll be around later. It'll just give me an extra hour to get my assignment sorted."

"Who are you going to see?" I said, moving the conversation on.

"Angus and Julia Stone at The Ritz in Manchester."

"Never heard of them," I confessed, "they're probably too young and trendy for me."

"No, you'd like them, Jay," Erica insisted.

"What sort of music?"

"Hard to describe, quite middle of the road. Australian indie folk."

"Not sure that's for me."

"It's better than it sounds! Alice and I both fancy Julia Stone, she has the best pair of legs I've ever seen."

"I fancy them both," Alice said, which was a definite gibe at Erika. Alice had previously told me that Erika felt threatened by her bisexuality.

With an atmosphere hanging in the air, I went upstairs, quickly changed and then felt a little reassured that Erika and Alice kissed their goodbyes before we headed out in the rain for our short journey home.

CHAPTER THIRTY SEVEN

<u>ALICE</u>

Jay was giving me a lift home after our rather embarrassing attempt to fix him up with Erika's Mum. I'd told Erika it would never work but she was pretty insistent that we gave it a go. I was a little annoyed with her for talking me into it as Britt was never going to be the one for him.

"So is that my level?" Jay asked as we pulled away up Erika's road.

"What do you mean?" I said, knowing exactly what he meant, "Britt's nice."

"She's very nice but she's pretty old too."

"Listen to you, Peter Pan! You're no spring chicken yourself. Anyway, I thought you weren't interested in anyone?"

"I'm not. I'm just interested in what you think my level is. It appears the bar isn't very high if you think NILFs are my thing."

"NILFs?"

"Nanna's I'd like to forget."

I laughed. I had got myself in a bit of a dark mood with Erika because of the blind date debacle but I could feel my frosty mood thawing.

"That's a terrible thing to say. She's not a Nanna!"

"No, but she's definitely old enough to be one."

"Jay, technically you're old enough to be a Grandad….Slow down, slow down!"

I instinctively made a grab towards the steering wheel which Jay didn't appreciate.

"What are you doing? I'm going slow!"

"The ducks," I said as a way of an explanation and pointed at our feathered friends.

From the side of our road, our beautiful mother duck, Deirdre and her now not so little offspring waddled into the road. The mother was followed by her nine children who had now grown to match her in size. She still proudly led the way though and they all respectfully followed.

"Aren't they cute?" Jay said with genuine fondness as the car pulled to a complete standstill to allow the ducks to pass in front of us.

"They're so big now. You should have seen them when they were tiny little chicks! They were so cute."

"I can imagine. They look ready to leave the nest now."

"Yeh, they must be almost there now. Erika and I love them so much, I won't eat…"

I never managed to finish that sentence. As I was saying it we saw a white Range Rover approaching from the other direction. I wouldn't say the driver was speeding, she was probably doing a steady thirty miles an hour, what caught our attention was the fact that she wasn't making any attempt to slow down. The ducks had now gone past Jay's car and were on the other side of the road. It seemed impossible not to see them.

"She hasn't seen them," Jay said with panic in his voice which was followed by a quick flash of his lights to warn the oncoming car.

For just a few seconds, I was calmer than Jay.

"Calm down, Jay, there's still plenty of time for her to stop....Jay beep your horn!"

I didn't see the moment of impact but my heart felt it. At no stage did the woman drop her speed below thirty miles per hour. She just kept coming towards the ducks at a constant speed oblivious to Jay's repeated sounding of his horn. As the Range Rover was about to impact on the helpless ducks I instinctively put my hands over my eyes and shut them tight. I don't know who that lady was or what sort of mental state she was in but I know she saw those ducklings. Something had made her heart so cold that she decided not to stop either before or after she ran over Deirdre's poor family. By the time I had taken my hands from my eyes, Jay was opening his car door, his hazard lights were already on and the back of that Range Rover was disappearing into the distance. I froze for a few seconds, scared of what I was going to witness, but then gathered enough courage to get out the car too.

It was a scene of total carnage. Blood and feathers were everywhere. One or two of the young ducks seemed to have been killed outright but others were on their sides frantically flapping their wings. Deirdre was one of them. She seemed to catch my tearful gaze, pleading with her eyes for help I could not give. I wanted to be brave, I really did but when Jay picked her up and cradled her in his arms, I noticed her broken wing and burst into tears.

"Look at them! Just look at them!" I screamed as tears cascaded down my face, "how could anyone be so wicked?"

As Jay carried the distressed mother duck in his hands, he was moving from one of her offspring to another to see if any of them were still alive. I think five were already dead and the other four were barely clinging to life.

In all the commotion, I hadn't realised that another car had pulled up facing Jay's. It was a red car, I can't recall what make it was but do remember that it looked expensive. The lady driver had also come over to tend to the ducks.

"Oh my goodness! The poor little things, have you hit them?"

"No, someone else did. She didn't stick around," Jay explained.

"How cruel! I have a large cardboard box in my boot and a picnic blanket. Shall I put the blanket in the box and maybe we could put the injured ones in there?"

"Good idea."

And so began the process, in earnest, of distinguishing between which birds had now succumbed to their injuries and which ones were still fighting for life.

The lady was a beautiful, immaculately dressed woman in her thirties. She was wearing a knee length dark green checked coat with a black faux collar but was untroubled by having her expensive clothing covered in duck feathers and blood. After retrieving the box and blanket from her car, she helped Jay and I carefully place Deirdre and three of her injured ducklings into the box. She spoke soothingly to them and stroked them gently. It felt like Jesus had sent an angel down from heaven to reduce the impact of the Devil's work. I was immediately in awe of her grace, her beauty and her general sense of calmness.

"We need to get them to a vet's," I stated, in broken tones, through my tears.

"Do you want me to drive back down to Erika's first, Alice? She might help you through this," Jay suggested.

"No, no, I don't want to disturb her. She's got work to do."

"Are you sure?"

"Yes, Jay, we need to get them to the vet's as quickly as we can.

Can you Google local vets?"

"It's OK," the lady said, "you don't need to Google it. If you guys want to follow me there's a vet's on the way to Bury where I know they can get emergency treatment."

"Because they're badly injured?"

"Well that and also because the vet is my ex-boyfriend."

CHAPTER THIRTY EIGHT

JAY

I don't think I have ever witnessed anything quite as horrific as seeing that woman's car plough into a family of ducks. It appeared callous and wicked but the only way I can process it is to think that the lady must have been mentally ill. No-one of sound mind could surely wilfully choose to drive through a whole family of ducks without stopping. I really don't think it could be possible to choose to be that unkind. For twenty four hours after that, my emotions were everywhere but not just because of the despicable actions of that woman.

Picking squashed dead ducks up off the road is second in my lifetime lows only to being told, by a nurse at a hospital I was unable to visit, that my wife had passed away. When Mary arrived at the scene of the carnage though something very strange happened within me. I have thought about it a lot since and I can only describe it as the feeling of someone using a defibrillator on my broken, romantic heart. It felt like it was being shocked back to life. I didn't want it to happen but I was powerless to stop it.

My wife, Amy was, to me and probably to many others whose path she crossed, so beautiful that she could take your breath away. The same can be said about Mary. There is so much more to feminine beauty than facial features. Mary is beautiful because of her poise, the manner in which she walks, slow, straight backed and elegant; the way her blue eyes seem to constantly gleam; the way she talks in a soft, calm, comforting voice – all these things combine to set pulses racing and palms sweating even before you get under the surface of who she really is. A tiny part of me loved her as soon as I saw her and a larger part of me hated her for the sense of betrayal I immediately felt. Up until that moment I would have insisted that it was impossible for me to find any other human even remotely attractive.

Alice was hit hard by the completely unnecessary attack on the ducks. She had watched them grow from little chicks and her attachment to them had grown steadily over several months. When we followed Mary to her ex-partners vets, Alice sobbed uncontrollably for the first five minutes of the journey before managing to bring her tears, her breathing and the flow of mucus from her nose under control aided by a few spare tissues I had in my glove compartment.

"Why would anyone do that, Jay?"

"I'd like to think that her mind was elsewhere and she just wasn't concentrating on the road."

"I don't buy that. I think she was just being an evil bitch. I think she was having a bad morning, saw the ducks in the road and just thought 'sod it, I'm not stopping'."

"Maybe," I said, unable to think of anything more comforting to add.

"It feels worse that it was a woman who did it. We're supposed to be the compassionate ones. We don't start wars and get off on killing things like men do. We're supposed to be the 'good guys'."

"Alice, there are bad women as well as bad men. Maybe nowhere near as many but it's not like they don't exist."

"I know, I get that but I just wish it wasn't true. I know from first hand experience that women can be bitches but just to plough through a whole family of ducks....words fail me."

I needed to move things along.

"This other lady is very nice though."

"Mary, yeh, she's an angel."

I knew her name was Mary, we had done very brief introductions amidst the chaos but I felt a wave of guilt sweeping over me when I was about to acknowledge her by name so deliberately avoided it. For an atheist to be imagining his dead wife looking over him with a mixture of confusion and disgust was a bizarre feeling.

"Let's hope her boyfriend can do something to save them."

"Ex-boyfriend," Alice said, correcting me.

There was a bit of a silence after that so I was left to ponder whether Alice was matchmaking again. Regardless of whether or not Alice intended to pull back cupid's bow for a second time in a day was immaterial – I was 100% sure that Mary would have no interest in me. I was also 100% sure that I didn't want a relationship with her either but part of me felt good that I still had the capacity to find someone attractive. I thought those feelings had been buried with my wife. I was intrigued to see Mary's ex-partner though, just to get an indication of what sort of man could attract a woman like that. I already knew he was a rich, intelligent one. Vets didn't tend to be poor or stupid.

I have to admit when we were subsequently introduced to Austin Pearson, I momentarily stopped thinking about those poor injured ducks. I was too busy cursing the fact that as well as the intelligence and the money, Austin had been blessed with incredibly good looks. Good enough to advertise after shave with his top off in a women's magazine. He was slim and chiselled which gave him the initial appearance of being a tall man but I subsequently realised he was probably only six feet tall at most. He just looked like the type of guy who spent all his leisure time drinking bottled water, eating a vegan diet and running ultra marathons. In the same way I always imagined gay men's ejaculate would be rainbow coloured, I imagined his would have little gold stars in or fragments of diamond. He certainly wasn't a pie and chips man like me.

Alice and I had to wait for our introduction to Austin though. Mary had asked one of the ladies on the counter for him personally when she had entered the surgery carrying a box full of distressed ducks. She was ushered through a door that had a sign saying 'Staff Only'.

"Are we supposed to follow her?" Alice asked as the doorway closed behind Mary.

"Maybe we're best just taking a seat in the waiting room," I suggested, so we sat and waited amongst a collection of people with a variety of animals; barking dogs, cats, mice and reptiles in a variety of cages, a man with a bird in a shoe box and several people with animals that were hidden from prying eyes which I imagined to be snakes and spiders.

"Do you think any of them will make it?" Alice asked about the ducks, still with watery eyes.

I wasn't in a position to gloss things up as I knew that before we left that surgery we would be aware of their fate which could only be a slow, painful recovery or death. I wasn't hopeful nor did I pretend to be.

"I've no idea, but they all looked in a very bad way."

"If I ever get my hands on that woman, I'll grab her by the scruff of the neck and throw her in front of a passing car and see how she likes it!"

A few of the people glanced over with concerned looks on their faces thinking they were sharing a waiting room with a maniac.

"You're too nice a person to actually do that."

"I'd like to though."

"So would I. Did you happen to see what she looked like?"

"I don't think so, but maybe if I saw her again I'd realise it was her. I'll certainly be checking out any white Range Rovers that come down Erika's road."

We sat silently for a while and then I noticed out the corner of my eye that something was amusing Alice. It started as a smile and then became repressed laughter.

"What's funny?" I asked quietly.

It makes me uncomfortable when someone starts laughing when I'm around. Paranoia dictates that I assume they are laughing at me. I start imaging I have a big ball of snot hanging down from my nose or someone has drawn a penis on my fore-head in lipstick whilst I have been sleeping or something randomly illogical.

"I can't say," Alice replied, still stifling her laughter.

"Why not?" I whispered.

"Just because."

"Tell me," I urged, if it was something to do with me I was desperate to know.

"Jay, we have an audience," Alice replied now whispering too.

"Can you whisper it in my ear then?"

"Yes."

"Go on then," I said impatiently.

Alice kneeled on her seat, cupped her hands and whispered into my ear.

"See the guy who has just come in at eleven o'clock?"

She meant his location rather than his time of arrival but it took me a split second to realise that. I looked over. There was a young lad, probably in his early twenties, with a pug on his lap. The lad looked like he was wearing a little light make up and the pug had a diamond studded pink collar and a pink bow. Pugs always looked sad but this one looked particularly miserable.

"Yes."

"He's gay."

"And you can tell that just by looking?" I whispered back sarcastically.

"Well, yes, but he is gay. I see him out around Canal Street regularly. He's always hammered so he probably doesn't remember me but he's a right laugh when he's pissed."

"So you were thinking of some of his antics, were you? What sort of thing does he get up to?"

"Oh no, I wasn't thinking about that at all."

"Why did you point him out then?"

"I don't know, I can't remember."

"Great. Well thanks for clearing that up."

"Hang on, it'll come to me. What was it? Oh, I know now - gay sex! Seeing him made me think about gay sex and that's what made me laugh."

"Why?"

"I was wondering how it works."

"Surely you know how it works!"

"I mean when it stops."

"Age wise?"

"No!"

"What then? I'm confused."

"When they stop. Two women having sex carry on until one gets tired. A man and a woman having sex carry on until the man orgasms. If he's made a particularly bad job of it, he might make a half hearted attempt to carry on for thirty seconds but then everything starts shrinking so he has to give up pretty quickly. Men are either too selfish or it's just a design flaw but either way they have absolutely no interest in continuing after they come so what happens with gay men? Do you think they carry on or do you think they just pack in after the first one comes?"

"I can honestly say I have never thought about it."

I didn't tell her I had thought about rainbow ejaculate but maybe this prior conversation was what made me think about it when we met Austin.

"I must ask Steve and Andy," Alice concluded.

"Well, I'm glad that thought has brightened your day."

"I have to admit it has been a temporary distraction."

"Have you text Erika yet?"

"Shit, no! I'll do that now."

We didn't speak again until Mary re-emerged with Austin in tow. Alice spent the following ten minutes texting at mesmerizingly lightning speed and when I wasn't transfixed by her million words a minute typing, I was watching the shenanigans of our fellow waiting room inhabitants and totting up the total amount that was being paid at the counter. It was an astronomical sum. If I had my life again, I would have put the extra effort in at school and made sure I achieved the grades to study veterinary science at University. This set me thinking about how my life would have been different. I may never have got together with Amy if I'd have stayed indoors swotting. I started considering whether that would have been a good or bad thing. Was the magic of being married to such a wonderful person worth the pain of losing her at such a young age? I had just decided it was definitely worth it, when Mary re-appeared followed by Austin. He walked purposefully into the centre of the waiting room. Given everyone else there was sat with animals, he pinpointed that Alice and I were the people he was looking for, probably aided by a description from Mary.

"Jay and Alice?" he asked us.

"Yes," I confirmed.

"Please to meet you both, I'm Austin," he said in a softly spoken, privately educated tone, reaching out his hand allowing Alice and me to shake it, "please follow me through."

As well as his movie star looks, I concluded Austin spoke exactly how an American would expect an English Prime Minister to speak, like David Cameron or Hugh Grant. He led us through a passageway to a side room where Mary was sitting in a corner. Her half-hearted smile indicated that either the news was unlikely to be positive or she had just had a massive row with her ex-boyfriend. I hoped for the latter but that hope didn't last.

"I'm afraid it's not good news," Austin began.

I caught sight of Alice's expression and my heart sank. I desperately wanted it to be one of those 'X' Factor moments when a smile suddenly broke out on Austin's face and he followed up with 'it's great news' but knew it wasn't the time for a stranger to be playing with our emotions.

"The ducks suffered catastrophic injuries and after a thorough assessment of all four of them, I'm afraid the only humane option available was to put them to sleep."

"They're all dead?" Alice asked, her voice quivering with emotion.

"I'm afraid so," Austin explained, "rest assured if there had been anything I could possibly have done, I would have done it without hesitation, but they were all suffering very badly."

"So that bitch has wiped out the whole Deirdre Duck family. If I ever get my hands on her…"

Alice's voice trailed off. She sat down next to Mary and started to cry. Mary put a comforting arm around Alice and hugged her.

"We did all we could Alice," she said soothingly, "we couldn't have left them in that much pain."

Austin directed his gaze towards me.

"Mary is right. You all did everything you could. I'm awfully sorry that didn't turn out to be enough. As you saw for yourself, we are dealing with a whole host of sick animals this morning so I'll have to leave you. If you want to remain in here until everyone is ready, you're welcome to, then just make your way back through to the waiting room."

"OK, thanks for trying to help us."

"Not a problem."

Austin turned towards Mary.

"Lovely to see you again, Mary. I'm sorry it was in such sad circumstances. Hopefully we'll speak again soon. Take care."

"Thanks so much for everything, Austin."

I watched their interaction. There definitely felt like there was some unfinished business between them as it appeared to me like love was still in the air. After Austin left the room, it all went quiet, only interrupted by Alice's gentle sobbing and occasional reassuring words from Mary. We probably stayed in there for about ten minutes, with Alice and Mary remaining seated and me standing, pacing aimlessly around the room.

"Do you need to be anywhere?" I eventually asked Mary, partially just to break my own silence, "You must have been heading somewhere before all this happened."

"Not particularly, I'd just nipped out to Spar to get some milk and a loaf of bread."

"No plans for the rest of the day?"

I was discreetly prying.

"Bit of washing and ironing to catch up on. Probably catch up with 'Bloodline' on Netflix too."

This was wasted on me as I had no idea what 'Bloodline' was. I presumed though, based on her answer and the fact that we had just ventured into her ex-boyfriend's vets that she must be single, she didn't have a wedding band on and at that stage had made no mention of children. Following this line of logic, unless she was a Lottery winner or from an extremely wealthy family, she must work somewhere to be able to survive.

"Not working today?"

I knew it was a Saturday but a lot of people work Saturdays these days.

"No, a bit of paperwork to catch up on this afternoon but that's about it."

"What is it you do?"

"I'm a financial adviser."

This wasn't a shock. She had a professional manner so I had anticipated that she would have some sort of professional job.

"Are you out tonight?"

"Not sure yet, some of my friends are off into Manchester, I might go with them but I'll see how I feel later."

Mary stood up. She hadn't asked any questions back so I presumed she had revealed as much as she wanted to reveal and had no interest in my life. Alice then stood up too.

"Well, I hope you have a great night if you do go out," I said with a polite smile before directing my gaze towards my tearful young friend, "Come on then, Alice, let's get you home."

"OK, thanks for everything, Mary. We've crossed paths with a bitch and an angel today."

"Some of my exes will tell you I can be both," Mary said almost laughing at her own joke.

"Well," Alice replied, "that's because men are idiots."

"True," Mary agreed, "anyway, you get yourself home. I'm sure your Dad will take good care of you."

Alice and I looked at each other.

"Jay's not my Dad," Alice started to explain.

"Oh, I'm sorry. I just presumed with the generational difference and everything that he…"

"He's my husband," Alice blurted out.

I don't really know why she said it. It was a very odd thing to say. Perhaps it was just another attempt to lighten her own mood or maybe she thought Mary would know instantly that it was a joke and would laugh but Mary didn't laugh at all – in fact, quite the opposite. She looked mortified. She tried to speak but words weren't coming out of her mouth, just embarrassed noises. She spluttered some incoherent nonsense. I wasn't comfortable seeing her look so ill at ease.

"Alice! Take no notice of her, Mary. We're just friends. Alice's brother, Dominic is best friends' with my son, Hunter and Alice and I get the train to work together. A lot has happened over the last twelve months and…"

"And Mary doesn't need to hear our life stories," Alice stopped me mid-ramble, "Sorry about the husband thing, I just sort of said it without thinking then immediately felt bad about it. Jay would make a lovely husband but I don't think my girlfriend would be too delighted if he married me."

"You're rambling now," I said to Alice with a degree of satisfaction.

"I know, sorry!"

"Don't be silly, I enjoy hearing a bit about you," Mary responded kindly, "It has been genuinely lovely to meet you both, it's just a shame it's been in such horrible circumstances."

After a further bit of small talk we kissed our goodbyes. Alice got a hug too. I must admit I felt I needed one as well but I was subsequently glad that it wasn't forthcoming. I knew there was something special about Mary and it scared me how much her introduction into my life had had on my equilibrium.

PART TWO

CHAPTER THIRTY NINE

<u>Twelve Months Later</u>

<u>JAY</u>

Alice and I often found silly ways to pass time on our train journey. This particular morning was no different. We were discussing which famous people we found attractive.

"What about Carol, the BBC weather lady?" I asked.

"No, come on! Far too old for me! Isn't she about sixty?"

"I'd say mid-fifties."

"Ooh Jay, do you have a bit of a thing for her?"

I could feel myself blushing. I couldn't remember the last time I had felt myself blush. It must have been at least twenty years before.

"Well, there's definitely something about her I find attractive," I confessed.

"Two things I would imagine, her boobs are pretty amazing."

"I was going to say her jovial manner and her Scottish lilt."

"Of course you were!"

"Anyway, why are you looking at her boobs? You just said she was far too old."

"It's impossible not to notice her boobs, they sort of come out the screen like they're three dimensional. I have a lot of boob envy going on when it comes to Carol Kirkwood. God has been over generous there."

"OK, what about Kate Lawler?" I said, moving on from the wonderful Carol.

"Who's Kate Lawler?"

"Come on! Surely you're not too young to know who Kate Lawler is?"

"I seriously have no idea who you are talking about."

"She's on Virgin Radio…"

"Still no idea."

"She won 'Big Brother' years ago…"

"I've never watched Big Brother."

"Well, have a look on social media."

"Just describe her for me, I can't be bothered Googling her."

"Blonde, pretty tall, skinny, a bit girl next door type, pleasant looking but not all that amazing, but her voice is the sexiest voice I've ever heard."

"Really? I want to hear her talk now."

"She's on Virgin when I drive home. People think Nigella Lawson has a sexy voice, but it just sounds to me like a snobby woman failing to be sexy in an embarrassing fashion."

"Harsh."

"But true. Listen to Kate Lawler - drive time on Virgin - a voice for the loins."

"What's so sexy about her voice then?"

"I don't know really, it's sort of Southern but not posh and not chavvy, a bit husky but not full on Mariella Frostrup."

"Jay! You know I have no idea who Mary-Ellen Frostrup is. You just say all these people from years ago because you enjoy confusing me."

There was more than an element of truth in this. I defended my corner though.

"Confusing you? I have to listen to you and Erika talk about tattooing eye brows and lips and shellacking nails, whatever the hell that means!"

"Shellac is just a manicured polish with a high-shine finish."

"Are you still speaking English? Anyway, it's Mariella Frostrup, not Mary-Ellen."

"I'm not really bothered."

"Me neither, I've bored myself now. Let's move on."

"OK, Erika wouldn't like me playing this game anyway."

"Why not?"

"She'd accuse us of objectifying women."

"She takes herself too seriously sometimes. It's just a bit of fun trying to find someone we both find physically attractive. It wouldn't work with men."

"True."

"Is being physically attractive a burden?"

Alice gave me a quizzical look along with a frown.

"Are you being serious?"

"Of course I am, why?"

"I'm not exactly Adriana Lima."

I had no idea who that was but presumed it must be a 21st Century version of Cindy Crawford. I would normally ask but I let it go. I still don't know.

"You must know you're pretty though."

"Maybe if you catch me on a good day."

"Stop being so modest! It's a compliment, take it without objection. All I was wondering was whether being physically attractive can sometimes work against you as people could maybe try and befriend you before they know who you really are."

"Did you?"

I hadn't thought that accusation could have been directed at me but it was a point to ponder.

"I certainly didn't start talking to you because I wanted a relationship with you but maybe subconsciously if you hadn't been pleasant looking I may not have struck up that initial conversation. I'd like to think I'm not that shallow though even subconsciously. I'm talking more about young lads or young lesbian girls, do you ever feel strangers just start randomly attempting to strike up a conversation because they ultimately want to date you?"

"Well if they have, I've been totally oblivious to it. People make more of a beeline for Erika anyway. She's the one with the looks that make peoples jaws drop."

"Is she not so good looking that people are intimidated by her though?"

"It doesn't work like that these days. One lad said to me that he only ever goes for girls with looks that are ten out of ten. He said most of the time he gets knocked back but occasionally the girl likes him and then all his mates ask him how he managed to pull a girl that's a rocket!"

"A rocket?"

"A beauty."

"OK. So, on the subject of rockets, how is Erika?"

"She's good. I'm going over to Leeds on Friday to see her."

"Do you miss seeing her every day?"

"Erm…not really."

"Hang on a minute! What's going on here?"

"What do you mean?"

"Well, that doesn't sound like the infatuated Alice of last year."

"No, no, I'm still in love, I just meant that I see her loads and there's something nice about having a few days apart and the excitement building as the day nears when you will be meeting up again. I'm going there this weekend, she's back home the following weekend, we Facetime loads and I'm really busy at College with my assignments so I feel like the balance is just right."

"How's her Mum?"

"Britt? She's good. It wasn't cancer. I've told you that, haven't I? It was just a cyst."

"Yes, you told me."

"She still asks about you each time I'm there. I reckon you'd just have to wink or nod in her direction and her big Granny knickers would be around her ankles."

"I don't imagine Britt is the type of more mature lady who wears big knickers."

"True. Posh thongs?"

"I'll never know but I would imagine so."

"Not even attempted to release some of that pent up sexual frustration with a no strings attached night of passion with a classy old bird?"

I smiled.

"Stop winding me up! You know only too well that I'm not interested."

"Sorry, you're right I am just winding you up…..I'm looking forward to next Saturday night."

"The big Chorley pub crawl for Hunter's 17th?"

"Yes, I can't wait."

"I can, it's going to be a nightmare. He's going to be an absolute mess. He shouldn't even be going out boozing at his age but I can't seem to stop him."

"Me and Erika will look after him."

"We'll see. I think he's beyond control these days."

CHAPTER FORTY

<u>**ALICE**</u>

Hunter's 17th birthday celebrations were incident packed and not entirely for the right reasons. The issues were, like they so often are, compounded by alcohol intake. We were all incredibly drunk. When I say all, I'm not including Jay, as he hadn't been out all afternoon like Erika, Dom, Hunter and me. Although Erika and I both suggested inviting Jay along, Hunter wouldn't let him come. I think he felt his Dad would cramp his style and he probably couldn't let himself go with his Dad watching over him – he certainly didn't struggle in his Dad's absence.

To ensure Jay wasn't totally left out, we agreed to meet him in a bar behind the bus station in Chorley called 'The Ale Station'. Jay likes to nip in there for a couple of pints on a Saturday afternoon. It's become his little routine over the last six months. He said if we nipped in there for an hour, he'd buy us a drink.

I still find it weird going into Chorley with my kid brother even though I've probably been into town with him and Hunter a dozen times now. He still seems too young to be out drinking and technically he is, but he has managed to get himself a false ID and seems to get away with it in the majority of places.

Dominic is a funny drunk. Hunter is too. They get all childish and giggly. Dom keeps himself to himself but Hunter is a little wilder. I feel under some sort of weird obligation to keep an eye on him though. Jay's been through enough shit without something happening to Hunter and drugs are rife around here on a night out. Cocaine seems to be the main drug of choice but you wouldn't know what shit's been put into it. You'd have to be thicker than a porn star's cock to think Colombia's finest would end up on the streets of Chorley. Anything that ends up on the streets of Chorley is probably watered down with whatever crappy white powder scummy dealers can get their hands on.

Hunter's actual seventeenth birthday had been the day before. Jay, Hunter and several family members including Amy's parents, Jay's parents and a few Aunties, Uncles and cousins had been for a meal at 'The Malthouse', a family pub and restaurant in Whittle-le-Woods by the canal. Apparently it went well, there were pictures of Hunter sat in Jay's car with 'L' plates on, driving them both home afterwards, which were cute, although Jay was looking a little petrified in the passenger seat. Hunter didn't do so well in his GCSE's so is working as an apprentice for a builders firm, so apparently chipped in a few quid to get himself on the insurance.

Erika, Dom, Hunter and I had a Saturday session planned for weeks. Hunter knew he had the family 'do' on the Friday, which he said he just wanted to get through rather than look forward to. It was only his second birthday without Amy and he said having her family around him made it tougher. The Saturday was therefore earmarked as a real opportunity to let his hair down and party properly. We certainly did that.

I had stayed the night at Erika's Mum's on the Friday after Erika arrived home from University. Sober, getting re-acquainted sex is lovely, tender and warms the cockles of your heart but given a straight choice, I'd always opt for the drunken, passionate, sordid, no-holds barred, saucy sex that you end up having after a drunken night out. Sex that takes you to places that you'd probably be too embarrassed to venture in sobriety. 'Did we really do that?' sex that makes you both blush and smile when you wake up the following morning. That's where we went on Saturday night, bizarrely in a spare room at Jay's house and even more bizarrely he didn't arrive home until Sunday morning.

Before all the naughty sex in Jay's spare bedroom, as I say, there were plenty of goings on. Erika drove us up from Bolton to Euxton on Saturday morning and after an awkward cup of tea with Mum and John, we got into our party clobber and ventured out. When I say awkward with Mum and John, I specifically mean John. I think he's a bit mesmerised by Erika. He tries to tell jokes to make her laugh but Erika is laughing more because they are crap jokes and they're badly delivered rather than because they are actually funny. Erika doesn't mind but it just makes me squirm and I'm glad when I get her out of there. I love John, I really do, but I don't like the person he becomes around Erika.

First stop on our marathon session of pub crawling was 'The Talbot' – my old work place. With the amount of assignments I need to do this year, I knew I'd be knackered if I continued to work there so asked them to take me off the rota back in September when I started the College year. They still ring me up if someone calls in sick or they need extra staff for a shift due to holidays or because they have a singer or a band on so I still do the odd shift from time to time. It's becoming less and less often now though. It has been useful extra money for travelling backwards and forwards to Leeds though, which isn't cheap.

The Talbot was a good place to start. I obviously know all the staff there and I enjoyed introducing them to Erika as she was looking particularly stunning. She had a tight white crop top on and white jeans and was more heavily made up than I had ever seen her before. I could see the lads behind the bar drooling like hungry dogs. Like most of us, she has her good and bad days looks wise, but on her bad days she still looks gorgeous and on her good days she looks out of this world. On Hunter's birthday, Erika was at her finest.

Dom and Hunter were supposed to be meeting us at midday in The Talbot but when it had turned half past and they still hadn't arrived, I text Dom.

'Where the hell r u?'

'Still at Hunter's.'

'Y?'

'He's been shaving and he's cut the head off a spot and it won't stop bleeding!'

'Gr8. Tell him 2 wet a piece of loo paper and stick it on top until it dries.'

'OK. How do u know that?'

'Works on my beard,' I text jokingly, subconsciously rubbing my chin after I text it.

'Ew. I'm your brother, I don't want to be thinking about your lady beard.'

'I didn't mean that. Knob. Just hurry up.'

'OK, how do you really know?'

'Remember Dad doing it when we were kids. I repeat hurry up.'

'OK. C u soon.'

Half an hour later they showed up and we kissed our hellos.

"Happy Birthday! Only an hour late for your own celebrations you big pussy," I teased Hunter moving towards him to rub his hair. He stepped back protectively.

"Take the piss but don't touch the hair," he said jokily but I knew he was serious, "it takes time to look this good."

I wouldn't say Hunter was a particularly good looking lad

but he was developing a confidence and ability to flatter that could charm young, impressionable girls.

"OK," I said, running a hand down the side of his face, "good to feel it's bum fluff free."

"I have to tone down the masculinity for the benefit of Chorley's female population. The full-scale Hunter is too much of an Adonis for Chorley to cope. The local paramedics couldn't cope with all the swooning."

"It's not doing anything for me," Erika commented in a tone that indicated that she was less than impressed by Hunter's arrogance.

"Yeh, but you're a big, fat hairy lezza," Hunter said jokily but nobody laughed.

"You've still got some bog paper stuck to your neck, Hunter," Erika replied stoically.

"Shit! I haven't, have I?" Hunter said panicking and running around his neck, "Where is it?"

"Oh sorry, did I say toilet paper on your neck, I meant a dick on your head."

Erika and Hunter were normally fine with each other but could sometimes clash as they were both strong minded and opinionated. Jay was far more modest and self-deprecating than Hunter.

"So what are you lads drinking?" I asked trying to ease the tension that I could feel building.

"E-strella," Hunter said.

"It's pronounced E-streya," Erika corrected him.

"OK, Miss Know-it-all. We'll have two pints of that."

"You can say please sometimes, Hunter."

"What's with the attitude, Erika?" Hunter asked.

"Just don't spoil the day by being a prick."

"Don't you mean 'Happy Birthday Hunter'?"

"Happy Birthday Hunter but don't be a prick."

"I won't. I know how much you hate pricks."

"OK then," I said, the lads had only been there two minutes and already you could cut the atmosphere with a knife which didn't bode well for the rest of the day, "another Gin & Tonic, Erika?"

"Please."

Erika made a point of looking at Hunter after she said the word 'please'.

"Kiss and make up though children, it's a celebration."

We probably only stayed in 'The Talbot' for another hour or so but it was long enough for the initial tensions to die down. Despite him being too cocky for his own good some times, Hunter was also incredibly funny and the more he drank the more he needed to be centre stage. Erika calmed down though and just let him do his thing. Once Hunter and Dominic had had a couple of pints they were itching to head up into town.

Dom ordered a Cooper's taxi on his phone. The driver who turned up looked a bit peeved that it was only a fare that took him a mile and a half back into town but it was raining and neither me or Erika wanted to arrive in town looking bedraggled. The lads would have been knackered too, they don't do anything to keep fit these days having stopped playing football, as they prefer to spend their lives drinking lager or playing on their X-Box, so the climb up the hill would have seemed like a marathon to them. Anyway, we gave him a fiver for three minutes work so as long as he picked up another fare relatively quickly in town it won't have worked out too badly for him.

The rest of the afternoon slowly descended into an alcoholic mist. I remember going into Sir Henry Tate when the taxi dropped us off and the lads went into the bookies to have a bet on the football. Funny what sticks in your head after a heavy session though, I clearly recall two old boozers at the bar asking us whether we knew who Sir Henry Tate was. We looked at each other, shrugged and confessed we hadn't the foggiest. One of the blokes then said he was the Scouser who started a sugar company that went on to become 'Tate & Lyle' and funded the art gallery that became known as the 'Tate Modern' in London.

"Impressive but what's that got to do with Chorley?" Erika asked the main bloke who was telling us the story whilst his mate ordered them both another pint.

"He was born and raised in Chorley," the gap toothed boozer explained.

"White Coppice to be exact," his mate shouted over from further down the bar, they had dispersed to double the chances of getting served.

"So Bradley Wiggins has a gold post box and Sir Henry Tate has a pub," I pointed out, "we know how to look after our own around here!"

"I bet Joseph Gilgun wouldn't mind a pub named after him," Erika observed.

"Fair point," I conceded, "the Sir Joseph Gilgun would be a cool name for a pub."

"Who's Sir Joseph Gilgun?" the old blokes both asked simultaneously.

"Chorley's finest ever actor," I answered.

"I've never heard of him," the guy further down the bar said, heading back towards us with two wobbly pints of Bitter.

"Not as smart as you think you are, pal," Erika said as we moved to a corner table with our Gin & Tonics.

I remember that first drink, I remember the lads coming in and getting us a second Gin and then after that, the afternoon disappeared into an alcoholic black hole until we headed over to 'The Ale Station' to see Jay. Apparently, when we tried to piece our afternoon together, we had frequented several other bars in between but what we discussed and who entertained us with their witty banter has been consigned to history. All I remember was noticing that Hunter was absolutely caning the drinks and thinking it would all end in tears. It did too but if you'd have given me a million guesses, I would never have guessed how. I just thank God Dominic isn't quite as stupid.

CHAPTER FORTY ONE

JAY

I enjoy a quiet pint in 'The Ale Station' on a Saturday afternoon. Coronavirus took more from me than most, but I think most people realised how much their local bar or pub meant to them once the lockdown was lifted. My natural reaction after Amy's death was to hide inside my shell whilst I tried to adjust to life without her, but as time passed and I learnt the painstaking process of how to cope, time spent within the warm community atmosphere of 'The Ale Station' became important to me.

Mick the barman at 'The Ale Station' or to give him his rightful title, 'The Owner', is a bit of a beer aficionado like myself and always ensures he has a range of good quality guest ales for me to sample. There are no doubt other places in Chorley that have just as warm an atmosphere and a wider variety of beers but I have come to know Mick, his staff and also his family over the last few months so have no intention of spending my Saturday afternoons anywhere else. They are all good people and it has that clichéd feeling of being like a second home.

I may know Mick's family but one of the comforts of being there, at that point, was that I always felt, rightly or wrongly, that he didn't know mine. I don't mean that he doesn't know Hunter, he vaguely does, as Hunter does pop his head in occasionally. I mean he didn't appear to know about Amy. I think he made a comment once about me sneaking away from the wife for a crafty pint and I just didn't correct him. I hate seeing people's faces drop with an unnecessary guilt when I explain that I'm a widower so I just hadn't told Mick. I think most people around here see me as 'Poor Jay' and I would just prefer to be seen as plain old 'Jay'.

On that Saturday of Hunter's 17th Mick got to meet all the people I now consider to be my 'close family' and despite them all being perfectly pleasant, I felt it was a bit of a shame that he didn't get to see them at their best. Alcohol doesn't enhance anyone's character it just magnifies all their personality traits so makes them a cartoon version of their real selves.

Alice, Erika, Hunter and Dominic had arranged to meet me for 'one swift pint' (as Hunter put it) in the interim period between their afternoon drinking session and their evening one. I had put the plan in place with Alice, really just to check Hunter was OK. He has become a fairly regular drinker over the last twelve months which I have felt powerless to stop, but his capacity to tolerate alcohol doesn't appear to be improving and I am often awoken in the early hours of a Saturday or Sunday morning to the sound of 'heaving' emanating from the bathroom. The bathroom if I'm lucky anyway. Sometimes Hunter is sick off the side of his bed, sometimes all over the sheets and he has been known to both vomit and urinate in his bedroom cupboards. He is a kid trying to be a man and at this stage he's still failing.

To be fair to all four of them, although they were all evidently drunk when they semi-staggered into 'The Ale House', they all came across as the pleasant, friendly, polite kids that they actually are. The two girls weren't in anywhere near as bad a state as the lads and were both capable of coherent conversation whilst Dominic and Hunter just seemed to mainly just communicate with each other in a strange 'Lord Of The Rings' type language.

I have a lot of time for Dominic and think he is a good influence on Hunter. He's a quiet lad but when you engage him in conversation he tends to have a lot of interesting things to say. He isn't one of these kids who comes out of his shell under the influence of alcohol but it does bring out in him an element of contentedness and self-satisfaction that isn't as visible when he's sober. In drink he smiles to himself almost constantly and finds everything incredibly funny. Dominic's laugh actually makes me laugh. It's a very deep guffaw. It reminds me of how Frank Bruno used to laugh when interviewed by Harry Carpenter in the 1980's.

Hunter, however, is different. Alcohol makes him brash and, I hate saying this, but even as his father I find him annoying when under the influence. He is too self-assured for his tender years and it worries me that he'll say some smart arsed comment to the wrong person in a bar and end up getting a taste of someone's fist.

Erika offered to buy me a drink.

"Just get me a half of the 'Indian Pale Ale' please Erika, but ask Mick if he'll do you two pints of tap water too for the lads. I said I'd get a round in but I'll wait to see what sort of shape these reprobates are in after they've had a while to sober up."

"Come on, Dad!" Hunter protested, "It's my birthday. I wouldn't have come in here if I'd have known you were going to get all arsey! I'm not drinking water on my birthday."

Dominic muttered something to Hunter but it wasn't clear enough for me to hear.

"What did he say?" I asked, pulling a confused face at Hunter.

"It doesn't matter," Hunter said dismissively.

"No, go on, what did he say?"

"He said a pint of water might help us get through the night!"

"That's right! Good lad, Dom! You need to listen to him, Hunter, he's obviously the one with all the brains. You want to be enjoying yourself later rather than puking into a toilet at half past nine."

"I never puke!"

"We must have a ghost with a bad gag reflex in our house then. A ghost that only haunts at weekends."

"Very funny."

Erika followed instructions. She went to the bar then made two journeys back, the first with two pints of water and my Indian Pale Ale before returning a second time with some sort of short for herself and Alice."

"What are you drinking?" I enquired.

"Gin & Grapefruit tonic."

"Very nice."

"There's a woman at the bar who keeps looking over at you lot like she knows you," Erika said as she passed Alice her drink. I looked across and knew immediately who it was. My heart started beating like I was giving Usain Bolt a race. Confused by alcohol, Alice was a lot slower on the uptake.

"Which one, hun?"

"The blonde one. She's waving now."

"Oh yeh, I recognise her. Who the bloody hell is it? Oh, I know! It's MARY!"

Alice stood up, raced over to Mary and gave her a big hug. After the pandemic, people were split into two camps, those who hugged more and those who never hugged again. Alice was a hugger. Erika looked confused and a little perturbed by Alice's exuberant reaction.

"Who the hell is Mary?" Erika asked.

"I've no idea but my penis seems to like her," Dominic said in clearer tones than he had spoken since he arrived.

"Yeh, she's a MILF rocket." Hunter added.

These observations seemed to darken Erika's mood.

"She's not all that great," she sniped.

"Oh, but she is," Dominic replied.

"Mary is the lady who was there when the ducks were run over," I explained.

As I was elaborating on the duck story, filling them in on who exactly the mysterious blonde lady was, Alice was bringing her over to where we were sat.

"Everyone, this is Mary," Alice announced, "this is the angel that tried everything she could to save Deirdre Duck and her little family."

"Hi Mary," Hunter, Erika and Dominic said collectively, Hunter and Dom with more gusto than Erika who seemed evidently jealous of the angel in our midst.

"Hello again, Mary," I said once a bit of initial commotion and pleasant chit chat had died down, "are you here with someone or would you care to join us?" I asked, ready to grab a chair at a moment's notice.

"I'm actually on my own so if you wouldn't mind me briefly joining you that would be lovely. I'm only staying for the one drink though."

There was a lot of collective encouragement for Mary to grab a seat with us, which I noticed Erika didn't partake in, but ignoring her sullen mood, I grabbed a spare seat from a nearby table and our circle was widened to accommodate our new guest.

"Thank you," Mary said as I offered her a seat and then sat down beside her.

"How come you're here on your own then?" Erika enquired.

"I was escaping," Mary replied mysteriously with an embarrassed smile.

"Escaping from who or what?" Alice asked intrigued.

"From a bad date," Mary replied coyly.

"Oh no! What happened?" Alice pressed.

"Well, in a nutshell it started badly and became progressively worse. I gave it a couple of hours out of common courtesy but if I ever set eyes on that man again I'll know I've died and gone to hell. I've concluded Chorley men definitely aren't the greatest."

"Watch what you're saying! You're talking to three of us. We aren't all bad," I tried to say this in a jokey, friendly tone but once it had come out, I started worrying that it may have sounded something like a come on, which felt awkward so I found myself pulling back from the conversation and allowing the others to ask the questions. In summary, Mary had been on a date, arranged via Tinder (why she had to resort to Tinder for a date is beyond me) with a bloke from Chorley. It turned out he wasn't much of a gentleman though , he had turned up in a jacket that he'd been out fishing in during the day and was still giving off an aroma of pond water and dead fish. The conversation had largely been about carp, roach, rolling your own cigarettes and Chorley Football Club.

"Facially he was beautiful," Mary explained, "but he was rude and boring. It was never going to work."

"Sounds like a disaster. You're very brave using Tinder. I could never do that. You can't see a soul in a photograph," Alice observed.

"What are you on about? Of course you can." Hunter said, screwing up his face to signal confusion whilst implying Alice had said something ridiculous.

"Soul spelt S-O-U-L not S-O-L-E, you retard!" Alice bit back.

"Rug muncher," Hunter replied, before taking a gulp on his water.

Alice glared at him. I could tell Hunter was starting to grate with everyone with the smart arsed comments that were starting to become more common place when he spoke to the group. In this case, however, he picked up on Alice's look.

"It was meant in a lovable way," he said defensively and almost apologetically. Hunter thinks a lot of Alice and wouldn't want to upset her.

"Anyway, two hours was long enough," Mary continued, ignoring the bickering, "so when he suggested we head back over towards his place in Eccleston and have something to eat in an Italian over there, I decided it was time for me to make a hasty exit. I said I was nipping to the Ladies and never returned. I felt a bit mean doing that but I was just overcome with an urge to escape. I was going to just jump on a train back to Bolton but just missed one so was just nipping in here for a quick glass of wine to settle my jaded nerves when I spotted you guys."

"You should come out with us," Alice pressed.

"No, I might run into my date and don't want to have to provide an explanation."

"Just be honest and tell him he was boring. It might sting a little but he might be a bit nicer then on his next date," Alice suggested.

"No, no, I'm going to head home."

"Come on, it's Hunter's birthday, we'll have a great laugh," Alice persisted.

I couldn't help but glance over at Erika who was making no effort to look as encouraging.

"No, I don't think so, Alice."

"Come on, please," Alice begged with puppy dog eyes and cupped hands.

"Thank you for thinking I would contribute positively to

your night out, Alice but honestly, after the day I've had, I'll be happier to be home and back in my pyjamas and slippers by nine o'clock."

"Oh Mary, you're a young, single woman, you should be letting your hair down," Alice said with frustration.

"Not that young anymore! It's flattering that you are being so persistent but I won't be coming. This white wine is going down very nicely so I may well stay around for another glass but after that I'll be off home no matter how much effort you make to try to persuade me otherwise."

Mary did stay for another glass. Mick came over collecting glasses and I introduced him to everyone. The bar had quietened down briefly at that point as a big group of lads who had come down from Chorley Cricket Club had just left so he poured himself a pint and sat with us for twenty minutes. The conversations broke off into two groups, ours involved Mick, Mary, Alice and myself whilst Erika and the boys drifted off into a separate conversation about Marvel characters I think. Our conversation was largely about how the Coronavirus had changed all the human race that had lived through it. Most people had lost someone, whether it was a neighbour, a family member, a friend or a work colleague, they had suffered loss. They had also, for a period of months, lost their freedom and regaining it had made them value it more.

"Jay and Hunter know that as well as anyone," Alice said, then stopped herself elaborating probably realising Hunter's birthday celebrations were not the time to be discussing our loss, but it was too late, the revelation had been made.

"How come?" Mary asked.

It wasn't an innocent ask, if someone mentions someone else has suffered loss, you know you are walking into a substantial conversation when you enquire about it.

"Hunter's mother, my wife, died of Covid-19."

"Shit! I'm sorry. Did she have underlying health conditions?" Mary asked sympathetically, somewhat horrified but still with an inquisitiveness. I've noticed people tend to be horrified by Amy's death but some can't help wanting to know more. It's like rubbernecking when driving past a motorway pile up.

"No, perhaps that would have made things a little easier to come to terms with but she was actually one of the healthiest people I've ever met. If you remember, at the outset, all the media explanations were indicating it was just going to be like a harsh dose of flu for most people other than the elderly with underlying health conditions but that isn't how it worked out. Older people obviously did make up the vast majority of the fatalities but the amount of young people, like Amy, that died was shocking. We thought we had escaped it unscathed too as she took ill on the second spike. It was such a weird thing, it was all very mild at first and then there was this swift deterioration….anyway, it happened, we cope as best as we can, Hunter's birthday isn't really the time to be going into this in any detail."

"I'm so sorry to hear that," Mary said, placing her hand on top of mine and saying it with such sincerity that I felt I might cry.

"Thank you. The sense of loss never leaves you but sunshine often breaks through the clouds these days. These young folks have been a massive help."

"We love him," Alice said with a kind smile and it was my turn to take a big swig of my drink, briefly hiding in my glass as I regained my composure. These were the type of moments I felt like curling into a foetal ball and breaking down but I was becoming better at fending off these waves of grief. Whilst Hunter hid behind the mask of drunken bravado, I hid behind my mask of steely composure and between us we did our best to fool people that we were managing when the real truth was that we were still drowning in grief but kept finding our way up to the surface for brief gulps of air.

CHAPTER FORTY
TWO

MARY

It was time for me to go. Meeting Alice and Jay again had been a plus in a day of minuses but I had a train to catch so I could get back home, get my bra off, put my pyjamas on and contemplate crying myself to sleep. I quietly mentioned to Alice that I was heading off and she tried, possibly for about the thirtieth time that evening, to persuade me to go around town with them but when I politely declined once more and stood up, she stood too and gave me a big, tight hug.

"Well, it's been lovely seeing you again Mary, it really has. I've got your mobile number now and I'll add you on Insta and Facebook so I can celebrate in the future when you tell me other dates have gone much better than tonight's disaster."

"If it had gone well, I would never have wandered into here, so it's not all bad."

"Exactly!"

I didn't hug anyone else in their group or even shake their hand, social distancing during the pandemic had changed peoples' willingness to share in physical contact and I respected that but was pleased that Alice was prepared to make an exception. Erika, Alice's girlfriend, could barely bring herself to say goodbye. I hadn't taken to her, there was something about her that I didn't like. She definitely didn't have the natural warmth that Alice had. She seemed somewhat aloof like a pampered cat. She was stunningly beautiful, fair haired and impeccably made up with an incredible figure but despite barely speaking to me had managed to throw a few dirty looks in my direction. Some pretty girls are like that, they get used to getting their own way without having to try too hard. I definitely hadn't done anything wrong but at the same time, I wasn't prepared to make a big fuss of her.

Jay offered to walk me down to the train station.

"No, honestly Jay, you don't need to do that, it's literally just over the road."

"It's no trouble then, is it? These lot are all heading off to some bar where they've paid for a table now anyway and I'm not invited so I'm heading home. I may even be lazy and jump on a train to Buckshaw if one's due."

"Well, if it's no trouble," I said, largely because I wanted some protection if I happened to run into Steve the fisherman.

"It isn't."

So that was how Jay came to be walking me over to Chorley train station. It was literally a two minute walk.

"So your date was a bit of a disaster then?" Jay said as we walked along.

"Yes, it was already going completely wrong anyway but when Steve asked halfway through my first drink whether I took it up the backside, and he didn't say backside, then I knew there was never going to be a second date."

"He sounds charming."

"Apparently his ex-wife never let him do it so it has to be agreed at the outset second time around."

"Well, that sounds like a perfect platform to build a relationship on," Jay pulled a crazy face in case I hadn't picked up on the vibe that he was being sarcastic, which I obviously knew he was.

"I don't understand why men have this weird obsession with trying to reduce sex to something crass. It's a loving act of togetherness, not a crude thing solely about depraved self-gratification."

"Mary, I totally agree."

"Good."

I temporarily felt a little awkward after that. Jay was pretty much a stranger and I don't know what made me blurt out the most disgusting moment of my horrendous date. I suppose it might have been because he just gave the impression that he was a nicer breed of man and I needed persuading that there were still a few of them out there. Jay wasn't a physically attractive man, he was an untidy, slightly overweight, middle aged man who permanently had a look of sadness in his eyes but he just seemed like an old fashioned gentleman at a time when they were almost extinct.

"Have you ever checked whether Mary is in the dictionary between Marx and marzipan?" Jay asked randomly.

I thought I had heard him but because it was such a weird, random question I thought I may have heard what I wanted to hear rather than what he had actually said.

"Say that again!" I said with a little laugh.

"It doesn't matter," Jay said in an endearingly shy way.

"No, go on!"

"It was stupid. I asked whether you'd ever checked whether Mary was ..."

"...in the dictionary between Marx and marzipan, which I have but Marx wasn't in and nor was Mary...not in the dictionary I checked in any way!"

For the first time, I saw Jay's whole face light up, like someone had switched a switch to his whole inner self. It was a lovely thing to witness.

"Wow! You knew what I was on about. I am seriously impressed!"

"Billy Bragg's 'The Short Answer' from the wonderful 'Workers Playtime' album."

"I can't believe you're into Billy Bragg! You really don't look like a typical fan," Jay was saying with a real high pitched excitement to his voice.

"I'll have you know 'Talking With The Taxman About Poetry' and particularly 'Workers Playtime' are amongst my favourite albums of all time. I'm a sucker for a broken heart. They still rank a long way behind Lana Del Rey's 'Born To Die' and 'Norman Fucking Rockwell' by quite some distance by the way but they probably make my all time 'Top 10'"

"No fucking way! Sorry, excuse my language," Jay said ignoring the fact I had used the very same word only seconds before.

"No problem. Honestly it's true. Do you like Lana Del Rey?"

"I've not heard much by her, I thought 'Video Games' was beautiful."

"You need to start listening to her. Everything she's ever done is beautiful but sometimes with thorns in the stem. Tomorrow, if you do one thing, download all her albums. You will thank me for the rest of your life. A life without Lana Del Rey music in it is definitely incomplete."

"I am still stunned about the fact you like Billy Bragg, stunned in a good way. What got you into Billy Bragg?"

"An ex-boyfriend."

"The vet?"

"No, a passionate socialist long before the vet, a teenage

sweetheart, back before life got complicated....I need to go over to the other side of the platform."

"How long before your train's due?"

"It's due at twenty five past so just less than ten minutes."

"Let me get a ticket, I'll see you get home safe."

"No, no, I wouldn't want you to do that. There's no need, I'm a thirty four year old woman who is perfectly capable of getting herself home."

I felt a twinge of guilt for chipping a bit off my age as I find myself doing too often these days. Jay gave me a friendly smile.

"There is a need. You feel the world is short of gentlemen at the moment, I just want to show you that I'm one."

I tried to talk Jay out of getting a ticket but he was insistent, saying he would much prefer a ride on a train with a kind hearted Billy Bragg fan than heading home alone to be left to fret about what sort of state his seventeen year old son would come home in. Being escorted home by a seemingly friendly man may seem like a noble gesture but it came with an element of concern too. I barely knew Jay and for all I knew, he could be the mad murderer type he was supposedly protecting me from. The fact that I had run into him twice doing kind things with good people was a reassurance but I was still a little on my guard. I had a 'Personal Attack Alarm' key ring in my handbag which I always took with me on Tinder dates so whilst Jay bought his ticket I transferred that from the bag to my pocket, just to be on the safe side.

It turned out that the element of caution was unnecessary in this instance. Jay is a lovely, lovely man and four hours later as we sat drinking a bottle of red wine around my kitchen table, I was opening up to him in a way I hadn't opened up to anyone for a long time. I appreciate it was probably a little foolhardy to have let him in the house in the first place as that personal alarm would have been of no use in there, but thankfully as I say it turned out my instincts were fine. I was being completely candid with him about my romantic history. The fact I was pretty drunk was no doubt a contributory factor.

"I'm thirty five years old, Jay. I have a sixteen year old daughter, who is at her father's in Cheadle this weekend, in case you're wondering…"

Jay held his hand up.

"Hang on!"

I thought he was going to pick up on my mention of a daughter. Amazingly it was the first time I had mentioned her in conversation. I don't know whether it was a conscious attempt not to discuss her, I'm not sure.

"Thirty five? You told me you were thirty four before."

"Did I?" I said innocently, "I might have forgotten one. I can be anywhere between thirty two and thirty five on any given day. I don't like thirty five, it sounds so much older than thirty four."

"It sounds a year older."

"To me it sounds a lot older. Odd numbers sound older than even ones. Thirty five sounds older than thirty six."

Jay laughed.

"Mary, it really doesn't. Does eighty six sound younger than twenty three then?"

"No, of course not, you know what I mean."

"I really don't!"

"Shut up, anyway, I was about to tell you something important."

"Sorry, I won't say another word."

"I have a sixteen year old daughter, Tilly, she's at her Dad's in

Cheadle."

"I remember."

I held my finger to my lip.

"I honestly mean this, ever since the moment of her conception when her father pulled out no longer wearing the little rubber overcoat that he had been wearing on the way in, things have not gone to plan. Now I know I may not be the best looking woman in the world…"

"You're a beautiful looking woman, Mary," Jay commented with a frankness that a bottle and a half of red wine delivers. Given the type of man he is, I don't suspect he would have come out with that statement sober.

"Why thank you kind sir. Anyway, I was going to say, I may not be the best looking woman in the world nowadays but I wish I hadn't been oblivious to how pretty I had been at eighteen, maybe if I'd have known I'd have held out for someone really nice rather than just dating the half decent boys who asked me out. Some good came of it though. I wouldn't have Tilly now without that lack of self-worth!"

"How long did you date Tilly's Dad for?"

"Alex? About a year all told. Don't get me wrong, Jay, he's been a great Dad to Tilly, but he lives in cloud cuckoo land. He always has. Spends more than he earns, likes a pint or six, likes to bet until his wallet is empty and he can't say 'No' to a lady who flutters her eyelashes in his direction. If he'd have been smart enough to keep his condom on his codger, he would have just been a sweet teenage memory but instead I have him popping in and out of my life every fortnight."

"If you were together a year in total, does that mean you'd split up before Tilly arrived or after?"

"Before, not long before though. I sort of knew it wasn't going to be a lifetime thing even when I first found out I was pregnant but I wanted to at least try to make it work. Turns out it was only me that was trying to do the right thing. One of Alex's many conquests phoned me when I was eight months pregnant to reveal he'd been seeing her for four months without ever mentioning that he had a pregnant partner. I should have been horrified but I don't even remember feeling surprised. I saw it coming. I didn't shed a tear and took some sort of perverse pleasure in being able to split up with him without my family and friends thinking I was a fool."

"Where did things go from there? Any subsequent knights in shining armour?"

"No! I didn't date anyone else then until Tilly was five and then, for the last eleven years, I've had numerous disastrous dates and relationships culminating in tonight's fish stinking, anally obsessed, charmless moron."

"What about the vet guy, he seemed like a decent bloke?"

"Austin? He was by no means the worst but was incredibly vain, definitely had some level of OCD and was very controlling so not quite as perfect as he looks once you've scratched below the surface."

"Sounds like you've had some bad luck."

"I really don't think it is a case of bad luck, Jay. I really think there is a shortage of good men out there. Fifty, sixty, seventy years ago, women just had to tolerate the mediocre hand they were dealt but nowadays we go searching for more but then struggle to find it."

"Which is better?"

"What do you mean?"

"I mean is it better to be married for sixty years to a mediocre man or have a string of disasters like you've had?"

"Without a doubt, 'a string of disasters'."

"Why do you say that?"

"95% of the time I'm perfectly happy. I have a wonderful daughter, I have a good job which I enjoy, I have enough money to feed us and to go where I want when I want. I am absolutely fine in my own company. I would have hated to have been stuck with a man I didn't love in an era which dictated that he was the boss."

"So if you're happy 95% of the time, why are you unhappy the other 5% of the time?"

"I'm not saying I'm unhappy 5% of the time, just that I'm not happy 100% of the time. 5% 'not happy' rather than 5% 'unhappy'."

"OK, there's probably a subtle difference I suppose. Why are you 'not happy' 5% of the time?"

We exchanged smiles when Jay stressed the words 'not happy' in the way that he did. I would say that was the first time I realised there was a bit of mild flirtation passing between us. I think it was because I was finding him mentally attractive. He was interested in me and my history.

"I really don't know. Everyone chases perfection, don't they? Perhaps it's not possible. Perhaps it's only possible to be 95% happy."

"What do you mean?"

"Well, as we've established, I'm happy 95% of the time now. I'm happy in my job, when I'm at home I cook what I want when I want it, I choose what to watch on my TV, I choose where I go on holiday to, when I go and for how long. I decide when I go to the cinema, the theatre or to the pub and when I return home. I only have a small element of compromise in my life which involves fitting in with Tilly's plans but she's not a stereotypical teenager, she's pretty adaptable. Now, if I met Mr Right and he was everything I had ever dreamed of in a man, self-sufficient, kind, funny, good company, the whole shebang then if we moved in together everything in my life would change. I would suddenly have a whole new set of com-promises that I never had to consider before, like what we both wanted to eat, what to wear, what to watch on televi-sion and where to go and when. I would have a whole new set of friends and family to accommodate into my plans. Friends and family of his that I may not be particularly fond of. Now if he just let me choose everything we did, that would make me unhappy as I wouldn't want a doormat as a partner. If he chose everything, then it would be me that was sacrificing too much and I would resent that but if we struck a happy medium then neither of us would be 100% happy. I appreciate relationships are all about compromise but I can't seem to find one that takes me beyond the 95% happy I am when I'm on my own. The more often I try and fail, the more often I convince myself it isn't possible."

"Interesting concept but I completely disagree with every word you've just said!"

Jay said this calmly not in a disagreeable or argumentative tone. I was interested to hear him out. I filled his wine glass back up and smiled.

"You are aware that one blunt statement disagreeing with every single word I've just said isn't going to suffice. You're going to have to explain why."

"OK. Perhaps, just perhaps, when I look back on my time with Amy, I do it with my rose tinted spectacles on and it may not quite have been the perfect relationship my nostalgic mem-ories make it. Having said that, I definitely think I was happy more than 95% of the time."

"100% of the time?"

"Perhaps not, but almost."

"You would still have to make sacrifices and compromise

though."

"To an extent, I suppose, but compromise doesn't necessarily stop you being happy. We tended to like the same things on the television, we liked the same restaurants, the same holiday destinations, we liked each other's families, we had mutual friends and our own individual friends and could do our own thing without any resentment from the other partner. There were things Amy wasn't into when we met that she grew to love, like Hunter's football and there were things I would never have imagined I would enjoy like chick flick type box sets and West End musicals which I learnt to appreciate."

"If you ever did argue then, what would the arguments be about?"

"Hunter or sex."

"Why argue about Hunter?"

"Not really arguments. We would bicker about Hunter. He would play us off against each other about things like bed times and homework. I wouldn't consider them to be proper arguments though."

"And arguments about sex?"

"Nothing major. No betrayals and neither of us being into any weird stuff or anything like that. Just your typical me being a male and wanting a male amount of sex and Amy being a female and wanting a female amount of sex."

"Interesting."

Jay laughed really hard. Proper giggles. It was an infectious laugh that made me laugh too.

"Now it's your turn to elaborate, Mary! You could just as easily have said 'bullshit' as 'interesting'!"

"Was it that obvious?"

"It was."

"Do you want me to explain?"

"Of course I do."

"Well, you had me until the sex bit. I believe you saw this as the perfect relationship where you were both in tune with each other's feelings and both loved doing the same things but the sexual evidence doesn't back that up. I guess what you were saying is that you were wanting more sex than Amy, is that right?"

"It is."

Just for the record, I have always wanted more sex than every partner I have ever been with..."

I looked across at Jay and he was raising his eyebrows. I am not sure if this fact aroused him or whether he was sceptical but it's the truth, the truth with a caveat anyway.

"...so there isn't a male amount of sex and a female amount of sex, that's just a male misconception.," I explained, "it's down to individual people. My sexual interest tends to drop off in a relationship due to certain external factors and this may have been the case with Amy. Why do you think she wasn't feeling as sexual as you?"

"I don't know."

"You didn't think to ask in the midst of these arguments you say it caused?"

"I did ask sometimes but it created tension between us when I brought it up."

"You mean you felt the tension when you brought it up. Amy may have been feeling tense anyway at times and that's maybe why she wasn't in the mood for sex."

"Easy for you to make a judgement on someone you didn't know and a relationship you weren't in," Jay commented in a barbed way, the first time I felt he had moved away from a cool guardedness to a more natural sensitivity.

"I'm surmising as part of the conversation, Jay. There was, as you admit yourself, a sexual difference between you, I am just suggesting why this may have been. She was probably carrying a burden that she wasn't carrying with you. A work burden or something from your life, a tiredness, a concern or tiny little factors at different times in your marriage that were making her feel like avoiding sex. I'm not pretending to know the answers, Jay, I'm just saying whatever it was, that was Amy's missing 5%. You were missing it too. You just blocked it out your mind and tried to avoid the confrontation."

"Thanks for sullying the happy memories of my marriage!"

"That's not what I'm doing and anyway you prompted me for an explanation. I'm just pointing out that you were probably, at best, 95% happy."

"Fair enough."

"You look hurt."

"I'm permanently hurt, Mary, I just hide it pretty well most of the time. I didn't enjoy raking up the slight chink in a very happy marriage though."

"I'm sorry. How happy on a scale of one to a hundred would you say you are now?"

"Much less than 95% happy."

"How much less?"

"It's hard to put a figure on it but substantially less. As I said in the bar, this young lot have helped, particularly Hunter and Alice, but I'd probably be exaggerating if I said I was happy half the time."

"That's a real shame, Jay. It must be so hard at times. Do you think there'll be a way of becoming happier over time?"

"I don't know really. I know it's a bit of a cliché but time is a healer. I didn't think it would be but when Amy first died I thought I'd never be happy again so for me to say I'm happy nearly half the time is, as daft as it sounds, big strides for me. I don't think I'll ever be as happy as I was but I expect to be happier than I am now."

"Do you think you'll ever find someone to love again?"

"No."

Jay couldn't have said it any more firmly or with more conviction.

"Don't beat around the bush, Jay, say what you feel!"

"I just don't think it's possible."

"Of course it's possible," I insisted.

"No, I don't think it is. I think the guilt and suffering I would put myself through would outweigh any pleasure I would get."

I can't say I have known many widows and widowers in my life but of the ones I have, who are mainly people from my parents and grandparents generations, it is normally the surviving women who may opt to continue the rest of their life alone. Men don't normally do that. I know everyone is different but men generally seem to be more needy in relationships and after suffering loss, soon find themselves looking for companionship again. Jay was insisting this wasn't going to be the case for him. Whether it was true or not, I thought it was unnecessary.

"Obviously I didn't have the pleasure of knowing Amy, but if she was so special to you, surely she wouldn't have wanted you to be miserable?"

"No, of course not, but equally she wouldn't want me to be with anyone else."

"I'm sure that's not true."

"It is true. We had the conversation about what Amy would

expect of me if she went first and one of the expectations was that I would stay single."

"Wow! I'm definitely feeling the effects of that wine now so if I say something that's out of line then please tell me but is that not a little unfair?"

I was going to say 'bitchy' but I stopped myself. I'm not sure I would have got away with it.

"Possibly but it's fine. It's not like Amy is making the decision for me. I have no desire to be with anyone else."

"Yet."

Jay smiled, "You're sounding like Alice now, she says things like that but I have no intention of being with anyone else ever."

"Just keep an open mind."

"I don't need to."

"Well, on that bombshell Jay, I'm going to have to be a party pooper and retire to my bed. As you probably know you've missed the last train so you can either get a taxi home or you're welcome to sleep in Tilly's room. I've changed the sheets today so there's fresh bedding in there."

"Would that be OK? I can just jump on a train first thing in the morning then. Having said that, it might be best if I do ring a taxi, Hunter may get home and start throwing up. I might need to be there for that."

"He's a big lad, Jay. I'm sure he can look after himself."

"You'd be surprised."

"Well, why don't you text his mate and see if he'll stop over with him at yours."

"That's an idea!"

"OK, you do that and I'll go and grab you a fresh towel."

CHAPTER FORTY THREE

<u>ALICE</u>

Erika was in a mood about something, I wasn't certain what, she'd been in a funny mood all day but it definitely deteriorated when we met up with Jay at The Ale Station. When we walked through Chorley to Lost, which is without doubt our favourite club in Chorley, there was still an undercurrent. Sometimes, once Erika has had a drink or two, she will clasp hands with me or temporarily slip her arm around my waist as we walk along, sometimes for a bit too long for my liking which can, in itself, prompt an argument. I'm just not into big public displays of affection but Erika has argued it's more than that. She says it's paranoia about my sexuality and not wanting to risk an adverse reaction from bigots. I accept there is an element of truth in that but even when I dated lads I wasn't one to be seen slobbering all over some boy at a bus stop. I know there's a balance and I may sometimes fail to strike it but that doesn't mean I don't still think Erika is the most gorgeous woman on the planet because I most certainly do. Nevertheless, on that Saturday night of Hunter's birthday weekend, it wasn't a two way thing. On the walk down to Lost from The Ale Station, Erika kept at least six feet away from me for the whole way, acting as though social distancing had just been re-introduced.

We had booked a VIP booth in 'Lost', Erika and I had paid for it as a bit of a treat for Hunter but we'd only been in there for ten minutes, when the lads disappeared for what turned out to be about quarter of an hour. I had no idea where they had disappeared to and assumed they had bumped into someone they knew. Anyway, they were gone ages and in their absence I was able to try to establish what was wrong with Erika.

"What's the matter, honey?" I asked. Using pet names when someone is unhappy with you never works I don't even know why I do it.

"Nothing's the matter, I'm fine," Erika replied in a tone that implied she most certainly wasn't in the slightest bit fine.

"You clearly aren't."

"We're here to celebrate Hunter's birthday. I don't want to talk about it right now."

"Now would be the perfect time to talk about it because he isn't here."

"True, but we're in a public place and I know how concerned you get about us making a scene."

I was taken aback. I had no recollection of having done anything wrong but I was now being told by Erika that she was mad enough with me that she wanted to make a scene.

"What have I done now?"

Since Erika had started at 'Uni' I always felt there was something I was doing that wasn't quite right. It was nothing major but she'd pull me up on little things. I felt as though, now she was away, she wasn't 100% convinced that she wanted a long distance relationship and perhaps wanted the freedom of being single again. I could imagine every University student of either sex or any sexual persuasion lusting after her and it must be hard to have that level of adulation without questioning whether what you had was really what you wanted. The irony was that I was being accused of being the exact opposite.

"It's not a specific thing Alice it's just the whole way you act."

"I don't understand what you mean."

"You treat me like I'm your best friend."

"What's wrong with that? You are my best friend!"

"That's what I mean. You just don't get it."

"Explain it to me then."

"Our whole relationship just doesn't feel very passionate anymore."

"It does."

"Not to me, it doesn't. We've just sat in a bar with Jay and Mary for over an hour and whilst you were talking to them I don't think you looked over in my direction once. I could have stood up and walked home and I don't think you'd have noticed until tomorrow morning."

"Don't be ridiculous!"

"It's not ridiculous."

"Of course it is."

"OK, how many times did I get up and go to the ladies whilst we were in there?"

I was starting to see her point a little but I still didn't feel it was a rational one. She could have left the table six times or not left at all but having trust in your partner doesn't mean you aren't passionate about them.

"Erika, I was in a conversation and thought you were in one too so I didn't feel I had to be watching over your every move."

"You never used to be able to take your eyes off me."

"Erika, I still can't take my eyes off you."

"You just have! For an hour! I went to the toilet twice by the way. The second time I sat in a cubicle on my phone for ten minutes until someone knocked. I came back and you didn't even look up."

"I'm sorry," I said reaching my arm out to grab Erika's but she pulled hers away.

"You don't need to apologise. I'm just saying you used to be passionate about this relationship and about me but now it's just habit."

"That's not true."

"It is true, Alice. You were more excited about seeing some woman who tried to save the ducks than you ever are about seeing me. We're drifting apart Alice and the sad thing is, you're happy to watch me fade into the distance."

"That's so not true. I think you're just trying to spark an argument because you've given up on us without me even realising anything was wrong."

"You don't think there's anything wrong? We don't talk as much as we used to, you don't look at me like you used to, we don't kiss like we used to and we certainly don't fuck like we used to."

"It's not like we don't have sex, Erika, we had sex last night."

"I do things to you. You very rarely do anything back."

"I thought you liked taking the lead."

"I do, but not every single time!"

I could suddenly see my relationship dying in front of my eyes. I became desperate. Desperation is never good.

"I can change," I pleaded, "if that's what you want, I can change."

"That's not the point."

"I'm not really sure I understand what the point is. I've allowed things to go a bit stale. I need to put it right. Is that not your point?"

"No, I want you to feel passionate about me naturally without me having to tell you to do it."

"Well it's too late for that now, isn't it?"

"I agree. I think it probably is."

CHAPTER FORTY FOUR

HUNTER

I was a cooler kid at school than Dominic. There are kids who lead and kids that follow, I was a kid that led, Dom was a kid that followed. Each one needs the other though, I think Dom needed me to bring out his more adventurous side whilst I needed him to rein mine in. I would have spent every evening in detention if it hadn't been for Dom and no girl in school would have ever gone within a mile of Dom if it hadn't been for me. I gave him a certain level of credibility with the fairer sex that he would never have achieved otherwise. Dom is an incredibly kind and good person but he could easily have fallen into the hands of the nerds if I hadn't been around. I still remind him of this from time to time. We've left school now but things haven't changed all that much. I still help him get in with girls like before but now he isn't saving me from detention, we've moved on from that, now he stops me from getting arrested.

During our time at school, Dom may have looked up to me a little but we both looked up to Jacob Sharpe. Jacob was the kid Dom and I both wanted to be. At primary school, Jacob was a school year above us, so when we were in Year Five, he was obviously in Year Six but it was like he was 'King Of The School', he was captain of the school football team and walked around the school playground with a presence like he owned the place. There was good reason for his confidence, he lived in a huge house, wore designer clothes, looked like a young model and received Valentine's Day cards by the sack full.

Jacob didn't go to our Secondary school, his rich parents packed him off to some private school, I think it was Bolton Grammar, but we used to run into him around the Chorley area from time to time and he would always stop for a chat. Some good looking kids don't survive puberty with their good looks intact as their face gets ravaged by acne or soft childhood features become harsh adult ones, but if anything Jacob just honed his good looks as time passed. He joined the Gym so managed to side step the weedy stage. We jealously noted how he had ten times as many people following him on social media platforms than he followed back, most of them were girls and none of them were ugly. He could have just treated Dom and me like a pair of lesser beings but that was never the case. He always spoke to us like he was genuinely interested in what we were up to. We were shrewd enough to know that we were never going to be best mates with him, but we were happy enough knowing we were in his outer circle of friends. If Jacob Sharpe was having a party and was only going to invite his fifty best mates, we would never make the list. If he was looking to get two hundred there and needed to invite sixty or seventy lads, just to ensure it wasn't wall to wall teenage girls then we might be considered. We knew where we stood and we were more than happy to stand there. I wouldn't say we hero worshipped Jacob Sharpe but we definitely admired him.

After I left school, I wanted to start going out into Chorley on Friday and Saturday nights. I was never the brightest child and after Mum died I stopped even half trying with my school-work so was never going to stay on in further education. I managed to get a job working for a builders and discovered I was more than half-decent at grafting for a living so started to pick up a half-decent wage for a kid still living at the family home. All the older unmarried lads on site seemed to spend their whole weekend in the pub and keen to fit in, I was desperate to do the same.

Dom was much smarter than me. I wouldn't say he worked his socks off at school but was just naturally clever. Our school didn't have a Sixth Form so he moved on to the local College, Runshaw and seemed to like it there but as a result of his student life, he never had any money to spend or any real inclination to go out drinking. I just had to persuade him that it was the right course of action. The allure of the opposite sex was probably what did the trick but there were initially some doubts.

"We won't get in anywhere though, Hunter."

"Why won't we? We both look eighteen."

Dom was pretty dark skinned so had a bit of a moustache and not a flimsy, wispy one either, a proper moustache. I was also looking much older recently largely because the physical demands my job placed on me had caused me to fill out. We both definitely looked older than we actually were.

"Some of the kids from College say they pretty much ask everyone for ID - everyone who looks under twenty one anyway."

Granted even I knew we didn't look twenty one.

"We need false ID then."

"How are we going to get hold of that?"

"We'll ask Jacob Sharpe."

By 'we' I meant 'I'. I was our spokesperson. Dominic pretty much sat back and allowed me to take the lead on things like this. He isn't a pushy person and I am. Jacob Sharpe was definitely the solution to our problem. If you've ever seen Shawshank Redemption, you might remember that there was a bloke called 'Red' who could get things into prison. Andy

Dufresne famously asked him for a rock hammer. Well Jacob Sharpe was Chorley's answer to Morgan Freeman's character. Jacob Sharpe was the kid in Chorley who could get you things, things outside the letter of the law. I don't mean things that would involve a stretch inside if he got caught with them, like guns or knives but I mean things that were slightly beyond the letter of the law like false ID, alcohol for sixteen and seventeen year olds and soft drugs for anyone who wanted them. Initially, when we were in Year 11, we had just wanted the booze, our natural next step was the ID. We had gone beyond sharing a bottle of cider in Astley Park, we now wanted to enjoy our alcohol in the friendly environment of a public house.

Jacob's Mum and Dad had always known he was a popular lad so there probably seemed nothing untoward about a load of kids calling around at his house. He knew enough kids to only take on 'work' for people he knew so his parents weren't alerted by the coming and going of strangers. Fortunately we were in the familiar faces category. I text him asking if he could get ID for both me and Dom. I would have been about sixteen and a half at the time.

'When do u need it 4?' Jacob text back.

'No rush but soon.'

'I can probably get you a couple of provisional driving licences within a month. Dom is dark haired so they're pretty easy to get hold of but a fair skinned kid that looks like you will be a lot harder. I'll get one though. I charge fifty quid."

'Cheers m8'.

"Fifty quid! I can't afford fifty quid for ID!" Dom said in protest when I updated him on the text conversation.

"I'll get you it, just pay me back in instalments when you can."

Provisional driving licences were the most popular fake ID available. Once kids passed their driving tests they were issued with proper licences so had no further need for a provisional. The well behaved kids just threw theirs in the bin. The shrewder kids, however, were aware that there was a bit of a black market in provisional licences and would sell theirs on to the likes of Jacob for about twenty quid a pop. If you happened to know someone who was twelve to twenty four months younger than you who vaguely resembled you looks wise, you could cut out the middle man but not many people did. Jacob, on the other hand, knew everyone.

We had our false ID within a fortnight and an investment of £100 for the pair ensured we had aged almost two years overnight. If anyone scrutinised the photographs they could easily spot that the person on the driving licence only bore a passing resemblance to us but there was enough of a likeness if a bouncer gave it a quick once over on a busy night.

For the first three months of going out into Chorley we were turned away from bars and pubs as many times as we were let in, but thankfully no-one took our ID off us, so we kept going back. After three months, we had a strategy, make our faces familiar and arrive anywhere we want to go early, before the bouncers decide to properly implement their 'pick and choose' policy. It worked too and the occasions we were asked to produce ID gradually became less and less. By the time I was seventeen nobody asked. Coronavirus had put many struggling pubs and clubs out of business and although the surviving bars had a duty to ask for ID, they didn't want to turn regulars away and that's what we had become.

One of the knock-on effects of Coronavirus that was regularly spoken about by lads on the building site was how it had become much more difficult to 'pull' women. I hadn't been out there trying so had nothing to compare to, but I knew what they meant. Although people were no longer compelled to socially distance, it was regularly practised which obviously made it difficult to get close to a girl that caught your eye. Getting to a stage where you could actually kiss someone tended to involve a process of separating girls into two categories, the 'germ cautious' ones and the 'reckless' ones. Girls could move from the former category to the latter one as the night progressed and more and more alcohol was consumed but you had to be strategic about when you chose to make your move. I became very adept at watching women, picking up on their behaviour, smiling across, making friendly conversation and judging whether there was any value in chipping away at their defences. Like most things in life, success breeds success and if you manage something once, it gives you more confidence the next time around. I'm not saying I am the best looking lad in the world or pull the most women but if those SAS blokes lined up all the young lads in the country and asked us to get in line with the best at one end and the worst at the other, I would be much nearer the top than the bottom. Let's just say I often live up to my name.

By the time my seventeenth birthday came around, I was beginning to tire of the weekend routine of going out, getting drunk and trying to pull. Don't get me wrong, it was still fun but I was open to trying something different. Cocaine is the primary drug of choice amongst the young, adventurous party goers of Chorley and I felt I was missing out by not at least trying it once. I was round at Dom's house one evening in the middle of the week prior to my birthday weekend and revealed to him my intention of getting coked up to celebrate my seventeenth.

"Don't be so fucking stupid," Dom said dismissively. It was rare for Dom to swear so it showed how dismayed he was by my revelation.

"It's not fucking stupid. It's just letting my hair down a bit."

"Cocaine is for people with no personality who are trying to make themselves look more interesting than they actually are."

"Same could be said for alcohol."

"Yeh, but at least your pint of lager hasn't been up someone's arsehole going through customs and it isn't funding some drug gang in Columbia."

Dom's a legend but he is sensible with a capital 'S'.

"I'm not bothered by that and anyway it probably hasn't been up someone's arse, it'll have been hidden inside someone's shoes or in their toiletries but even if it has been up someone's arse it'll have been in a bag. We only live once. Where's your sense of adventure? "

"We only live once so I plan to do what I can to make sure I live to be a hundred."

"You get pissed."

"I'm sure getting pissed a few times as a teenager won't harm me too much in old age. Anyway, stop deflecting, we're talking about your mad plan to take cocaine."

"It's not exactly mad. Three quarters of the kids around here do it every Friday and Saturday night."

"I'm sure it's not three quarters."

"I reckon it is."

"Well, even if it is, they haven't all just lost their Mum's to Coronavirus. Your Dad wouldn't cope if he lost you too."

"Dom stop getting all anxious about it! People don't die of cocaine overdoses! They die because they take a dodgy 'e' or move on to heroin."

"Well, it's up to you. Don't be trying to persuade me to join you. I'm not taking that shit. Where are you going to get it from anyway?"

"I'll see whether Jacob Sharpe can get hold of some for me."

"He probably can, he's a right dodgy bastard."

"You weren't moaning about him when he was getting your ID."

"I'm not complaining now, just merely pointing out that he's dodgy."

I spoke to Jacob on the Thursday. He said I was in luck because due to high demand he had recently started supplying a small amount of cocaine to his most trusted clients.

"It's good shit too, pal. I have a little bit myself and it's the dog's bollocks," Jacob said with a real sense of pride like a pensioner who had grown his own marrow.

"OK great, if you can get me some I'll have that for Saturday night."

"I'll get it sorted, pal."

One of Jacob's many strengths is that he is incredibly organised. Whilst getting ready to go out on that Saturday session I nicked the head off a spot and the bastard thing wouldn't stop bleeding for ages. I was getting so mad with it but as I was stressing my phone rang. It was Jacob.

"Hello mate!"

"Hello Hunter. Everything good?"

"Great, other than a spot I've cut which won't stop bleeding."

"Can't help you with that, pal, never had a spot in my life. I can help you with that other thing though. I'm due to pick some stuff up about tea time. Where are you going tonight?"

"Lost."

"Great, I'll come in and find you just make sure you're in there before it starts getting busy. I'll be there before nine. As it's a new batch, I might join you in trying it out. Any problems with that?"

"Of course not."

"OK, I'll give you the nod and we can nip into the Gents. That's why I want you there early so we won't have shit loads of people coming in and out."

"No problem, we're always in early anyway."

We must have only been at our table in Lost for five minutes when Jacob came in. He just walked past, nodded at me and then headed straight towards the Gents. Erika and Alice were stropping about something, no idea what, I wasn't interested but I kicked Dom under the table."

"Come with me," I said quietly so only Dom could hear.

"I don't want to," Dom protested.

"I need you to," I stressed and when I stood up with a deep sigh Dom dutifully followed.

Jacob was sat up on one of the sinks when we went in. He looked relaxed. I was pretty pissed but I was still cacking my-self that someone might spot us and we might end up getting a beating or even arrested. Jacob, on the other hand, just looked like we'd gathered together for a friendly chat.

"Are you after some gear as well, Dom?" Jacob asked.

"No, no," Dom said with a nervous shake of his head.

"OK, you alright standing guard? Hunter and I will just nip into one of the cubicles, if anyone comes in just have a little chat with them so we know not to come out. If we walk out the same cubicle people are going to either presume we're on something or they are going to think one of us has been dish-ing out his love in a cheeky fashion."

"Alright," Dom said despairingly, "just stop talking about it and get a fucking move on."

CHAPTER FORTY FIVE

<u>**DOMINIC**</u>

I'm not one of life's risk takers. I've always hung around with the cool kids rather than the swotty ones and I enjoy going out and having a beer even though I'm not eighteen yet but I know my limits. Once I pass my driving test I won't be one of these kids showing off to their mates by overtaking on blind bends or doing a ton on the motorway flashing at everyone to get out of my way like 'Billy Big Balls', I know who I am and don't try hard to make myself look like someone else. I'm the sensible one. I'm the sensible one in our house because everyone else that lives there is a little bit crazy and the sensible one amongst my mates. I can't see that there'll ever be a time that I'll decide I need to be smoking, driving like a maniac or taking drugs, it's just not me.

To be honest, I'm not really that bothered about drinking either. I wouldn't really say I enjoy the taste of alcohol. A bottle of lager isn't disgusting but I wouldn't say I love it, wine is just plain disgusting and most shorts aren't great either. I don't mind vodka because you can't really taste it that much, whiskey and gin are pretty rank and some of the others like Amaretto and Baileys are OK but I could only have one or two. I often drink Summer Fruits cider which is about the nicest alcoholic drink out there. It's like drinking a fizzy Ribena that gets you pissed. Anyway, the long and short of it is that I don't go out at the weekend for the booze. I go out for the women.

I am respectful when it comes to women. I just think they

are amazing creatures. I'm not like Hunter who wants to shag every pretty girl in Chorley either, I just want to fall in love with one. If I could find one girl who I think is great and she thinks I'm great too, that would be perfect. Looks aren't a big factor but she couldn't be too outgoing (I already have a mother and stepfather who can be embarrassingly loud so I don't need another loud person in my life) and I wouldn't want her to smoke as I don't think I could bring myself to kiss someone who had nicotine breath. I mentioned this to Hunter once and he said after two or three seconds of kissing them you seem to clean their mouth for them but I don't fancy putting his logic to the test.

I think my biggest hurdle in finding someone at the moment is that I am absolutely clueless what to say when speaking to women. Hunter seems to be able to trot out any old waffle and they lap it up but I clam up around women and if I can string a sentence together without it sounding lame then I'm doing really well. Once I overcome the conversation issue, I know I'm going to struggle with the kissing bit. I have no idea whatsoever when the right time is to put your arm around a girl, hold their hand or kiss them. I'm not sure I'll ever know and I can just imagine that I'm going to balls it up and make myself look like a right tit. Hunter lost his virginity at fifteen but I can't see me losing mine any time soon. I'm not bothered about the sex thing for now, I just want a girlfriend. I look forward to every weekend hoping it might be the weekend that my luck changes but it never does.

Hunter has been my best mate for a long time. I love the confidence he has in himself. Some kids at school used to just think he was a complete bell end but I have always just found him funny. Nothing seems to faze him. If I have one spot, I feel like everyone can see it from a mile away and every girl on the planet will find me hideous but Hunter can have several and still think he's the best looking man on the planet.

"It's God's way of giving all the other lads a chance, Dominic," he would explain to me, "the Almighty probably regrets making me that much better looking than every other lad and he's just trying to make things a little bit fairer. The women will still flock towards me though. I still have my aura."

My sister, Alice, is bisexual and at the moment is dating a girl called Erika who is so impossibly gorgeous that I fall in love every time I so much as glance at her but I know Hunter fancies Alice something rotten and thinks one day, if he times it right, he'll persuade Alice to finish with Erika and start going out with him instead. I can guarantee it will never happen but I can tell he thinks it will. He thinks he is irresistible and you just have to admire anyone who has that much self-belief.

I do worry about Hunter though. He was born reckless but that recklessness has been exacerbated since his Mum died. His Mum was just the loveliest, friendliest person that you could ever hope to meet. She looked like an Olympic athlete too, tall, skinny, toned and beautiful so if you had told me beforehand that she was going to get the Coronavirus, I'd have been totally convinced that she'd have been asymptomatic or at worst would have fought it off with very mild symptoms but that wasn't how it worked out. I think I cried every night for a week when she died but I've never seen Hunter shed a tear. I'm sure he has, I'm sure he's cried buckets but in front of me he's wanting to give off the impression that this tragic event has just made him stronger and even more determined than ever to live life to the full. I'm just worried that below the surface he's really so miserable and storing up so much grief that he'll end up doing something crazy.

When Hunter started talking about getting hold of some cocaine on the weekend of his seventeenth birthday, I immediately began to have an uneasy feeling about it. I know loads of people take cocaine on a regular basis and they seem to be able to function reasonably well on it but those people aren't

Hunter. They don't all have a point to prove to themselves that they are undamaged by the shit that life has thrown their way. I wasn't worried about the coke itself, I've seen Pulp Fiction, I know it was the heroin that did her over and if it had been coke she'd have probably been OK, but if Hunter can be a bit crazy after a few pints, I couldn't bear to imagine what he was going to be like after a line of coke. I knew he would be wanting to tell all the bouncers to 'go fuck themselves' and wanting to throw bricks at the windscreens of police cars. I knew I would be the one who has going to have to stop him.

The afternoon part of the celebrations actually went pretty well. Erika was in a mood with my sister about something which dampened the vibe a bit but Hunter was really up for a mad session so we just let the girls strop around a bit and we concentrated on getting smashed. My plan was that if we managed to get absolutely caned Hunter might forget about meeting up with Jacob Sharpe for his line of coke but by the time we met up with Hunter's Dad in 'The Ale Station', I started worrying that I'd taken things too far and panicked that I'd just replaced one problem with another. Instead of Hunter getting arrested because of some coke fuelled antics, he'd end up choking in a pool of his own vomit. When Jay, Hunter's Dad, suggested that we have a pint of water each, I persuaded Hunter that it was a good idea but I realised I was in a Catch 22 situation, sober him up and he'd be after that cocaine or let him get really pissed and not only risk Hunter seriously damaging his own health but risk being in such a state myself that I wouldn't be able to look after him. I chose the former option.

I fell in love in 'The Ale Station' that night. Alice has been banging on for ages about some angel who helped her and Hunter's Dad try to save a family of ducks by Erika's that had been smashed to pieces by some speeding driver. Anyway, this angel, Mary her name is, happened to turn up in 'The Ale Station' because she'd walked out on a date. She was incredible. Age wise she's probably half way between our age and my

Mum's age but everything about her is just stunning. I don't think I have been so bowled over by a woman in my life. I had that same age old issue that it became hard for me to get my words out. I had only just mastered the ability to speak in front of Erika and now here was someone else to return me to the land of silences and gibberish. I started up a separate conversation with Erika and Hunter just so I didn't make a complete dick of myself in front of her. It was when I was in that conversation I spotted something. Jay was looking at Mary with that same sense of awe and admiration that I was. He was 'in love' with her too. I realised I was a seventeen year old kid who had absolutely no chance with her but that no longer mattered. My heart was broken every weekend and I just bounced straight back the following week but for Jay it was different. Jay was vulnerable. After Amy died he had already had one nervous breakdown and if his heart was broken by Mary he could well have another. I didn't think it was a problem I could solve but knew if there was a solution, I needed to find it.

People say you can drink yourself sober. I don't profess to be an expert on this, I'm still new to this game but I don't think you can. You can definitely come down from a peak level of being wasted though and an element of normal behaviour can return. Once we eased off that peak level of drunkenness on Hunter's seventeenth, I just wanted to sober up. Hunter, on the other hand, was looking to reach a new high.

To cut a very long story short, we left 'The Ale Station' headed down to 'Lost', Jacob Sharpe came in, who I now absolutely despise with a passion, he sort of nodded at Hunter and all three of us ended up in the Gents. Once we were in there, the two of them went into a cubicle with a straw, some foil and a bag of coke with me, muggins that I am, standing guard and wishing they'd just get it over with.

Sod's law dictated that a bouncer was always going to walk

in whilst I was pacing anxiously around in the toilets. The bouncer strutted through pushing each shoulder forward as he walked. He was a thick set bloke in his forties with a shaved head and a beard. A typical bouncer really not tall but square shaped like a muscular Sponge Bob. I headed over to the sinks to make it look like I just needed to wash my hands but since the pandemic I have become averse to using communal sinks without having a tissue to turns the taps off with. If Corona taught us anything, it was that germs lurk everywhere. I deliberately made a scene about the tissues to make sure Jacob and Hunter had heard we weren't alone.

"Shit!" I cursed.

"What's the matter with you, lad?" the bouncer asked.

"I need some bog roll to turn the taps off with."

"Do you not have hands?"

"Germs are everywhere."

"Not in here at eight o'clock, they're not. This place is spotless when it opens. By one o'clock in the morning, when a load of you kids have pissed, crapped and vomited everywhere, that's when you need a tissue."

"You can never be too sure," I added, as I fetched some bog roll whilst the bouncer flopped his weapon out at the urinals.

I returned to the sink and made a thorough job of washing my hands, on the top and the palms.

"How many of you lads came in here?" the bouncer asked in a matter of fact manner as he tucked his todger away.

"What do you mean?" I asked feigning innocence but probably with an element of panic in my tone.

"I watched you all come in. Some pretty boy first then you and your mate. By my reckoning that makes three."

The bouncer was a bit too intimidating for me to question

why he asked if he already knew the answer.

"I'm not sure who the pretty boy is but I came in with my mate who's having a crap."

He took a few steps towards me, looking at me sceptically as he did.

"Bit weird that, isn't it? Coming into the bogs with your mate who needs a crap? Not the done thing, is it? Two hip young lads out on the tiles and then one says to the other,

'I need a crap, do you want to come with me?'

He put on an effeminate voice whilst he did this mickey taking.

"I mean," he continued, "maybe it's just me but if one of my mates said to me that he was going for a crap and would I care to join him, I wouldn't be responding in the affirmative."

I needed to defend myself a little here to make my fictional story carry at least some weight.

"I didn't realise he needed a crap. I told him I was going for a piss, he followed me and now he's having a crap."

"So why are you waiting for him?"

"I'm not! I was just washing my hands."

"OK, well dry them then and then fuck off outside."

"I will."

I went to the dryer. The bouncer had moved over to the cubicle where Hunter and Jacob were locked in and was stood, arms folded, outside.

"I don't know what the fuck the pair of you are doing in there but if you know what's good for you, you should put an end to it right now and come out."

"What are you on about? I'm having a crap!" Hunter shouted.

"Well flush the chain and come out!"

"I haven't finished. My arse is in bits, I've been on the Guinness all afternoon."

"I don't believe you, sunshine. I suggest you come out right now before I have to knock the fucking door down!"

"I'm telling you, I can't come out. My stomach's churning."

The bouncer was too long in the tooth to be playing games with mouthy teenagers.

"Right, I've had enough of this bollocks!"

It looked like the bouncer was caught in two minds. I think his initial impulse was to charge at the bolted door but then realising he may damage property he went for an alternative option. He headed for the cubicle next to the one Hunter and Jacob were in. I knew immediately what he was intending to do. He was going to climb up on the toilet and peer over into their cubicle to see what was really going on.

I knew what I had to do. I followed the bouncer into the cubicle, stood inside, closing the door behind me just as the bouncer was peering over into Hunter's cubicle.

"Fucking cokeheads, I knew it!"

"Leg it!" I shouted and as I did so I heard Hunter and Jacob flush the toilet, release the latch on their door and run.

I knew the bouncer was about to jump down and give chase and also understood it was my job to stop him. Without much space to pick up pace, I ran full pelt at him whilst he was climbing down off the toilet and tried to rugby tackle him then wrestle him to the ground. It was a bit of a feeble attempt, I was still pretty drunk, wasn't much good at contact sport anyway and he was a big man so he didn't lose his balance at all. He tried to push me off him but I wasn't letting go so to ensure I loosened my grip on him he just delivered a hard punch to the back of my head. It bloody hurt which made me even more determined to hold on tightly and also made the bouncer even madder so he punched me a second time. The second punch was delivered with a lot more venom than the first. It knocked me downwards and I presume, from my subsequent injuries, that I must have hit my head on the lavatory as I fell. I was out cold.

I have no idea how long I was out cold for but I can remember the feeling of grogginess followed by the sensation of being carried. When I felt my senses returning, I made an attempt to open my eyes and survey my surroundings. The right eye wouldn't open at all but my left eye complied.

It took a number of seconds for my left eye to focus properly. It was like having a kaleidoscope eye and my brain needing to alter the settings. Once I could see, I realised I was on a settee in a room I had never been in before. The first person I saw was the bouncer, still with the same exasperated expression he had been wearing earlier. I knew from the general commotion as I was coming around that he wasn't alone. I gingerly turned my head and spotted a second bouncer, then a lady who looked like a member of staff, then a third bouncer and then a fourth. I took a couple of deep breaths as the head movement was making me feel nauseous but my enquiring mind wanted to know who else was there. I tilted my head further and sat in the corner, on four chairs lined up in a row were Hunter, Jacob, Alice and Erika.

"I've heard their version of events," said the punching bouncer as he looked angrily at me, "now sunny Jim, it's time to hear yours."

CHAPTER FORTY SIX

<u>**ALICE**</u>

Having just been told I had been a pretty lousy girlfriend for quite some time, I wasn't really in the mood for partying. People can accept that they can't sing, can't dance, can't cook or can't draw but no-one likes to be told they aren't much good when it comes to sex. It was particularly hurtful as I thought we were having the type of sex Erika wanted us to have but it turns out I was wrong. I just wanted to go home.

Having managed to get all her issues off her chest, Erika brightened up and it was now me that was miserable. It was as though we only had a certain amount of happiness that could be shared out between us.

"Alice," Erika said in a soft placatory tone, "Don't go all gloomy on me. I'm not saying we definitely can't get past this, I'm just saying I'm not sure whether we can or not."

"Because I take you for granted and I'm shit in bed."

"Not exactly what I said."

"It's what you meant."

"No, I just feel we need to re-energise our relationship or accept it's time to move on. Both of us need to, I'm not saying it's just you."

"Well, that's very noble of you. You've not exactly been perfect yourself you know, since you went to Uni. You've changed since you've been there, Erika and not necessarily for the better.....shit, was that our Dom?"

There had been a bit of a commotion on the far side of the bar earlier, involving lads and bouncers but Erika and I were too busy immersing ourselves in our own stormy waters to really take any notice of someone else drowning in theirs. You can't help but notice though when two bouncers are carrying an unconscious man around and that man bears more than a passing resemblance to your younger brother. I needed to get closer to see what was happening. I automatically left my seat and raced over with Erika soon following. The closer I got, the more convinced I became that the unconscious, bleeding man was Dominic. Once I was within a few metres, all doubt was extinguished.

"What have you done to him?" I tearfully asked one of the bouncers.

"We've done nothing, love. Apparently he tried to attack my colleague and he slipped and whacked his head."

"That's just bullshit! Dom wouldn't attack anyone. He's the most gentle person in the world. Bloody hell, he's bleeding!"

Dom had a cut and a lump above his right eye but he was making some groggy groaning sounds which gave me some re-assurance that he was going to be OK.

"How do you know him?" another mean looking bouncer asked.

"He's my brother," I replied.

"Your brother? Right, come through here."

I was whisked through into a side room. The bouncers tried to stop Erika following me in but she must have explained, probably in a no nonsense way, that she was my girlfriend so they let her through. The two bouncers carrying Dom had already taken him into the room and laid him down on a settee in what must have been their staff room. There was a small kitchen section with a kettle and a microwave, a table, several chairs and some CCTV. There were four bouncers in there and a lady who I immediately assumed was in charge. The walkie-talkie she held in her hand was a giveaway clue. She was a thick set woman with dark hair and glasses who looked to be in her forties. Sat in the corner on two wooden chairs were Hunter and Jacob 'Feely' Sharpe. Hunter was looking agitated and nervous. We were invited to take the two spare seats next to them.

"How's he doing?" the lady asked.

"He's coming round. The fact he's drunk has probably resulted in him not putting his hands out to cushion his fall," a bouncer explained.

"We've been with him all day, he wasn't drunk," Erika protested.

"So he's not been drinking?" the lady asked.

"Well yes, he was drinking but he wasn't too bad."

"He tried to attack me," a big bald headed bearded bouncer explained, "Based on the size of me and the size of him, do you think he would do that if he was sober?"

"I don't believe he would ever do that," I said still totally confused about what was happening, "Hunter, were you not with him when all this happened?"

"No."

"Why not?"

"We'd just left the toilets when he fell."

"They were making a run for it," the bald headed bouncer explained.

"That's bollocks," Jacob protested, "we just walked out of there and then a load of the bouncers just grabbed us."

"They'd been taking drugs," one of the bouncers added.

Both Jacob and Hunter did look like they had taken something. I looked at their eyes and each pupil looked like it had grown to the size of a discus. Jacob was being his usual cocksure self but Hunter kept fidgeting in his seat and kicking his shoes together. This wasn't the chatty, confident Hunter that had been with us earlier in the day.

"Do you know what I think?" Jacob Sharpe said standing up which was an indication that he was about to tell us, "I think this bouncer has just randomly kicked the shit out of Dom and now needs some excuse to justify his actions. Inventing this cock and bull story about drugs just serves a purpose."

I didn't believe a word of it. Jacob 'Feely' Sharpe was Chorley's biggest bullshitter. He was in the year below me at our Primary School but every single girl in my class (and every other class in that school) fancied the short pants off him. He was an incredibly good looking young lad, unfortunately he still is. He didn't go to our Secondary school. Chorley's state schools weren't good enough for him. His parents were minted so they packed him off to private school but when we were in our mid-teens he always used to go to the discos at Chorley Cricket Club. One time, when I was in Year Nine, in my childhood naivety I fell for his choreographed charm. That night, temporarily, he made me feel prettier than I had ever felt before.

Jacob was a good kisser, I had already kissed enough boys at discos to know I didn't like sloppy kissers or boys who were 'tongue focused' but Jacob had a kiss that made me tingle in all the right areas. On the whole, it wasn't seen as good form to be kissing a boy who was younger than you but Jacob was the exception to this rule. Kissing Jacob raised your social status to another level.

Even at thirteen years old though, Jacob Sharpe was not content with just having a passionate snog with a girl twelve months his senior. Beyond the cricket club is the tennis club and beyond the tennis club, down a slope is a small field of longer grass. I remember him leading me down there, hand in hand, in the semi darkness to the far side of the tennis courts and we sat down so our backs were against the fence.

When we first arrived down there, in our little secluded spot, he started up the charm offensive again, about how pretty I was and how he had fancied me since Primary school, but this time, once we started kissing again, his hands started wandering. At first, it was just attempts to have a sneaky feel of my boobs and I let him touch them briefly before removing his hand but when he started trying to slip his hand into my knickers his luck ran out. I removed his hand and then thirty seconds later, I removed his other hand. I was on my period anyway, so even if the same scenario had played out a few years later I'd have possibly done the same (or just said 'look mate you're wasting your time right now but you're welcome to come back to the re-opening in a few days' time') but rejection didn't sit well with Jacob Sharpe. Spoilt kids hate not getting their own way.

"Come on Alice! Don't pretend you don't want this."

"I'm not pretending, Jacob."

"Of course you are."

Looking back on this moment, which I have done many times, I'm still not quite sure what he did then. He sort of grabbed me and twisted me in one simultaneous move, pulling me down from resting my back against the fence so I was horizontal on the grass and he was sat on top of me.

"Get off, Jacob!" I said sternly, at this stage he was frightening me.

"Stop pretending, Alice, let's just get this done."

I'm not certain what he was intending to 'get done' but whatever it was I was certain it wasn't going to be happening. I started struggling but he restrained me.

"Come on Alice," he said again, leaning down to kiss me but I turned my head to the side.

"If you don't get off me in three seconds, Jacob Sharpe, I'm going to scream so loud that they'll hear me in Preston," I warned.

That did the trick. He reluctantly removed his body off mine and stood up. I stood up too, brushing myself off.

"Bloody hell, Alice, calm yourself down. I was just messing about. Can you not take a joke?"

"It wasn't funny. I'm going back in."

"Don't you dare tell anyone about this, Alice Moorcroft or else…"

"Or else what?"

"Or else I'll tell the whole of Chorley that you wanted me to be the first and when I wouldn't do it, because I'm just a thirteen year old kid, you got all moody, started crying and then started making up a pack of lies."

That's the sort of kid that Jacob Sharpe is, a slimy liar. After that, both that night and subsequently, he deliberately went all out to be particularly friendly with Dominic and Hunter. It was like he was trying to taunt me. He was trouble.

"Sit down, dickhead, this isn't the House of Parliament," one of the bouncers commanded of Jacob and he duly obliged, which was no surprise as he's full of shit but ultimately he's a coward.

"If it's all so innocent," the bearded bouncer asked, "what were you doing in a cubicle with this other lad? Wiping each other's arses, were you?"

Jacob Sharpe has an answer for everything.

"No, I went to Primary school with Hunter. He's always been a good kid. I just happened to bump into him in the toilets and he was pretty wasted, not drugs though, just booze. I started talking to him and he wasn't making much sense. His Mum died of Covid-19 and I'd heard he'd gone off the rails since then. Anyway, as we were talking, his body jerked and a little bit of vomit sprayed out of his mouth. I didn't want him just to be sick on the floor so I led him into a cubicle so he could be sick in the toilets."

"Is that the best you can come up with?" the bald headed bouncer asked.

"Well where are the drugs then if we're supposed to be druggies?" Jacob asked, continuing the pretence of being outraged by a false accusation.

"You probably took a line each and then flushed the rest."

"The only thing we flushed down the toilet was his vomit."

Hunter did look awful and Jacob's story may have seemed plausible if I hadn't seen Hunter prior to him supposedly bumping into Jacob in the toilets. He was drunk but he'd even sobered up a little since we had been in 'The Ale Station' with his Dad so to see him now acting like his mind was away with the fairies suggested Jacob had supplied him with drugs. Jacob put on such a convincing act that I even started to doubt my own verdict for a little while before realising his story just didn't add up.

"If it was all so innocent and you were just caring for an old friend, why did your mate here try to rugby tackle me?"

"As I've said, I honestly don't believe he did."

"Don't start calling me a fucking liar," the bouncer said getting even more worked up.

"Well if the boot fits," Jacob replied.

The lady from management who had been prepared to sit

and listen for a while now decided to play her part. She decided to question a sheepish, twitching Hunter rather than an arrogant Jacob.

"Is that true, love?" she asked Hunter in a friendly sympathetic tone, "did your Mum die of Corona?"

"Yes, she did," Hunter replied.

"I'm so sorry to hear that."

"Thank you. She had no underlying health conditions either," Hunter added.

"That's awful. Now I want you to be honest with me. Sorry, what's your name young man?"

"Hunter."

"OK, Hunter, I want you to be honest with me. Have you been taking anything in here that you shouldn't have?"

"No, I don't do drugs."

"That's good to hear. But you were sick?"

"Only a bit."

"OK, Hunter, look me in the eyes."

The lady moved really close to him and stared into his eyes.

"I want to believe you, Hunter, but I'm not sure your eyes are telling me the same story as your lips."

It was at this very moment that Dominic started to properly stir. Everyone was alerted to the sudden movements from the settee as he started using his arms to lift himself up so he could have a proper look around to see what on earth was going on.

"Perfect timing," said the bald bouncer as a confused Dominic started staring around the room, "I've heard their version of events. Now, sunny Jim, it's time to hear yours."

CHAPTER FORTY SEVEN

JAY

We had probably retired to bed before midnight but it had taken a long time to drift off to sleep. Mary's daughter's mattress was perfectly comfy, it was firm with just a little bit of give in and the bed was spacious for one, as it was a small double, but my mind was restless. It was the first time since Amy had died that I had not slept in my own bed. For several months it had seemed strange sleeping in that marital bed alone and now it felt even stranger not being there. Everything had been perfectly platonic with Mary but I still felt guilty. It wasn't because of anything I had done, it was because of how I felt. I had felt a real sense of joy to be spending some time again with an intelligent, attractive woman of a similar age to me. Whilst I lay there in bed though, I just couldn't shake off that feeling of betrayal. It wasn't just the fact that I had enjoyed Mary's company, it was far more than that, I had orchestrated a scenario where I was now spending the night at her house.

I have grown accustomed to being a restless sleeper since Amy died so with an active, guilt ridden mind it was no surprise that it took a long time to settle. Once I did sleep, I had strange dreams that I no longer recall that I kept waking myself up from and then had to begin the cycle of settling again.

In the middle of the night, probably about three o'clock,

something unexpected happened. My door slowly opened and after the light from the landing rushed in, I could make out Mary's silhouette.

"Is everything OK?" I asked, puzzled by her presence, she had come into the room but was rooted to the spot by the doorway.

"Not really, no. I'm so sorry to disturb you."

"You aren't disturbing me, Mary. I'm an insomniac. Every night I fight battles I can never win."

"Would you mind if I got into bed with you?"

I really didn't know what to say. I just knew, in that moment, the right answer was neither 'Yes' nor 'No'.

"Why would you want to do that?"

"It doesn't matter. I shouldn't have asked."

"No, no, it does matter. Why would you want to get into bed with me?"

"I'm frightened."

"Of what?"

"Oh, it'll sound really stupid if I say it out loud."

"I really don't think that it will."

Once I insisted it wouldn't sound stupid, I was half anticipating Mary was going to come out with something particularly random like she had had a bad dream about witches or goblins but even if she had said either of them I wouldn't have laughed. At that point my body was bereft of humour.

"Sometimes, historically once or twice a month but in recent times more often than that, I wake up in the night and I get really anxious and I mean REALLY anxious about the fact that one day I will cease to exist. Covid-19 has definitely not helped nor did that incident with the ducks," Mary's voice was cracking as she spoke.

"Get in, under the duvet," I instructed.

Those words just came out. I knew, for my own mental well-being, it probably wasn't the right thing to say but the words seemed to spill out before I could stop them.

"Before I do, I need to say a couple of things," Mary said.

I could make her out more clearly now. She was wearing a pair of shorts and a thin top that left her arms bare. It wasn't lingerie as such but it was sexy. I wondered whether this was 'every night attire' or whether it was the nightwear she reserved for nights when she had male visitors.

"OK."

"Firstly, I'm lonely, Jay and sometimes when I'm lonely I do stupid things. In the past, I have had sex with people I really shouldn't have had sex with to temporarily escape from that feeling of loneliness. Just to make it clear, I am not here right now to make that same mistake. I am genuinely just here because I'm anxious."

"OK," I was saying very little because I really didn't know what to say.

"Secondly, bearing in mind everything I have just said and I appreciate this is a bizarre thing for me to ask given we are almost strangers but once I do get in bed, please could you hold me?"

I stopped myself from just saying 'OK' once more.

"I can, but in the spirit of full disclosure, can I just point out that, as you may well be aware, nature does weird things to a man's body whilst he sleeps so anything you may be made aware of in the pelvic area was there before you."

"Understood."

Mary climbed into bed. She didn't say anything else. She just slipped under the sheets, faced away from me then angled her body into mine so her backside was barely touching my waist and her back was aligned to my stomach and chest. As she settled, I became conscious that I was breathing against the back of her neck. I tried to breathe both less deeply and less often which I discovered was physically impossible for me to do. I did not have to worry for long. The pattern of Mary's breathing soon indicated that she had fallen asleep.

I didn't return to sleep myself for some time. I had too many questions to answer. The main one being why I was 'spooning' a woman I hardly knew but had already established had anxiety issues and was sexually promiscuous. Did I not have more than enough problems of my own? This was madness. I had consistently told myself I would never have a sexual relationship again and yet here I was. I should have just told her I did mind. When Mary asked if I minded, I should have just said that I did. Yet here I was, scared to move, breathing down the back of a stranger's neck. What the hell was going on?

CHAPTER FORTY EIGHT

<u>**DOMINIC – 3am**</u>

We were all walking back to Hunter's house. By 'us all', I'm not including Jacob Sharpe in that group, that weasel had buggered off as soon as we left 'Lost', cursing the fact that he'd had to flush a shitload of cocaine down the toilet. Not a word of thanks was uttered. Jacob can be very charming when he's planning and scheming, trying to hatch a master plan but when things go wrong for him, he's a bit of an arsehole. I used to think he was OK but I'm starting to see him for what he really is now.

I was walking along with Erika. The whole episode between Erika and Alice that seemed to have gone on throughout almost the entire day and early evening had somewhat resolved itself through the course of the night but it still seemed like there was some tension there. They were being polite with each other but they weren't interacting like they normally did. They normally seemed besotted but throughout the evening they had just been tolerant. As a consequence of this, on the walk to Hunter's, I was walking along with Erika whilst Alice and Hunter had dropped back about a hundred metres behind us.

I don't think I'd ever had a proper 'one to one' conversation with Erika before. The majority of times our paths crossed, she was obviously with my sister but even during the moments I was alone with her, I previously couldn't get past her looks to hold up my side of the conversation. So much had happened that evening though that I was just too tired for my weary mind to allow my awkwardness to kick in.

"How's your eye?" Erika asked sympathetically.

"Sore."

"Let's have another look at it."

We temporarily stopped walking under the next lamppost so Erika could inspect it under the light.

"It's a proper shiner that."

"I know. I don't mind too much though, it makes me look hard."

Erika laughed.

"I don't think it does. If anything, it makes you look like a man who can't take a punch! Bouncers are bastards, aren't they?"

"On this occasion I think it would be a bit unfair to blame the bouncer. He was just doing his job, trying to stop two kids taking drugs and I charged at him."

"You're too loyal to Hunter, if you ask me."

We had all debated going home after the 'Lost' incident. It had been me that insisted that we stay out. I could feel the lump above my eye steadily growing and the cut kept opening up but it was Hunter's birthday weekend and I wanted him to have a night out that he'd look back on fondly rather than considering it a complete disaster. I insisted if he stayed out though, he calmed things down with the drink. He was behaving pretty erratically anyway and I'm pretty certain cocaine and alcohol aren't an ideal mix.

I had pointed out to them all that I might not get in anywhere anyway with my black eye but we developed a tactic whereby I went in everywhere arm in arm with Erika and tilted my head so my good eye was more visible. That was the tactic but, to be honest, it was a fairly quiet night in Chorley, which was a regular issue these days because of the fear of Corona and because of the dent it was making in people's finances, so I think, if you'll pardon the pun, they were just willing to turn a blind eye. Thankfully the rest of the night was a lot of fun and managed to pass off without major incident.

"Hunter's had a tough time," I said responding to Erika's comment about my excess loyalty.

"It doesn't give him licence to be a bell end or a crap friend. His Dad's a legend but Hunter just seems to be trying too hard all the time."

"I know what you mean about 'trying too hard'. I think he's struggling, even more than his Dad, to come to terms with his Mum dying. I think Jay is pretty transparent whilst Hunter hides his emotions underneath a show of bravado."

"Interesting observation. How come we're all going to Hunter's again?"

"I wanted to stay there."

"How come?"

"I'd just rather wait another day before explaining this black eye to my Mum and Step Dad. They're an unpredictable pair and I just don't have the energy right now to be dealing with their drama nor do I particularly want to face them with a hangover first thing in the morning. You two could have gone back but I think Alice was pretty keen to do her big sister thing and keep an eye on me, especially as Hunter isn't really in a fit state to keep an eye on anyone."

"I don't think cocaine agrees with him. I've taken a few lines of coke at Uni and it hasn't sent me as crazy as him."

"Hunter's starting point was probably a lot further along the line towards madness."

"True," Erika said, chuckling a little as she said it.

"Hopefully he won't ever do it again but who knows with Hunter."

"You really did get him out of a lorry load of shit tonight, you know that, don't you?"

Erika and Alice had been made aware of the whole story through the course of our night out. Having all been taken to a side room in 'Lost', Hunter and Jacob had apparently denied everything whilst I was still knocked out. Once I came around, the bouncers had wanted to hear my version of events, to see whether it tallied with theirs. I had seen enough crime dramas on TV to know the best way of avoiding incriminating your-self was to say 'No Comment' which always made the charac-ters sound guilty so rather than go down that exact route, I just feigned concussion and said 'I can't remember' to every question I was asked. I think the bouncer who punched me had only seen two lads crouched around a bog and little else so was presuming guilt rather than having any evidence to prove it. With a lack of evidence, they just kicked us all out and warned us that we wouldn't be welcomed back. No doubt we'll be back in there in a few months' time when the dust has settled.

"What's been going on with you and my sister then? You don't seem to be your usual selves," I asked, moving the conversa-tion on from Hunter and his cocaine experiment.

"I don't know, Dom, it's probably my fault. Your sister is a wonderful person and I love her so, so much."

"But..."

"But I'm really not sure we should be exclusive at our age. If I met her at twenty five, I know I would want to stay with her for the rest of my life but I can see everyone at Uni going out, being wild and having so much fun whilst I feel I'm not really having the same experience because I'm in this long distance relationship."

"It's not that long distance. Alice goes over."

"I know she does and when she's there it's great but when she's not there, that's when it's hard. I feel guilty for not having fun and guilty when I do have fun."

"You know I'm not going to advise you to dump my sister."

"I know."

"But at the same time I don't want you to make her miserable. If the two of you are going to meet up and act all weird with each other like you have been tonight, it's not worth it."

"I know. I need to get my head straight and decide whether I want to get back into this relationship with the same passion and commitment I've had before because if I can't, it's not fair on either of us."

CHAPTER FORTY NINE

<u>**ALICE**</u>

"Have you and Erika had a row?" Hunter asked as we watched Dom and Erika going further and further into the distance ahead of us.

"No," I answered as I couldn't be bothered getting into this discussion with a drugged up Hunter.

"You look like you have."

"We're fine. It's just been a weird night."

"Tell me about it."

"You're a fucking arsehole by the way."

"I am? Why?"

"Taking cocaine."

"Loads of people do it."

"Maybe but they don't all end up getting my brother beaten up."

"I feel bad about that. He knows I do."

"Your Dad would be horrified too if he knew."

"I can't say I'm overly bothered what my Dad thinks. Anyway, he won't know because no-one would be cruel enough to tell him."

This somewhat contradictory statement was an instruction to keep my big mouth shut.

"I won't tell him Hunter but Christ you of all people should keep away from drugs."

"You don't understand."

"You're right, I really don't. I just know your Dad is a top bloke and he didn't deserve to lose your Mum. Your Mum didn't bring her illness upon herself though. She caught a virus, she became incredibly ill and died. That's bad enough but if you died because you were taking drugs that would be even worse."

This set Hunter off.

"Bloody hell! You and your brother are so melodramatic about it! It's cocaine, Alice! Half the country takes it."

"Well I never would. I've read up on the shit that dealers put into it. You've probably sniffed a right load of crap up your nose not just cocaine."

"I don't care. I got a buzz out of doing it."

"Why do you need to do that to yourself?"

"I don't know. Sometimes I just want to escape from real life for a while and tonight I did that."

"I'm sure your Mum would be horrified if she knew you were using her death to justify taking drugs."

"You never met my Mum."

"I'm not saying I did. I know enough about her to know she wouldn't have wanted you to be taking cocaine."

"Alice, my Mum wouldn't have an opinion at all because last time I saw her they were putting her coffin into a fucking hole six feet in the ground. She really didn't look capable of stating an opinion but even if somehow she magically could, she would have to shout pretty loud for me to hear her."

I didn't have a natural response to that so we just walked along without speaking for a few brief moments. I don't think Hunter felt comfortable with the silence.

"I know you all think my Dad is a great guy," Hunter continued, "and deep down although he does my fucking head in sometimes, I know he is but he still isn't my Mum. My Mum was the one who brought the family together. She was the one who dished the hugs out, she was the one I could open up to about how I felt and she was the one who was just bursting with pride whenever I did anything. If I brought a painting home from school when I was like five or six of the dog, my Mum would put it up in the kitchen and rave about how marvellous it was whilst my Dad would just ask why I'd drawn it with five legs. She thought I was an absolute superstar, my Dad just thinks I'm hard work."

"Men just show their emotions differently, Hunter."

"I know and I know he's trying, he really is but as I say he's not my Mum and as far as my life goes, a line was drawn in the sand the day she died splitting my life into two. Everything that happens now she's gone is never going to be the same because she won't be around to share it. Alcohol numbs that pain a bit and, as I've discovered tonight, cocaine does it better."

"You need a girlfriend, Hunter."

"Are you offering?"

"I have my own girlfriend. Right up there."

I unnecessarily pointed her out.

"Does she make you happy?"

"She makes me incredibly happy."

"I don't think she does, not any more. You need someone who idolises you, Alice and Erika doesn't. She idolises herself."

I knew he was suggesting himself as the alternative.

"Let's get one thing straight, Hunter, you and I will never be an item, we will never sleep together and we will never share a kiss. That said, I'd love it if we could be friends and if you need someone in your life to open up to, a female, I would be more than happy to be that person temporarily until you find someone special but, to repeat, that someone special will not be me."

"Why? Cause you like fanny more than cock?"

"Not the most charming way of putting it but yes, I probably prefer women to men, all things considered, but that's not the reason. You are Dom's best friend and Jay's son. It would be like dating a family member."

"Maybe in a few years' time you'll see things differently."

"Believe me, I will never change my mind."

"You might."

"Hunter, I won't!"

"You might."

We could probably have continued disagreeing on this point for some time so it needed someone to stop making their point. I chose to do just that."

"Come on, let's walk a bit faster and catch the others up."

"OK. Anyway, you're missing the point."

"Which is?" I queried.

"You have something about you, Alice, that other people haven't got. I don't quite know what it is, I mean you're pretty but you're no Kylie Jenner but there's just something about the whole Alice Moorcroft package which is incredible. I've shagged far fitter girls than you and not been bothered if I ever see them again but you have this effect, like cocaine in some ways, that keeps pulling people back again and again. Loads of people, male and female, feel that way about you, I know they do. If Erika doesn't realise you're incredible then you need to bin her off because there's a bloody long queue of people out there who know your true value even if Erika doesn't."

CHAPTER FIFTY

<u>ALICE</u>

Erika and I had mind blowing sex that night. Unquestionably the most wonderful, orgasmic sexual encounter that I have ever experienced. As we both lay there naked afterwards, in a spare bedroom at Jay's, quivering, shaking and feeling a little bit sore, I knew our relationship was over. I knew it might not end immediately but I knew we had reached the end of the line. It was going to be heart breaking but it was time to let each other go.

CHAPTER FIFTY ONE

JAY

It was weird waking up the following morning. Subconsciously, my brain was aware that someone was next to me. For a split second, I was fooled into thinking Amy was alive and the time since her death had just been some horrible nightmare. Reality soon took hold.

"Good morning," said a voice from behind my head, I had obviously let go of Mary at some point during the night and turned over.

"Good Morning!"

"Is this a bit awkward? I'm sorry I came in here last night like a frightened child."

"It's fine," I said as I turned over to face her. Looking at her first thing in the morning re-enforced the opinion I already had that Mary was well out of my League. Without make up she still had a smooth complexion and mesmerising eyes that hinted at an enchanting soul. If I had never been married or was a lonely divorcee, I would have been so proud to have found myself in a situation where I was sharing a bed with her. To be totally candid, a little bit of me did have that small element of pride that somehow this forty something, out of shape, tired looking man with small man boobs could still end up in bed with someone so heavenly. Pride was mixed in the pallet with a whole range of other emotions including confusion, guilt, desire, shame and sorrow.

"It's such a weird sensation. From an early age we are told that we are mortal and it's something we tend to just accept but sometimes that grim reality just overpowers me and I find it very frightening."

"I'm sure everyone gets freaked out by the thought of their own death from time to time. You aren't religious then?"

"No. Can you remember Jonathan Edwards, the triple jumper?"

"I can."

"Well if you remember, he was from a religious family, I think his father might have been a Vicar or was that Matthew Pinsent, the rower, it could even have been both of them? Anyway, that doesn't really matter, the point is that Jonathan Edwards was a religious man. I think for a while, when he was a triple jumper, he wouldn't take part in events on Sundays. Then, once his triple jumping career was over, he was on religious programmes on TV like Songs of Praise, he really was a celebrity figurehead of the Christian church and then one day he announced he had been questioning his faith and had come to the conclusion that in all probability there was no God.

"I can't say I remember that."

"Well, the point is that I've had a similar experience to that. It just happened earlier in life. I had very religious, God fearing parents. I went to Christian Primary and Secondary schools, said my prayers every night and worried constantly if I was pleasing God. At seventeen though, I met Tilly's Dad, Alex who was a passionate socialist, hence the introduction to Billy Bragg but he was also equally passionate about atheism. He had a whole library of books about atheism written by people like Richard Dawkins, Sam Harris and Christopher Hitchens. He encouraged me to read them, which I reluctantly did, to dismiss them really but it turned out that they were intelligently written and I started to question all the assumptions I had previously made. I slowly came to realise that on the balance of probability there probably was no God. Thousands of years ago man sought a solution to the workings of the planet and God, in his many different forms, became that solution. As time passed though, science came along to challenge the status quo. The answers science provided were darker and more frightening so many people clung to their old belief system as the thought of lasting forever is much more palatable than thinking you are constantly moving along life's conveyor belt towards nothing.

I know I wouldn't have to contend with these anxious moments on a regular basis if I had remained religious but once what I now believe to be the most likely answer revealed itself, it was impossible for me to go back."

"I totally get it. I'm pretty much on the same page as you are now with religion but I've never really believed. Now I've lost Amy I do think it would be fantastic to think after a few more years I'll be joining her forever in some paradise elsewhere but I can't fool myself into it. In all honesty, I'm surprised anyone can in the twenty first Century, especially after Corona. Did anyone have their prayers answered on that one?"

"Sorry, that's a bit of a heavy way to start a Saturday morning! I just felt I needed to explain myself after wandering in. Normally when I feel like that it's Tilly that I cuddle up to, not a man I hardly know."

"Stop apologising! Honestly, it's fine."

"What about you? How are you feeling about being here? Have you shared a bed with anyone since your wife died?"

"I've not shared a bed with anyone else ever, to be honest."

"Wow! So you've only ever slept with your wife?"

"Well, before we were together, in my wild youth, I did have drunken, brief sex with a couple of different girls but they were one-offs at parties and I never actually ended up staying overnight with them."

"Shit, I feel really, really bad now. I'm so sorry."

"Don't be. It's not like anything happened last night. It did feel very strange though. You went to sleep very quickly and I was just lying there, holding you but thinking about Amy. It's funny what goes around in your head, isn't it? There was a song that Amy and I used to love by Anna Nalick called 'Knots' and that was going around and around in my head.

"By who?"

"Anna Nalick. She's not famous, well she was for a while in America, probably about fifteen years ago now. She's one of those singers that you think should be massive but somehow isn't but then you get a bit of a buzz out of being in on the secret. She was one of Amy's favourites. 'Knots' was Amy's favourite song by her. It's a ballad."

"Grab your phone from the side."

"What for?"

"Put it on 'You Tube' so I can have a listen to it."

"Nah, you don't want to listen to that."

"Yes, I do! Go on, grab your phone and put it on."

"OK."

So I grabbed my phone and we sat up in bed and listened. It's the type of song that pulls on the heart strings even when you aren't feeling emotionally vulnerable but at that moment I was an easy target. It raked up so many memories that by the chorus I was in tears. Mary started crying too. When it finished, we shared a hug. A long, tearful, snotty hug, then Mary passed me a tissue, I wiped away my tears, blew my nose and then we headed down for breakfast.

CHAPTER FIFTY TWO

<u>MARY</u>

Jay reminded me of the actor that was in Cyrano de Bergerac, Gerard Depardieu . He wasn't aesthetically pleasing but had this real manliness that had a certain charm. I didn't regret going into Tilly's room to see him after getting all anxious in the middle of the night but what I did regret, pretty much as soon as I said it, was blurting out about past sexual partners. There was absolutely no need for me to have said that. I'm not saying I am ashamed of my sexual history, I am a single woman and have the freedom to do what I want, but I think the way I put it across and the time I chose to discuss it wasn't right. That uncomfortable feeling was made even worse the following morning when Jay casually mentioned it was the first time in his life that he had shared a bed with anyone other than his wife. It just made him seem loyal and made me seem needy. As a self-employed, independent thirty five year old woman nothing could have been further from the truth.

I think about three minutes into the conversation that morning I realised I wanted this man to be part of my life. I wasn't sure in what capacity but I have met so many un-impressive men over recent years that to meet someone who came across as a genuinely caring and warm hearted man was a real rarity. I understood that he had been hugely impacted by his wife's death and our relationship may only ever be a platonic one but that didn't bother me. I enjoy sex but I can live without it but I think if you meet someone you truly feel a connection with, you owe it to yourself to allow that relationship to run its course. I wasn't going to let him walk out the door of my house without asking whether he wanted to keep in touch.

With the exception of my father, I cannot think of another male who has had an almost entirely positive influence on my life. A lot of chauvinism has drifted down from previous generations and I find men generally to be lazy and selfish. I am not saying I haven't met some decent men, because I have but I think the older you get, the harder it is to find one you would want to spend time with on an ongoing basis. I suppose Alex has been a constant in my life because he jointly created our wonderful daughter but his passionate nature lacked boundaries so I wouldn't say, all things considered, his influence on my life, Tilly aside, was a generally positive one. I blame him for a lot of the commitment issues I have with men. I'm not possessive or anything like that, I just go into a relationship expecting them to show all their flaws once their guard comes down so take what I need from them quickly. I would say the average length of my relationships since I re-entered the world of dating, when Tilly was five, is about a month.

I had only met Jay on two separate occasions but it was enough to suggest something about him was very different. Most single men, once they reach my age and beyond, come across as desperate. They are normally either desperate for a relationship or desperate for sex or both. Jay was the polar opposite of this. As long as he was telling the truth, and I have no reason to doubt his sincerity, he was desperate not to have sex or a relationship. This perhaps made him more appealing rather than less, it certainly didn't appear to be a shrewd plan to attract me through pity.

"So what happens next?" I asked him bluntly as I passed him smoked salmon and poached eggs at my kitchen table.

"With what?" he asked sounding completely confused.

"We've crossed paths twice inadvertently. Do we arrange a

third meeting ourselves or do we just let fate run its course and see if we bump into each other a year or two further down the line?"

"Would you like a third meeting?" Jay asked pushing me into being more candid than I would normally be.

"Very much so. Would you?"

"Yes, as friends."

"Of course, Jay. I know exactly where we stand."

I didn't really know what I wanted from this friendship. I wasn't sure if I wanted to try to break down his barriers or just have the sort of friendship Alice seemed to have with him. It was probably too early to tell. I just knew I didn't want to let go.

"So what do you fancy doing?"

"I don't know….maybe go for a nice walk somewhere?"

"What about the Lakes?" Jay suggested, "It's only an hour or so up the road but with the lockdowns and the personal stuff, I haven't been up there for a couple of years now."

"OK, that sounds good but can we not go to Bowness? Every time I go to the Lakes, I tend to go to Bowness. It's lovely but I'd prefer to go somewhere else."

"That's fine. When shall we go?"

"I've got a couple of things on next weekend," I replied without detailing that I was out with the girls on the Friday night and had another Tinder date lined up for the Saturday in Westhoughton, "so maybe the weekend after?"

"Sounds like a plan. How about I pick you up early on the Saturday morning, say about eight and I'll bring a picnic. Bring sturdy shoes."

"OK, it's a date…by which I mean a date in the diary, not an actual date," I said quickly backtracking.

Jay smiled, "I know. I will look forward to it."

CHAPTER FIFTY THREE

ALICE

"So I think I'm going to finish things with Erika," I deliberately said it in a matter of fact manner but I knew it was a major announcement.

Some woman spoilt this major newsflash moment by walking past us on the train and coughing without covering her mouth let alone into a tissue. Jay glared at her but still, despite everything he had been through, he still did not comment.

"That annoys me so much," he eventually said with annoyance once the woman was out of earshot, "hang on, you're doing what? Finishing with Erika? How come?"

"It just isn't working like it used to. Not since she went to University."

"Well it's not going to work like it used to, is it? The dynamics have changed, you just have to re-adjust."

"I don't think she wants to though. Not really. I think she's tried to find a balance but it's led to her picking fault in things I do and say, which I hate. I think I'm best just letting her go whilst we're still really fond of each other before it descends in to one of those crappy relationships where all you do is argue."

Jay pulled a sad face. It was like a real life emoji.

"Only you can make that decision but if you feel it's the right decision then I'm sure it is."

"Will you keep in touch with Erika if we split up?"

"It depends."

"On what?"

"Will you be severing all ties with her?"

"I expect so."

"Then I wouldn't keep in touch then. I'd be polite and send the occasional text initially, like on her birthday, but eventually I would let that just fizzle out. I love her and I think she's a wonderful human being but if we have to be 'Team Alice' or 'Team Erika' then my allegiances are always going to be with you."

"Thank you."

"Don't thank me, Erika's just easier to avoid than you are! She doesn't get my train every morning nor is her brother best friend's with my son."

"True! So it isn't that you and I are mates, it's just more convenient to take my side."

"Exactly."

"I hate you!"

"Ask me if I'm bothered."

"So spill the beans then, what happened with Mary?"

"Nothing happened with Mary."

"Don't give me that! You stayed overnight."

"Only because I missed the last train."

"Yeh, but what were you up to that made you miss the last train?"

"Nothing. Just chatting."

"Jay, I've seen how you look at her."

"Which is how exactly?"

"Like she's stunning."

Jay shifted a little in his chair when I said that. To me, his squirming indicated that I was right on the money. He didn't try to deny it either.

"OK, I appreciate that she's a fine looking lady but the world has many fine looking ladies so that doesn't mean anything. I just enjoy her company and would like us to be friends."

"Just friends? Not fuck buddies?"

"Just friends," he emphasised the word 'friends'.

"Well, that's disappointing."

"Well it shouldn't be."

"So is Mary happy just being friends with you? She seems to be searching for her Prince Charming and it sounded to me like she already has a lot of friends."

"It appears she has room for one more. We're going to the Lake District a week on Saturday."

"Very nice, very romantic too," I said with a huge grin.

"Forget what I said before, I'm going in 'Team Erika'."

My eyes started to well up. It was a shock to me but it was even more of a shock to Jay. He had a look of both guilt and concern.

"I was joking, Alice, I was just joking."

"It's not that. I'm just sad that it has to come to an end. I've loved her so much and I think she's really loved me too. I just don't see our future together anymore."

"Mary has some theory that people can only ever be 95% happy. She explained that every positive decision you make has some sort of negative consequence so you have to be prepared to make a small sacrifice. Really big decisions aren't about making small sacrifices though. They are about looking at the two pathways that lead to your future and deciding long-term which one is going to make you happier. There are major sacrifices and huge risks involved but based on the information you have, you have to choose what you think is the best route."

"What do you think I should do?"

"I think you should make the right decision not the comfortable one."

"Is that a hint that you think we should split up?"

"No, I've told you before I can't and won't give you relationship advice. I might chip in with the odd word of wisdom but nothing more. I was very lucky and had a relationship that worked very naturally the vast majority of the time. You just need to decide whether you can fix yours so it's as good as new or whether it's broken beyond repair."

"Well therein lies the problem. I don't think it can be fixed so it's as good as new nor do I think it's broken beyond repair so it's just a question of whether either of us want to make do with this patched up version of what we used to have."

"I can't help you make that decision but what I can do is let you know that I'll be there for you no matter what decision you make."

"I know you will. Thank you Jay! I love you."

"I love you too sweetheart…. Like a niece."

"Why did you add 'like a niece'?"

"In case any of this lot are listening."

No-one made eye contact but I'm sure one or two smirked.

"It's funny who you try not to upset, Jay."

"What do you mean?"

"I mean you worry too much about what your dead wife will think even though you're an atheist and what strangers on a train will think even though we will never see them again. If they want to think you and I are shagging, let them think that. I don't care."

"I do."

"I know you do but it's ridiculous. If you went in to 'The Bay Horse' and put ten grand behind the bar and said to the landlord that all the drinks are on me all night, most people would think you were great but some would still say,

'Who does that flash bastard think he is?'

Some people will hate you no matter what you do. With Mary, you aren't really worried about what Amy will think, you're worried what Hunter will say and what Amy's friends will say. Stop worrying about everyone else and start concentrating on what matters to you."

"Thank you for the lecture."

"No problem but if you follow it up by saying I've embarrassed you in front of all these people I swear I will never speak to you again!"

CHAPTER FIFTY FOUR

ALICE

I needed to see Erika face-to-face. A long-term relationship shouldn't be finished by text or phone, I felt it needed me to sit in front of her. We had exchanged regular texts over the two week period following Hunter's birthday weekend and we spoke every couple of days but it just felt awkward and unnatural. Our conversations were punctuated by long silences and our texts were informative and formal rather than the jokey and sexual tone that we used to adopt. Our relationship was on life support, there was no chance of survival and it now needed one of us to be brave enough to switch it off. I offered to go over to Leeds but Erika had said she'd forgotten to take a few clothes that she needed back to University last time she was home so needed to come back anyway. We agreed to meet in Costa in Buckshaw on the Saturday morning at 10am.

I was there first, took the liberty of ordering both coffees and sat at a table in the corner awaiting Erika's arrival. I watched her come in and despite everything that I knew was about to happen, my heart still skipped a beat when she came in. She was wearing her black turtleneck with a pair of faded blue jeans and looked as stunning as ever. We said polite 'hellos' and Erika took her seat on the two seater settee that was opposite the one where I sat. I momentarily recalled how we used to sit next to each other or if we did sit opposite we used to lean forward so our noses were nearly touching and we could taste the sweet smell of each other's breath. Our backs were now pressed firmly against the seats. It saddened me that we each had to visibly demonstrate to the other that it was over. We chatted in a friendly fashion for a few minutes about Leeds and College and then moved on.

"Jay is off to the Lakes today with Mary," I announced.

"I hope it works out for him, I really do but personally I didn't take to her."

"I don't think it was her you didn't like Erika, it was the situation you were in, in 'The Ale Station'."

"Perhaps but if roles were reversed I would have made an effort to bring her into the conversation."

"You were busy talking about Marvel films with Hunter and Dom."

"Only because I was being ignored."

"Whatever."

It was weird that since we had seen Mary we'd had a row, followed by amazing sex but had now reverted back to not getting on. I think, perhaps to an extent subconsciously, that sexual encounter was definitely us enjoying each other's bodies and one final intimate moment together knowing that it would never happen again.

"Anyway presumably you didn't want me home from Leeds to chit chat and bicker. Presumably you wanted me back here so you could tell me we're finished."

"Erika, it doesn't matter if you say it or I do but we both know it."

I was then caught completely off guard. Erika didn't say anything for a few seconds, moved her mug of coffee unnecessarily, inhaled deeply and then exhaled so her whole body sagged slightly before delivering her body blow.

"I know. I've fallen in love with someone else."

This was a development I had just not anticipated. I could cope with us splitting up, in fact I had very much got my head around it but the fact that Erika was declaring that she had already given her heart to someone else just made me feel insignificant.

"A female?"

I don't know why I asked that. I guess it was just because I was in a state of shock and my brain wasn't working properly but the question just pissed her off.

"Of course it's a female, Alice. I have no question marks about my sexuality, you know that. I can't believe you even asked that."

I was being lectured by someone who had cheated on me before we had even split up. I may have asked a daft question but she had just declared she loved someone else yet I was the one being made to feel guilty. I came to my senses and struck back.

"I apologise for asking. So is she a good fuck?"

This was a dig at Erika for criticising me for being below the necessary standard.

"It's not just about the sex. I just love her. Really love her. The way I used to love you."

"Is she at Uni?"

"Sort of."

"Surely she either is or she isn't."

"She's a lecturer at my Uni."

"Oh right," I said, I hadn't been expecting that development either, "how old is she?"

"Thirty five."

"Christ."

"Thirty five isn't old."

"I didn't say it was, just a lot older than us."

"She's one of my sports lecturers."

"Is that even allowed?"

"What? For a lecturer to have a relationship with a student? I'm not a kid at school."

"No, but it's hardly professional, is it? I mean if you have a dissertation to be marked by the woman you're sharing a bed with then surely that puts you at some sort of unfair advantage."

Erika didn't like this. I think because it was a valid point.

"This is a conversation we don't need to be having."

Erika stood up to go.

"Hang on! Just sit down a minute and do me the courtesy of hearing me out."

Erika pondered for a moment and then sat back down.

"Thank you. How long have you been sleeping with her?"

"Fuck! Do you really need to go there, Alice?"

"You brought it up. You could have just turned up here and we could have just amicably split but you wanted to get in, as a parting shot, that you were already over me. So answer the question, how long have you been sleeping with her?"

"I don't want to answer that. You and I loved each other, we stopped loving each other and once that happened I found someone else."

"More than two weeks then. All that shit you were spouting off when we were out for Hunter's birthday was just to ease your conscience because you were shagging someone else. You were jealous of me talking to Mary because you thought I might beat you at your own game."

"It was early days then. I wasn't sure what I wanted then."

"And you know now?"

"Yes, I do. The last two weeks have been extraordinary."

"What's her name?"

"Lucy."

"Presumably Lucy doesn't know we had incredible sex when you were last home. Did you have to avoid sleeping with her for a few days so she didn't see the scratches on your back and the teeth marks on your arse?"

Erika rolled her eyes.

"It wasn't all that mind blowing. Lucy is a mature woman, she understood my relationship with you was fading out whilst my relationship with her was gathering pace."

"Well I hope you are very happy together. It's weird, isn't it, there's poor Jay who can't bring himself to have a relationship with someone despite his wife being dead whilst you're hopping into bed with a middle aged woman before our relationship is even over. Reflects how much Jay's relationship meant to him and how little ours meant to you."

That was a good time to leave. I had nothing else to say. I could have just sat there and cried but I didn't want to give her the satisfaction. I just stood up and left. I wanted to make that dramatic exit before she did. Ten minutes later, Erika sent me a text,

'Alice, our relationship meant the world to me. I was completely faithful and only ever had eyes for you until the romance started to fade. I will always look back on what we had as something special. I hope we can still be friends."

I didn't reply. I very nearly replied with 'You've tainted everything' but instead I blocked her number, blocked her on social media and wiped her out of my life completely. I have never seen her since but there are times when I long to. It was a wonderful relationship for a long time but it still scares me how quickly it derailed.

CHAPTER FIFTY FIVE

JAY

Based on Mary not wanting to go to Bowness, I decided Keswick would be the perfect place for us to visit. It was a sunny, slightly breezy, Spring day when I picked Mary up from her home but the further North we headed, the stronger the wind became and the more the clouds gathered. It took us about an hour and three quarters to get up there but the time passed quickly as the conversation flowed naturally. The two previous times we had met, Mary had been fairly serious but this time I found her really funny, quick witted and self-deprecating.

"No, honestly I am one of the worst dancers in the world," Mary was explaining as we drove up the M6, "it doesn't bother me that I'm awful but I'm glad I didn't actually know when I was growing up. It was only when I started dating Alex that I realised. He just casually mentioned it once on the way home from a nightclub,

'You do know you have completely no rhythm, don't you?'

I thought it may have been because I was drunk because my peripheral hearing goes after a few drinks but it turns out I'm equally hopeless when I'm sober."

"I'm surprised by that. Good looking people are normally great dancers because they've had the confidence to step on to the dance floor from an early age."

I was comfortable with throwing a compliment about Mary's

looks into the conversation. It wasn't as though she wouldn't have heard it a million times before. It was probably so commonplace that she didn't even pick up on it.

"No, straight up, I'm completely crap! I'm that bad I've been at weddings and complete strangers have started recording me dancing on their phones. As I say, it doesn't bother me, if my terrible dancing puts a smile on people's faces then that's fine with me. Too many people take themselves far too seriously."

I quickly judged my own ability on the dance floor.

"I'd say I'm pretty average. Good on you for not caring, I'm too sensitive a soul to be like that. I reckon if a stranger was filming on their phone and I knew it was to have a laugh at my expense then I'd probably stop dancing immediately and not get back up on the dance floor for the rest of the night."

Mary smiled sympathetically.

"He's got the better of you then though, hasn't he? It's not my job to be good at dancing. I just enjoy doing it socially for a bit of fun."

"Amy was a really good dancer. She did ballet and modern dance as a kid and she'd do different dance classes as an adult to keep her fit. Everyone used to comment on how great she was. She was one of those people who spent her whole life being showered with compliments. I used to think how lucky she was and then one day her luck ran out."

As I finished saying this, I decided to make a conscious effort not to talk about Amy constantly. I was pretty sure Mary would understand that it was natural for me to do it as we had gone through life together but it didn't feel like the right thing to do.

"You'll have to show me a photo of her. I have an image of how I think she looked so it'd be interesting to know if I'm right."

"I have one in my wallet, I'll show you it when we get to Keswick. I promise I won't bang on about Amy all day though."

"Just say what it feels natural to say, Jay. Don't hold back on my account."

"Thank you."

I enjoyed showing people photos of Amy. Lads would always say things like 'You're punching well above your weight there' or 'How did you manage to pull her?' whilst women tended to say 'She's lovely' or 'She's beautiful' or 'She's so pretty'. Both sexes definitely thought more of me because of the wife I had.

As I say, we found plenty to chat about and I enjoyed finding out more and more about Mary as the day went on. We parked up at the 'Theatre By The Lake' car park, changed from comfy shoes to sturdy shoes and put on our waterproofs just in case before following a pathway down to Derwentwater. The Lake is much smaller than Windermere being only about three miles long and one wide but I would say it's equally beautiful with smaller crowds of people making their way around it. We continued along the pathway by the Lake's edge before stopping probably halfway along the Lake for our picnic. We managed to find an empty Lakeside bench with stunning views across the water. The wind and clouds combined with the odd spot of rain, made it a little too cold for us to take our coats off but once in a while the sun would break through, sprinkling beams of light across the lake and giving our cheeks a temporary warm glow.

"Did you want more than one child, Mary or were you always intending to only have one?" I asked as I tucked into some salt and vinegar crisps.

"Hmmm, tough one to answer that. I think when I had Tilly I knew I didn't want to have another child for a long time because I wanted to devote all my energies and finances towards her but when I reached thirty I did start to think if I met the right man I would like to have another child but then I never have so it's sort of immaterial. What about yourself, did you just want Hunter?"

"No, we would have liked more children but it never happened. We were just in our early twenties when Hunter came along and didn't anticipate that we would ever have difficulties conceiving but sadly we did."

"Oh, I'm sorry to hear that."

"It's just one of those things. Sometimes life doesn't allow you to plan ahead. Do you still think if you do meet the right man in the future you may have another child?"

"Possibly but I doubt it. Work wise I'd be OK..."

"What is it you do again?"

"I'm a self-employed financial adviser so I do think I could find a work-life balance if I had a baby but the hard part is finding the right man. I think, adapting the Forrest Gump analogy, men are like a box of chocolates, women pick the good ones in their twenties and then all that's left by the time they reach forty are the crap ones nobody likes or the ones someone else has chewed up and spat out."

"Is there not an element of taste involved? A lot of people hate coffee creams but some people love them."

"No, I'm saying all the Cadbury's chocolates get taken out the box straight off when it comes to men and all the cheap, nasty supermarket brand stuff is left behind. I reckon I'm pretty close to giving up on the dating game. I'm going to be one of those lonely old spinsters who takes loads of breadcrumbs to the park to feed the pigeons."

I doubted very much this was ever going to happen.

"I'm sure you have a long list of admirers and eventually the right man will come along."

"Don't get me wrong, Jay, if there was suddenly a load of Cadbury's Dairy Milk men in that box of male chocolates, I would not be that desperate to eat him."

"You know that sounds sexual, don't you?"

"I only realised once I said it," Mary replied as we exchanged a shy smile, "but as I think we discussed the other week, if I found the right man I'd have to make significant sacrifices to my way of living and I'm not convinced I will ever want to do that."

"Maybe you'll change your mind once he does turn up."

"Maybe, perhaps seeing how my Dad treated my Mum meant I set the bar too high."

"Are your parents still alive?"

"Yes, still going strong. They aren't old, Dad was sixty last year and Mum's fifty eight. Still working, still keeping well and still very much in love. Yours?"

"Yes, still alive. They are in their seventies now. My Mum is in the early stages of dementia but she's fine. She's just not been mentally aware enough to have helped me through this dark period of my life. Dad's good though. I also have a brother who is a policeman in New Zealand but we only really exchange the odd text and speak at Christmas. He was six years older than me and moved there when he was twenty one so we've never been that close. I've been over there a couple of times though, it's like two islands worth of the Lake District. Without doubt the most gorgeous country I've ever been to."

"I've heard it's wonderful. Sorry to hear about your Mum."

"Thank you. It's brilliant to hear about your parents though. Any brothers or sisters?"

"I have a sister in East Anglia called Sophie, she's two years younger than me. We're really close. She has two little boys who are four and two, Archie and Wilf."

"Cool names. Shall we start walking again? It's lovely when the sun comes out but it's pretty nippy when it goes in."

"I can tell you don't work outdoors!"

"I know. I'm very nesh!"

"Me too! Shall we stop at the café next to the theatre and have a coffee to warm us up?"

"Sounds perfect. I might have a little bit of space in this chubby belly for a piece of cake too."

"Why not? We're on our holidays!"

We stood up and started walking back towards Keswick.

"I need to invest in a flask if this is going to become a regular thing."

"I think you do."

I smiled a little to myself. I felt happy. I felt really, really happy.

CHAPTER FIFTY SIX

<u>HUNTER – One month later</u>

When my Dad shouted up to say someone was at the door for me, I have to admit I hoped it was Alice. With hindsight, why I even thought it could be Alice was ridiculous. Alice and my Dad are so close that if she came knocking on our door, which she does from time to time, he would just invite her straight in. This was someone Dad didn't know, hence the reason they were kept waiting on the doorstep and I was called down.

On the basis I hoped it was Alice, I checked myself in the mirror, corrected a few out of place strands of hair and then walked down slowly, avoiding the temptation to run, so I wouldn't appear at the door appearing breathless. Alice and Erika had split up and I was unsure how much this was influenced by me telling Alice that she could do much better. I wasn't ruling out the possibility that she was actually interested in me but was doing that girl thing of playing hard to get. Alice was one of those complicated girls that I knew would drive me crazy in a million different ways but I still couldn't help falling in love with.

To discover, on arrival in the hallway, that it was Jacob Sharpe standing there was a massive disappointment. It made sense why Dad would keep him there, my Dad wouldn't have had a clue who Jacob was. Mum may have remembered him from Primary school but not Dad. Still, it was strange that Jacob had come to ours. He had never been to ours before and normally relied on his 'clients' to go to him. My immediate thought was that I had ordered a shitload of cocaine at some point when I was wasted and it had merited a trip out for him.

"Oh, it's you Jacob. Dad, this is Jacob Sharpe, we went to Primary school together. Jacob, this is my Dad."

They just mumbled their hellos and nodded heads at each other. Before Mum died, certainly in the happy days before Corona, Dad would have offered a firm handshake. Nowadays only a select few benefitted from anything other than the head nod. Having discovered who our visitor was, Dad wandered away into the lounge or the kitchen.

"Am I alright to come in?" Jacob asked, in what immediately seemed like quite a low key tone for him. He was normally outgoing and upbeat. Once again, this led me towards thinking he was carrying a large consignment of cocaine and was nervous about completing the transaction on our doorstep.

"Of course, yeh, come in, come in. We'll go upstairs to my room.....Dad – Jacob and I are heading up to my room if you need me for anything."

I made a mental note to listen out for Dad coming up the stairs before I had the chance to hide the cocaine. Why I thought Jacob was going to leave this massive consignment of coke without taking payment was anyone's guess. I led the way up the stairs and Jacob followed me through to my room.

"Sorry about the mess," I said as we entered.

It was a fucking mess too. I think I'm normally blind to it when I'm on my own but when you have an unexpected visitor you notice the empty mugs and chocolate wrappers, the dirty clothes crumpled on the floor, socks that don't match and the weird patterns that masturbatory tendencies have made on your bed sheets. I immediately picked the duvet up off the floor and smoothed it over the bed.

"Sit down, pal," I encouraged once a brief tidy up had been

completed.

"OK thanks," Jacob said, still in that tone that didn't seem quite right.

"How come you're here? If you're bringing me anything you'll have to hold fire for payment mate. I don't carry cash these days. It's a germ thing, mainly."

"No, no, you've not ordered anything, Hunter."

"Oh right, I thought I'd forgotten. I was pretty wasted the other week. Been pretty wasted a lot recently but just on the booze not the coke."

Perhaps he'd come to apologise for the trouble at 'Lost'. He had certainly landed us in it. We should have just met up somewhere less public.

"Have you heard of contact tracing, Hunter?"

From feeling confused, I now started to feel a sense of dread. Contact tracing meant one thing to me and that was Covid-19. It was a means of tracking and tracing the movements of people with the virus to warn others who they may have come into contact with that they need to be tested and potentially put themselves into quarantine. If Jacob was Covid-19 positive and he had the nerve to come to our house to tell me, I was going to punch him as hard as I possibly could.

"Yes."

"Well obviously you know it's been used for Corona."

I was ready to fucking kill him.

"Yes. Spit it out, Jacob. I'm not being funny but if you've come here because you've tested positive for Corona, I'll give you a good kicking and my Dad will probably join in too."

"No, I haven't got Corona. Contact tracing is also used for H.I.V."

I know I'm not the most intelligent person in the world. I'm not thick, I just don't have much interest in education or current affairs. I watch the news occasionally but only certain stories grab my attention. Being completely honest, without Covid-19, I probably wouldn't have been able to tell you who the Prime Minister was. I'm still not 100% sure what party Boris Johnson is in, I know it's the Tories but I'm not sure if they're the Brexit Party or the Conservative Party. Anyway, I didn't have a clue what H.I.V was. A part of my brain was telling me it might be a sexual disease but I really would have just been guessing. People mentioned chlamydia a lot and syphilis a fair bit but not H.I.V at all.

"OK. Sorry to sound a bit thick here but what's that?"

"It's a virus."

"Like Covid?"

"I don't know, Hunter, sort of. The day after I saw you in Chorley, I started feeling really shit. I initially thought it was a bad batch of coke but then I developed a rash, started burning up and my throat was really bad so I naturally started to shit myself that I had Corona. In my line of work, I don't exactly social distance. Anyway, I had a test done and although it came back negative, I continued to feel like shit."

"But you have got this other virus?"

I couldn't remember the letters. I was going to say HGV but realised that's a bloody lorry.

"H.I.V – I might have."

"For Christ's sake, Jacob, what are you doing here breathing all over my room if you've got that?"

"You don't catch it from breathing."

"Are you sure?"

"I'm 100% positive."

I relaxed when he said that.

"You don't look ill now."

"I don't feel ill anymore."

"OK, well I'm sorry you've had that but what's it got to do with me?"

"I'm coming to that. After I tested negative for Corona but still felt terrible, my Doctor was asking me loads of different questions about things and I ended up owning up about taking drugs. He suggested I do these tests for H.I.V and the first one has come back positive."

"But you said you are OK now?"

"Only for now, pal. I have to go for another test to confirm it in six weeks' but, going back to the contact tracing thing, my Doctor suggested I speak to everyone I have had sex with or shared drugs with and encourage them to get tested too."

"I'm not ill though, Jacob. I've not had a temperature or a sore throat and it's not like we shared a needle."

"We used the same straw."

"A fucking straw! So what? It's not like it's the same needle puncturing into your skin and then into mine."

"Apparently it can be transmitted from one person to another by sharing a straw - something to do with the blood vessels in your nose. Apparently HIV growth is highest amongst kids using coke."

"I'm not getting tested. I'll be fine."

"You should, pal."

"If I get a bad cold, I'll get tested then but if I don't and you can't pass it on through breathing then I'm not going to my Doctor's. I know our Doctor pretty well. After my Mum died he was around at ours a few times to see my Dad so I am not going to tell him I've been taking cocaine. Not a chance! I just won't take coke again so even if I get it I can't pass it on so I'll be fine."

Jacob stood up.

"Look pal, you do what you want. My job was to tell you and I've done that. The thing is, you can get it by shagging too so if you've got it and you shag someone then you can give it to them too."

That put a different slant on things.

"OK shit, that's different. I might not take drugs again but I'm not going to stop shagging. It's not serious like Covid-19 though is it? I mean the Government aren't locking everyone down twice a year to avoid us all getting it, are they?"

Jacob started heading to my door and then turned back towards me.

"Read up on it, Hunter. You aren't going to die of it in a couple of weeks like Corona, but it's still serious shit. Read up on it and get yourself tested."

"What's it called again?"

"H.I.V."

"H.I.V. OK, I'll read up on it."

I saw Jacob out, went to the kitchen fetched myself a bottle of water from the fridge and then went back up to my bedroom. I sat on my bed and Googled 'HIV' on my phone. Within five minutes, I was in tears. This was no cold. I had just spent the last twelve months trying to claw myself out of a massive hole and now, just as I was about to reach the level ground, I had stumbled and fallen right back in but this time it felt like someone was at the top shovelling the soil right on top of me.

CHAPTER FIFTY SEVEN

<u>**ALICE**</u>

Mentally I didn't react to the split from Erika the way I thought I would. I thought I would be devastated, would cry constantly for weeks and would have to fight the impulse to drive over to Leeds to plead for a second chance. I was far stronger than I had anticipated though and the majority of the time I was completely fine. I'm not saying there weren't teary moments or times I wanted nothing more than to spend an evening cuddled up with her but those moments passed.

One thing that splitting up from Erika made me realise was that I no longer had any female friends. Sometimes I missed those chats with other women. There is a level of intimacy and depth to a real conversation between two women that a conversation with a man can't replicate. Jay was a good substitute sometimes, he could tap in to his feminine side on occasion but at times he deliberately fought it off.

My social circle was now made up of just three men, Jay, Hunter and Dominic. If I wanted to go for a coffee or lunch with someone it would always be Jay, if I wanted a night out, then it was always with Hunter or Dominic. Once he'd had a few drinks, if he hadn't managed to pull, Hunter still needed reminding from time to time that I was strictly off limits but most of the time he behaved himself. I didn't want to encroach too much on the friendship between Dom and Hunter so I tended to just go out with them once a week. After the 'Lost' incident we tended to go to a few pubs early on in Chorley and then move on to the clubs of Bolton, Preston or Wigan.

One Sunday afternoon, I was in my room doing some College coursework when my phone started vibrating on the bed. I had put it on silent so the notifications wouldn't disturb me but I was curious to know who it was calling so I sneaked a look. It was Hunter. I wasn't quick enough to answer it, I had probably been too caught up in what I was doing to notice it straight away, but I thought it was weird that he was calling me. Hunter never called me. Occasionally he texted but normally any arrangements for going out were done through Dominic and Sunday wasn't a day for making arrangements. I called him straight back.

"Did you just ring me?" I asked, which in itself sounds like a stupid question but phones do sometimes go off in people's pockets and it was unusual for him to be calling. He didn't actually give me an answer but just went straight to his point.

"You know on my birthday you said if I ever needed a female to open up to, you'd be there for me?"

I was drunk at the time but I had both said it and meant it.

"I do but I'm surprised you do. You were coked up to your eyeballs. Are you OK? You sound like you've got a cold."

"No Alice, I'm not OK. Did you mean it when you said you'd be there for me?"

I thought he was probably having a bit of a crisis about his Mum's death.

"Of course I did, Hunter."

"Can you come round to ours then?"

"Right now? I'm trying to get some coursework done."

"Please. It's important."

"Important enough to need me to put all my work down and come straight away?" I probably sounded a bit exasperated when I said that. I realised I was already not being quite as generous and accommodating as I'd offered to be.

"Yes."

"OK then. Is your Dad in? He'll think it's weird if I come to see you."

"Why would he? He knows we're mates."

"Yeah but...oh, it doesn't matter, it's fine."

I was going to tell Hunter that his Dad was more my mate than him but it sounded harsh so I stopped myself from saying it.

"He's out anyway. He's just walked up to 'The Ale Station'."

"On a Sunday?" I said sounding shocked, Jay was very regimental about his trips to the pub and Sunday wasn't normally his day.

"He's started going occasionally on a Sunday. I encourage him. He always comes back a bit happier after he's been to the pub. I don't know if it's the company or the alcohol but whichever it is, it works. On the basis he's walked there, he'll be out for ages."

The way Hunter said this worried me slightly in case he had ulterior motives.

"I won't need to remind you where we stand again, will I?"

"Of course you fucking won't, Alice," he barked back sounding emotional and annoyed, "Look it's important. Will you come around or won't you?"

"I said I would, didn't I?"

"Reluctantly."

"I was in the middle of something, Hunter. Anyway, it doesn't matter. I'm on my way."

CHAPTER FIFTY EIGHT

JAY

Alice and I were on a walk along by the River Yarrow between Euxton and Eccleston. It had become a regular thing for us on a Sunday morning, I would drive to hers, leave my car there and then we'd walk up to Back Lane then along a pathway that cuts across farmers' fields that lead through to the river. We would follow a trail that would then take you through woods next to the water's edge, past some little waterfalls before bringing us past some quaint old cottages and then back on to the main road by Euxton Methodist Church. Alice called it 'Our Weekly Walk Into Paradise'.

All in all, our circular route was about four miles long. Alice said she was gradually going to build my fitness and stamina up so I could start doing parkruns with her on a Saturday morning. She had been doing them most weeks since Erika had gone off to University and although I had printed off my registration, I had yet to be persuaded to turn up. I explained to her that there is a competitive side to my nature and I didn't want to turn up until I could confidently run the whole 5k, it was called parkrun not parkwalk after all. I just didn't like the idea of struggling around at the back. I knew there was no shame in it and finishing last was better than watching tv with a coffee and a croissant but some sort of strange masculine pride wanted me to try to keep up with Alice.

The main reason I think Alice was trying to get me into some sort of shape was because she had concluded that Mary and I belonged together, but my middle-aged, knackered, out of tune body was an obstacle to her fairytale romance. Admittedly my friendship with Mary really was blossoming. We had started seeing each other three or four times a week, had met each other's children several times without a hint of awkwardness and thoroughly enjoyed every moment we spent together. For some reason this wasn't enough for Alice, she wanted to transform it into the romance of the century and for us to be like Mia and Sebastian in La La Land, conveniently forgetting that they didn't end up together. She had formed an opinion that my thirty eight inch waist was a significant stumbling block. No matter how hard Alice tried and no matter how fit she got me, I was never going to be Ryan Gosling.

I'd like to think, despite the fact that there were no sparks of romance, that Mary was the type of woman who could see beyond the looks of a man. She was a highly intelligent, well read, strong minded woman who had more depth of character than anyone I'd ever met so I'm sure a bit of flab would not have been a deal breaker if she ever met a slightly chubby man she romantically connected to. By saying Mary had depth of character is not, by any means, a criticism of Amy who was always refreshingly uncomplicated.

I was enjoying the life lessons Mary was sharing with me though. My musical knowledge was as strong as hers, if not stronger, especially on eighties and nineties stuff, although her twenty first century musical knowledge was miles better than mine. There must be a subconscious agreement that interest in 'pop culture' disappears the day you get married. It was Mary's literary knowledge that was far superior to mine. I read a bit, especially in an attempt to get some sleep but Mary was a voracious reader who spent as much time as possible with her nose in a book or her Kindle. She wore reading glasses too which I think every hot blooded male on earth would have found incredibly sexy. Her choice of books was very eclectic but would regularly find its way back to highbrow twentieth century authors like Virginia Woolf, George Orwell, James Joyce and Franz Kafka.

Mary was the primary focus of our conversation as Alice and I walked past the waterfalls on a wonderful sunny Sunday with blue skies littered with a few thinly spread white fluffy clouds.

"So how was your night on the tiles with Mary?" I asked.

Alice had probably been split from Erika for about six weeks at that point and had decided she was missing female company so had text and phoned Mary to see if the two of them could have a night out together. Mary readily agreed.

"Do you know what Jay, it was fantastic! I knew I needed a night out free of creatures with testicles but I didn't realise how much until Friday night. If you don't sweep that delightful woman off her feet soon, I'm going to see if she'd be up for a bit of woman on woman action. She's far too lovely to be single."

"Perhaps she's happy being single."

"Come off it, she's just searching for her handsome Prince and because she can't find him, she might get desperate and be prepared to opt for you."

I didn't say anything. I knew my silence would be interpreted by Alice as me taking offence.

"Jay, that was a joke," she said reaching out and gently placing her hand on top of mine as we walked.

"I know, it's not the jokes about my appearance that bother me, it's the obsession with trying to generate a love story out of this friendship I have with Mary. We're getting on really well so don't curse it by meddling and trying to turn it into something it isn't."

I'm sure Alice's bottom lip quivered.

"The two of you are just so good together," Alice said sounding like a frustrated child who was being told there was no pudding.

"Talking about friendships, how much have you seen of Hunter recently?"

Alice eyed me suspiciously perhaps she thought I was going to try to match make with the pair of them. I wasn't. I reckon soap and chocolate go together better.

"Why?"

"He's being very reclusive at home, more reclusive than normal. I'm concerned something's wrong. Has he said anything to you?"

"Not a word."

Alice seemed to blush when she said this perhaps there was more to this romantic thing than I thought.

"I don't suppose it would be you he would confide in anyway. It'd be your Dominic. Any chance you can check with him if Hunter's OK?"

"Dom wouldn't tell me anything. He's very private."

"Oh ok. Maybe he's just missing his mother, it tends to hit him in waves."

"Just leave him to sort himself out. I'm sure, as you say, when the time is right, Hunter will come and talk to you."

"Do you think?"

"Definitely. He may put on the act of finding you annoying but he loves you dearly."

"I wouldn't go that far!"

"He does!"

"So you've not noticed anything suspicious then?"

"Not especially."

Alice was definitely blushing.

"Maybe I'm just worrying about nothing."

"He could just find it strange seeing you spending so much time with another woman."

"Shit, yeh, I hadn't thought of that. Maybe I should speak to him."

"Just leave it, Jay and I'm sure if he does have a problem, he'll come to you."

CHAPTER FIFTY NINE

<u>**MARY**</u>

We had been watching 'Eternal Sunshine Of The Spotless Mind' at our house. All three of us had watched it, Tilly, Jay and me. I had seen it before, years ago, but hadn't really remembered too much about it other than the fact that I loved it. Someone at College had recommended it to Tilly and she had asked whether we wanted to watch it with her. She wasn't one of those kids that tried to distance herself from her mother, very much the opposite in fact.

It was strange watching films with Jay. We were in this space, this no man's land, between romance and friendship and I think Jay was quite happy pitching tent and staying there. I was comfortable with that. He had an emotionally complex background and if he could find safe ground then I could understand why he would want to settle in. It just meant that in scenarios such as watching films, he wouldn't position himself next to me, like a boyfriend would, but would make the armchair his own and would let Tilly and I share the settee. It wasn't because Tilly was present either. He would do the same if it was just the two of us.

"Wow, that was some film," Jay said as he stretched out when the credits came up. He is a fidget, most men seem to be, they can't seem to find a comfy spot.

"I remember enjoying it last time but I think I enjoyed it even more this time. I thought it was brilliant. What did you think, Tilly?"

Tilly looked like a junior version of me. Tall, blonde, fair complexion, blue eyes, we probably looked like we had emigrated to the UK from Sweden with Ulrika Jonsson. She didn't have the arrogance some pretty girls have though. She was polite, very friendly but a little shy. Most of our conversations involved me doing three quarters of the talking. She wasn't monosyllabic, she was just a more comfortable listener than a talker.

"It was OK. I thought he was going to be funny like in 'Dumb and Dumber'".

"Have you seen him in anything else?" Jay asked.

"No, I don't think so," Tilly answered.

"When you've seen him acting crazy in lots of different films, like your Mum and I have, it's good to see him in a more serious film. Have you not seen 'The Truman Show' then?"

"No, what's that about?"

"I won't tell you, it'll spoil it a bit if I do, just watch it, it's really clever."

"Is it funny?"

"Not funny like 'Dumb and Dumber' but funnier than what we've just watched."

"I might watch it over the weekend, thanks Jay....Mum, I'm going up to my room."

"OK, love....Jay would you like a coffee and a piece of home-made cheesecake?"

I was enjoying baking again. I had stopped for a while as Tilly wasn't really a dessert type of girl so it was a bit pointless making cakes for one. Jay had a very sweet tooth though and was always delighted when I'd baked something.

"Ooh, yes please! Just don't tell Alice next time you see her."

"Why?"

"She's trying, unsuccessfully as you may have noticed, to turn me into a finely tuned athlete."

"How come?"

"Well, one reason is that she wants me to start doing parkruns with her, which is fair enough, but the primary reason is to make me more attractive to women."

"I do the odd parkrun at Bolton. It's hard though, there's a massive hill that you have to run up twice. Tilly comes too sometimes. So go on, explain to me why Alice is wanting to make you more attractive to women, I thought your objective in life these days was to avoid attracting women!"

Jay seemed to look a bit hurt by this. He had been slouching in the armchair and sat up straighter when I made this observation.

"That sounds harsh!"

"You know what I mean you want to avoid having a relationship. Why would you try to make yourself attractive to encourage interest from women you don't want a relationship with?"

"Exactly! You need to have a word with Alice."

"Jay, you're a big boy now, I'm sure you can fight your own battles with Alice."

"I'm sure I can…" Jay paused and then changed tone, "are you OK with this?"

"With what?"

"This thing with us."

"I didn't realise we had a 'thing'!"

"You know what I mean our friendship."

"So are you trying to say, in a very round about way, that Alice is working on your athletic physique to make you more attractive to me?"

"Yes, in a nutshell."

"OK and what do you want from me? Re-assurance that I'm happy with things as they are?"

"That would be nice. I'm happier than at any point since Amy died but friendships are a two way thing so it's no good me being happy if you're not."

"Why would I not be happy?"

"I don't know maybe you might think that if you spend too much time with me it could stop you meeting someone else."

Sometimes men ask one question but they are really trying to unearth the answer to another. To me, it felt like this was what Jay was doing. I'm not someone who has the patience to partake in things like that.

"Is that what you're really asking, Jay?"

"What do you mean?"

"Are you actually fishing to see if my 'end game' in all this is to have a full on, physical relationship with you?"

"Well is it? I still don't think that's something I will ever be in a position to provide."

I decided it was time for the full-on, 'no bullshit' speech. I had sort of felt this coming for a while and had been thinking how to word it. I don't think it came out quite how I'd planned but the message was clear which was the main thing.

"OK...I'll put my cards on the table then...I'm a big fan of sex, Jay. Down here, in this region between my legs are a whole host of sensory nerve endings that once in a while, when the mood takes them, send messages to my brain that they want to be touched. They aren't like a dick which is a very needy creature that sends messages to the male brain every two minutes but more like an old friend who you touch base with every once in a while because you need that interaction in your life to put a smile on your face.

Now as far as my body goes, to be blunt, I don't need you to satisfy those urges. Hidden away at the back of a drawer in my bedroom, is a little battery operated miracle worker that can take me to places that no man has ever managed to. Having said that, the miracle worker doesn't compliment me on my baking skills, share a bottle of wine with me or suggest new films for my daughter to watch. I can find alternative ways of satiating my sexual desires but I can't conjure up a friendship with a household object unless you count Alexa which is a very 'master & servant' type friendship anyway as she only ever does what I want and I don't like friends who are pushovers.

Six weeks ago, early in our friendship, I have to confess I didn't knock the Tinder thing on the head straight away. I went on a date with a guy in Westhoughton and although he seemed like a very pleasant, well turned out guy who was much better looking than you and a fair bit younger, it didn't feel right with him. It feels right with you, Jay. There is a certain flow to our friendship, whether we are chatting or chilling that just feels right. We may never go on to kiss or have sex because you have a sense of loyalty to your wife and I get that, but whatever way you look at it, this is becoming a relationship I want to hold on to. You're not holding me back from meeting someone else because I don't want anyone else and I'm not over thinking the physical or romantic side of things because in the whole swing of things it's just a minor bump on a scenic road."

"I would love to say you had me at 'I'm a big fan of sex' but in the circumstances I guess it's not overly appropriate."

"Probably not but there is one thing I would ask."

"Go on."

"That you stop avoiding physical intimacy. I know that night I got into your bed probably scared you but it doesn't mean you have to sit on the armchair when we watch a film or say goodbye and drive home without a hug or a kiss. Lighten up a bit, Jay. Embrace your huggy-feely side. I'm assuming you have one."

"I would argue it's been you that's been avoiding hugging me."

"I have not!"

"You have! Ever since the ducks were run over, you've been hugging Alice but never me which is a shame as I'm naturally very tactile."

"OK, let's stop being coy with each other and start sharing some proper hugs. We're becoming good friends and any friendship that involves at least one woman requires hugs. It's the law."

"Would you like a hug now?"

"That would be nice."

"OK."

We hugged. It was lovely. I don't think I hugged him like a friend though. I was in love with him and I think he knew.

CHAPTER SIXTY

<u>HUNTER</u>

I think it's Alice's eyes that make me go crazy for her. She has really dark brown eyes. She has quite a heavy fringe the tips of which almost dip into her eyes, a small nose, small lips (not those pouty cosmetic duck lips everyone seems to have these days) but then she has big cheeks and these wonderful eyes that keep giving me this fuzzy feeling that repeatedly tells me, no matter what, that we belong together.

"If everything turns out OK today, Hunter, there are two things you should learn from this. One is to steer away from drugs and the other is that Jacob Sharpe is a Grade One prick."

"You don't sound too sympathetic about him potentially being HIV positive," I reflected, it now seemed an age since I didn't know what HIV was, yet it was probably less than a week.

"I am Hunter and I wouldn't wish that on anyone but if you keep trying to take the baked potato out the bonfire with your bare hands then eventually you're going to get burnt."

I laughed. It was probably a nervous laugh as I was absolutely bricking myself at that point.

"What are you on about, you? I reckon if you tried to take a baked potato out of a fire with your bare hands you'd get burnt every single time!"

"I know, I just couldn't think of the phrase and that just popped into my brain for some reason. My Dad used to put baked potatoes in tinfoil and put them on the bonfire when we were kids on Bonfire Night, that's where it's probably come from. What's the actual phrase? Something to do with matches?"

"I think it's 'You play with matches, you get burnt' – nothing to do with baked potatoes!"

"I think mine's better."

"Maybe it'll catch on," I said pulling a face to indicate I thought Alice was a complete lunatic, which she sometimes is, but a lovable one.

We were in the waiting room at the GUM clinic at Royal Preston hospital. I still don't remember what 'GUM' stands for but it's something to do with genitals. When I confided in Alice on the Sunday the week before about Jacob's visit and me potentially having 'HIV' she was brilliant about it. She stayed for a couple of hours, told me the little she knew about it, held my hand, hugged me, cried a little and helped me look into ways that we could go about discovering whether I was 'HIV positive' or not. Turns out there's a few different ways, one of which is a self-test kit but we quickly ruled that one out as Alice wasn't confident enough in the pair of us to get an accurate result and I was more concerned that my Dad would stumble across it. After half an hour on-line, we decided the best thing to do was book an appointment at a 'GUM clinic' so that's what we did. Alice promised she'd come with me to provide the necessary moral support as I was gradually learning this was a lot more serious than flu.

During the week before the appointment I gradually built up a bit of understanding about what 'HIV' was. It seemed to be a disease that had the world running scared about thirty years ago especially gay men, needle sharing drug addicts and people who regularly received blood from others but since then the drugs to treat it have got better and better so although it's still a terrible thing to have, it's nowhere near as terrible.

I'm not going to start pretending I'm some sort of expert on 'HIV' after a few days of reading up for ten or fifteen minutes each night but I did take a few things in. 'HIV' can become 'AIDS' which is when the immune system in your body breaks down and once that happens simple infections can become fatal as your body doesn't have the antibodies to call on to fight them off. It's like an aggressive nation with a load of soldiers attacking a country without an army. There were a lot of mentions on-line about the human body's 'CD4' count which I think are the cells that fight infection so the more of those guys you have the better. I won't bore you with the finer details though because I know if I wasn't living with the threat of it, I wouldn't be interested either.

I suppose with the threat of being diagnosed with a serious illness hanging over me, I should have had more important things to worry about, but my main concern about being diagnosed with 'HIV' was whether it would end any glimmer of hope of me getting it together with Alice. I know she kept telling me I had no chance but sometimes we would share a look or smile at each other in a certain way that indicated that there was some chemistry there. I'm not saying things will happen soon, it may take years, but I reckon one day she'll give me a chance. I was worried that 'HIV' might strip that chance away though. I am not scared of dying, I am not scared of being ill but I am scared of having an illness so serious that it would rule out any romantic interest from Alice. I'm not saying Alice is superficial because she most certainly isn't and I'm sure if she loved someone and they were subsequently diagnosed with 'HIV' it wouldn't be an issue but I still needed to win her over and I knew 'HIV' would make it harder to get things off the ground.

Alice didn't come into the room for the appointment with me. She did offer but I wouldn't let her, I wanted to deal with that part on my own. My name was called and I just went through to this little side room where a friendly, warm hearted black nurse with a comforting smile and a Caribbean accent explained that she was going to do a simple 'point of care' test. She explained this just involved her taking a pin prick of blood from my finger and then testing it to see if I was 'HIV' positive. She said if I went back to the waiting room and bought myself a hot drink the results would probably be back before I had chance to drink it. It was at that point, after the explanation but before the pin prick that I completely lost control of my emotions and just broke down. I had pretty much taken everything in my stride that morning until then but the reality hit and I just went to pieces.

"Hey, hey what's the matter my sugar?" the nurse asked putting a comforting hand on my shoulder.

"I'm scared."

"What is it you're scared of sugar? A big man like you shouldn't be scared of a little pin prick!"

The nurse knew that pin prick wasn't what I was scared of. She knew full well that I was scared by the prospect of the life changing news I was soon to be hit with but she was just lightening the mood. It worked too. I laughed a little through my tears and snorted a bit too I think.

"I'm scared of the unknown. I don't know how much my life will change if I have 'HIV'."

"It might not change very much at all for a long time."

"I might not get ill but it'll still change my life. I'll have to tell my Dad and we've not long lost my Mum, my sex life will be ruined and I'll have to track down everyone I've shagged recently and put them through what I've been through in the last ten days."

"Honey, let's get the results back first and if it is positive then we'll deal with all this, if it isn't you can stop all your worrying and crying. Now give me your hand."

"Which one?"

"It doesn't matter, the blood is the same in both," she joked as I put my left hand forward.

"Oh my goodness, Hunter," she added laughing with a deep laugh, "I don't think I've ever seen a hand tremble as much as that!"

The nurse put her thumb across my four fingers and the rest of one of her hands behind mine and then once the trembling had eased took her hand away, did the pin prick and took a tiny sample of my blood.

"Ok sugar, we're done. Go back in the waiting room, grab yourself a coffee and I'll call you through when we have the results. We'll take things from there."

Alice bought herself a coffee and me a sugary tea and we sat nervously waiting for me to be called back through to see what my future had in store.

"You OK?" Alice asked in a soft, sympathetic tone.

"I'm shitting myself."

"I bet. I'm petrified for you."

"I just need to start growing up."

"Hunter, you're seventeen, it's not about growing up. You just need to calm things down."

"I know. I wish my Mum was here. I don't mean right here, I'm glad you're here with me but at home, alive, around for me to talk to about all this shit. She would have listened, stroked my hair and told me everything was going to be OK. Dad won't. He'll just tell me I've been a fool."

"Hunter, you don't know what your Dad will say. If it is bad news, you need to sit him down and just open your heart up to him. He's a good man, your Dad, he'll help you deal with this, I know he will."

"I miss my Mum, Alice."

I could feel myself welling up again. I didn't want to start crying in front of her. I was two years younger than her so crying would just make that gap seem bigger.

"I know you do. Come here."

Alice hugged me really tightly. She smelt of skin and perfume. I wanted time to stand still. I didn't want those results. I just wanted to be in Alice's arms forever. It was crazy how much I was falling for her. I wanted to taste the sweetness of her kiss and share hugs with her every single day. I wanted to show her I had the capacity to love her more than anyone else in the world. As I was savouring every second of that hug, she pulled away.

"Are you going to be OK?"

"Depends what they tell me in the next few minutes."

"No, it doesn't, Hunter. No matter what you'll be OK. Me, Dominic and your Dad will make sure of that. I promise you."

"Thank you. God Alice, you don't know how much I love you."

Alice smiled at me like she had been inside my head and seen every thought I had ever had about her but was flattered rather than cross.

"I think I do. How the hell do you even get 'HIV' from sharing a straw anyway?"

"I'm going to surprise you by sounding quite clever here…"

"You're the only person that thinks you're stupid, Hunter."

"Anyway, when you snort coke, the blood vessels in your nose can rupture and tiny drops of blood can go onto the straw then if someone else uses the same straw, like I did after Jacob, not only does the drug enter their nasal passage but the blood of the other person does too."

"Shit!"

"So, if you ever snort cocaine, young lady, don't share a straw."

"You know I'll never be stupid enough to snort cocaine."

"You're indirectly calling me stupid already!"

"I'm not calling you generally stupid! I'm just saying on that night you were very stupid."

We shared that look again and smiled with a shared sense of embarrassment which was unusual for both of us.

"Same difference!"

It seemed to take forever, but because it was forever with Alice I didn't mind too much, but eventually that same Caribbean lady re-appeared and called me through. Alice and I exchanged another look, she whispered 'Good luck' and I made my way through to hear my fate. I was still petrified but I wasn't shaking as much second time around.

The Caribbean lady gestured for me to take a seat.

"OK, Mr Hunter Cassidy, I have your test results back and I am very pleased to tell you that you are 'HIV negative' which means there are no signs of 'HIV' in your blood."

In my mind, I stood up, took that Caribbean lady's hands and we were transported to a beach in Jamaica and as the sea kissed our feet on the wet sand, we danced in the evening sunshine to 'Lovers Jive' by Neville Esson, Clue J and His Blues Blasters, with a smiling Jools Holland guest performing on his piano. Halfway through the song the Caribbean lady moved aside and it was Alice that joined me on that beach, the pair of us dancing seductively, rubbing against each other's bodies, before sharing a long, tender kiss as the music faded.

In real life, I just let out a deep breath and said 'Thank God for that!'

Joyful tears followed and I quickly mopped them up with a tissue the nurse tactfully passed me.

"Now hang on a minute, I need to add a note of caution here. Sometimes, not very often but sometimes, it can take a little while for your body to register as 'HIV positive' so we would recommend that you come back for a repeat test in three months' time."

I felt like that nurse had lifted me up to the ceiling then dropped me face first on to the floor.

"So hang on, you're saying I might still have it?"

"I'm just saying, sugar, that you can't totally rule it out just yet but it's still good news at this stage. As good as you could get today."

I smiled at her.

"It is very good news."

"Now before I leave you, there are just a few other questions I need to ask you."

I wasn't expecting more questions.

"What about?"

"Sex, drugs and rock 'n' roll. Well, actually, there are no questions on rock 'n' roll."

CHAPTER SIXTY ONE

<u>**ALICE**</u>

We had been at Papa Luigis in Euxton for Mary's birthday, just the three of us, Jay, Mary and me. I love Papa's, it has the added benefit of only being ten minutes walk from Mum and John's so I can have a few glasses of wine without having to book a taxi and just as importantly the food is delicious. Both Jay and I had been many times before but it was new to Mary. She loved it, which I thought she would, that woman has fine taste. It was one of those nights when it felt like all three of us were on top form and we just chatted, laughed, ate great food and drank wonderful wine. Jay insisted the night was on him. I have no recollection of exactly how many bottles of wine that we got through other than it being a lot, probably at least five. We had all three courses then Jay insisted we finish off with Irish coffees. In fact, having never had one before and not being sure whether I would like whiskey, Mary suggested I have a Bailey's coffee instead. It was heaven. I will definitely be having one again, maybe even after every meal I ever eat. Once Jay finished his, he announced that he was nipping to the loo and would pay the bill on his way back.

"It's been a lovely night, hasn't it?" I said to Mary, she was sitting opposite me, so I held her hand as I said it.

"It has. I love to see Jay like that. It doesn't happen too often but sometimes he lets his guard down, forgets his troubles and is just a joy to be around."

"I always enjoy being with him."

I am always fiercely defensive of Jay. I can't help it even when he's not under attack. It's like a reflex action.

"I do too, Alice, you know I do, but you know only too well that he often looks troubled and it's fantastic to see him acting carefree."

"I love him. I think he's probably the best, sweetest man I have ever met."

I knew I was drunk and it was exaggerating my emotions but it was exactly how I felt.

"I love him too, Alice. He's one in a million."

I moved my face towards hers before saying, in a conspiratorial tone,

"You two aren't shagging, are you?"

"Us? No!"

"You'd tell me if you ever were, wouldn't you?"

"Alice, I promise you, you'd be the first to know but don't hold your breath."

"Would you though?"

"Alice!"

"Go on tell me when I'm drunk as I probably won't remember in the morning."

"Well, strictly between the two of us."

"Of course."

"I definitely would. I really love him, Alice, not in the way you love him, like your favourite uncle, I mean I really love him."

"Wow! He's so lucky to have someone like you loving him. I mean look at you, you're amazing."

"Thank you, Alice – straight back at you."

I grabbed her hand again.

"You should tell him!" I urged.

"I most certainly should not! What Jay and I have is special, Alice. If it only ever remains on a 'best friend' level then that's still special and I am not prepared to jeopardise that."

"You're just so lovely, Mary. I love you, Mary!"

The drink was making me emotional and a little teary.

"I know you do sweetheart," Mary said squeezing my hand tightly, "and I love you too."

We noticed Jay returning to the table.

"Are you ladies OK?" he asked as he sat down, noticing we had been sharing a moment.

"We are brilliant, aren't we Mary?"

"We are. Fierce."

"What have you been chatting about?"

"How much we love each other," I announced proudly but perhaps with a slight slur in my voice as it prompted Jay to start laughing at me.

"Alice Moorcroft, I don't think I have ever seen you this drunk. Mary and I will walk back up to yours with you."

"Don't be silly, I'm fine," I insisted knowing I clearly wasn't.

"No, Jay's right, Alice, we'll walk you back."

"You're both so lovely."

I think I may have squeezed their cheeks at this point.

"Shall we head off?" Jay asked, but I think it was a question directed at Mary rather than me as they'd both now judged that I was beyond making competent decisions. I wasn't really all that bad, just very tiddly. Sometimes when I'm drunk I play on the fact that I'm drunk and then realise I'm overdoing it and reel it in by trying to hold a serious conversation.

"Oh Mary!" I exclaimed, probably a little too loudly, my pitch isn't great when I've been drinking, "I've been listening to Lana Del Rey! Where has she been all my life? Isn't she incredible? I think she's my all time favourite artist ever. She's just so fucking cool, isn't she?"

"She so is. What albums have you listened to?"

"I've no idea. I just say 'Alexa, play Lana Del Rey and lo and behold, she does."

Out of nowhere, Jay started singing a Lana Del Rey song. It wasn't just a line either, it was about two verses - the one about Bacardi and going to the races. He hasn't got the greatest of voices but I don't think he was trying to impress us with his voice. He was trying to impress Mary by showing her he'd been listening to her music.

"Jay Cassidy, you big show off" she chided jokingly but it was more a tone of admiration than a telling off.

"I've been practising. I've been listening to Lana a lot recently."

"And what do you think?" I asked.

"Well I'm not as blown away as you guys but that's not to say I'm not impressed."

"I'd love to see her live. She had to cancel her last UK gigs because she lost her voice but when she comes back, if Corona ever allows that to happen, I'm going to move heaven and earth to get tickets."

"We should all go!" I said excitedly.

"I'd be up for that," Jay said, surprisingly going along with my suggestion too.

We started making a move towards the exit. I must have done enough within the course of the previous conversation to convince Mary that I wasn't too drunk as she stopped in her tracks as we passed the bar.

"Do either of you want a night cap before we go?"

Jay and I looked at each other. I gave him my best puppy dog eyes.

"Oh go on then," Jay said with a smile, "I'm already going to have a hangover in the morning so I might as well make it a good one!"

CHAPTER SIXTY TWO

JAY

As a young adult I meddled a little bit with drugs. When I say 'a little bit', I mean just that. On nights out when Amy was doing her own thing with the girls and I was out with the lads, over a couple of teenage years, I tried the occasional drug. I smoked a bit of pot, went through a spell of experimenting with poppers and took speed a few times. I called it quits on my minor league drug habit when I found it was screwing up my sleep patterns for the whole week afterwards. The immediate short-term high was not outweighing the longer-term low that followed.

One thing I remember with 'speed' was that I had a euphoric feeling of being the luckiest man in the world. It made me appreciate that I had the world's most beautiful girlfriend and a group of friends who meant the world to me. When I look back now, as well as being desperately sad about Amy no longer being with us, I feel sad that those friendships ebbed away over time as we all went our separate ways with jobs, marriages and children. In our late twenties and thirties, with the rise of social media, we started re-connecting but we were still socially distancing long before it was imposed upon us by Covid-19.

The point is though, I felt that same euphoric feeling of immense gratitude whilst I was out with Alice and Mary at Papa Luigis to celebrate Mary's thirty sixth birthday. My drug of choice was now Irish Coffee rather than speed but as I was walking back to Alice's parents house with the two of them busily chatting about books and music, I realised how lucky I was. I had lost the person who had been my everything for over twenty years but had found new friendships that were helping me deal with my immense loss. I understood life would never be the same again without Amy but it was still good and I had never expected it ever could be. Life was still very, very good.

Mary and I saw Alice safely back into her house and then turned around to head back towards Papa Luigis. We had walked ten minutes in the wrong direction so now had a half hour walk home. Everything was fine though, we had alcohol in our veins and it was a beautiful late Spring night with a still-ness and warmth in the air.

"Alice is a wonderful girl, isn't she?" Mary said as she took my hand in hers.

I didn't read too much into the hand holding. It had hap-pened quite naturally after our chat about me being more tactile. We wouldn't hold hands in front of anyone that knew us like Alice or Hunter (especially Hunter) but if we were out on a countryside walk or were just walking along alone at night, we would hold hands or put our arms around each other. It felt compassionate rather than romantic.

"She's a star," I replied.

"Have you ever noticed how Hunter looks at her?"

"It's impossible not to notice. I think she was his first real crush and he has never really shaken off his obsession with her."

"Even though she's into girls?"

"That might be part of the appeal!"

"Bless him. Human nature though isn't it to chase the things that are slightly beyond our reach?"

"It is, but you never know she may succumb to his charms one day. He's a good looking lad and she's had boyfriends in the past."

"I can't see it happening, I think she's too savvy for him. If it did though, how would you feel about it?"

"Mixed."

"How come?"

"I love them both but if they split up it would make it very difficult for me to stay friends with her. You lose the loosest link in the chain, don't you? My loyalties would always be with Hunter."

"All true. Let's hope they never get together then."

We carried on chatting until we reached the bridge between Euxton and Buckshaw Village. It's a fairly steep road bridge that goes over the Preston-Manchester railway line. The pedestrian part is pretty wide and late in the evening it is usually pretty quiet around there. The fact that it was deserted probably influenced Mary's next sentence.

"What are you like at Gymnastics?"

"Not the best. I could do a decent handstand on the grass as a kid and I can do a forward roll but that's about my limit. Why?"

"I used to do Gymnastics as a kid. I reckon if I could gather enough speed running down this hill, I could do a really good handstand and somersault combo."

"In your heels?"

"No, dumbo, I'd take them off."

Having said it, Mary let go of my hand and sat herself down on the tarmac at the top of the hill and began to take off her shoes.

"You can carry these down," she said as she passed me her shoes.

"Mary, how old are you today?"

It was a rhetorical question but she answered anyway.

"Thirty six."

"So do you not think your days of running down a hill doing cartwheels and somersaults are behind you?"

"No. Sometimes in life you just have to take a chance."

"And other times you have to ask yourself 'what's the point'? What are you doing now?"

Mary was doing various leg and neck exercises on the floor.

"I'm limbering up. You can't do a somersault without stretching out first."

"You're pissed, Mary!"

"Don't be so daft, I'm not pissed, I've just had a couple of glasses of wine."

"A couple of bottles."

"Have some faith in me! I can do this, Jay."

"I believe you, you don't have to prove it. Now put your shoes back on and let's walk back to mine whilst we're both in one piece."

"WATCH!"

Mary started running down the hill. I'd call it a sprint but it wasn't fast enough to be a sprint. She had a weird run too, a real ungainly motion with arms and legs everywhere. She ran like an ostrich trying to fly. It made me briefly laugh out loud. It felt like watching a car crash about to happen but also, as Mary was wearing a long skirt, the schoolboy in me wanted to see her knickers. Given she was thirty six I wasn't expecting them to be navy blue. Perhaps if I hadn't drunk a couple of bottles of wine myself, I'd have been less focused on the elegant lady's silly run and the colour of her knickers and would have concentrated more on the impending disaster. At no point did I ever think it was going to end well.

Just before the bottom of the hill, running as fast as her silly run would allow, Mary tucked her neck in, put her arms down and did, what looked in the cover of darkness to be a pretty decent handstand. I'm not sure, as everything remains a bit fuzzy, exactly what went wrong subsequently but I think she just didn't gather enough momentum to transform her handstand into a somersault. She flipped over but instead of landing on her legs vertically, Mary landed horizontally, on her back with a thud I could hear from the top of the hill. There was silence for a couple of seconds and then I heard her groan.

"Oh shit!" I said to myself, panic now replacing all sense of amusement.

I ran as fast as I could down the hill. I had visions of her having knocked half her teeth out or having broken a bone in her back. If memory serves me right, I might have fallen over once myself as I ran towards her which would go a long way to explaining the hole in my jeans and the cuts on my right knee that I discovered later. Halfway down I thought I could hear groans of agony as she remained motionless on the floor but as I got nearer I realised it wasn't a groan I could hear but laughter. I managed to stop my frantic running just in time to avoid falling over her.

"Don't try to get up if you've hurt yourself," I commanded.

"I'm fine, Jay, I'm just a bit concerned that I may have wet myself a little by laughing so hard."

"Too much information," I replied, in all seriousness.

Women talking about bodily functions made me feel a bit queasy. I remember being very concerned when Amy was in labour with Hunter that the strain of everything might lead me to witness an accident in public that I desperately did not want to see. Our family has never been one that parades around naked and leaves all the bathroom doors unlocked.

"Can you help me up, please?" Mary asked, still laughing a little.

"Are you sure you are OK?"

"I'm fine. Just a bit bruised. Did it look good?"

"It looked almost Olympian at first, well the run didn't that was very Bambi on ice, but the handstand was great."

We were having this conversation whilst Mary was still on the floor. I can't multi-task at the best of times so wasn't going to try to pull her up and talk at the same time.

"Do you think if I'd have been running a bit quicker I'd have managed the somersault?"

"Maybe."

"Shall I go back up to the top and try again?"

"Don't you dare!"

"Are you going to pull me up or what?"

I did try to pull her up. The difficulty wasn't that Mary was heavy, she has a tiny frame, I just think that as she moved her bodyweight forward, I leaned in to get more of a grip and a better pull but just lost my balance and collapsed clumsily on top of her. A fifteen stone man smothering you probably isn't ideal when you've just had a fall but Mary just burst out laughing again as I made awkward, fruitless attempts to get myself off her. I have no idea what we must have looked like to passing cars but can only imagine that it didn't look good.

We disagree about what happened next. My version, for what it's worth, is that as I regained my sense of equilibrium and was pulling myself up, Mary put her two arms around my head and pulled my face towards her. She kissed me. It was definitely that way around. I'm not saying I didn't kiss back briefly because I know I did, but the guilt soon stopped me.

"I'm sorry," I said apologising to one living woman and one dead one simultaneously, "that should not have happened."

We both awkwardly got to our feet.

"I'm sorry," I remember repeating.

"Don't apologise and don't overthink it. It was just a birthday kiss."

It was not just a birthday kiss though. We both knew that was not what that kiss represented. It represented an outpouring of pent up feelings. We didn't hold hands for the rest of the journey home.

CHAPTER SIXTY THREE

<u>**MARY**</u>

As a child, my two favourite films were Grease and Sound of Music. I've never kept count of how many times I've watched each of them but I imagine it is in the dozens. In each film, I found myself drawn to the most attractive actress. I appreciate that is perhaps a little shallow, but as a young child, you are just drawn to who you're drawn to and you don't politicise it. In Grease, the most attractive character was undoubtedly Sandy who was the star of the show. In the Sound of Music, however, Maria was played by the pleasantly attractive but by no means gorgeous Julie Andrews so I was more drawn to Captain Von Trapp's eldest daughter, the stunning Liesl.

In the film, Liesl's stand out scene is singing 'I am Sixteen' with Rolfe, her Nazi loving boyfriend. At the end of the song, Rolfe kisses her and after he departs she squeals with delight. On my thirty sixth birthday, when Jay kissed me drunkenly on Buckshaw Bridge, my mind was taken back to that scene in the gazebo and in my mind I gave out that same little delighted squeal despite being twenty years older than Liesl.

From Jay's perspective, everything was different. I can say with a great deal of certainty that he would not have been internally rejoicing after sharing that kiss. As we walked back to his house, he acted like it was a huge mistake, making a point of walking a distance away from me and barely speaking. I understood the background but I still didn't like that I was made to feel humiliated and emboldened by drink, I wasn't going to let the matter drop once we reached his house.

"Would you like a coffee?" Jay asked as I sat on a settee in his lounge.

There was no friendliness to his tone, it was more just matter of fact and I was feeling increasingly irritated that I was being made to feel like a naughty schoolgirl. We are adults, it was just a kiss and although I appreciated it was the first kiss he had shared since his wife had died, I would rather we discuss it than watch him sulk about it.

"A tea, please, I'll come into the kitchen whilst you make it," I said standing up and following him in.

It had always been the arrangement for me to stay over at Jay's after my birthday meal. As our friendship had developed, I had stayed over a few times previously and given we knew we would be drinking, it was just logical to drive up, leave my car at his and then drive home the following morning.

"So, are we going to talk about that kiss, Jay or are we just going to skirt around it forever?"

Jay has this funny thing going on when he's uncomfortable. He can't look me in the eye and talks in a much less expressive tone.

"I don't think there's a great deal to talk about. As you said, Mary, it was a birthday kiss between friends."

"Only it wasn't, was it? I know I said it but I'd only accept that from your perspective if you had continued to hold my hand on the rest of the walk back like you had been doing prior to the kiss."

Jay looked even more flustered.

"I was just a bit taken aback that you'd kissed me."

"OK, but you initiated it."

"I did not! You put your two arms around my..."

I held my hand up.

"Just shut up a minute."

"OK."

"Let me have my say here and then once I've finished you can have yours," I announced firmly.

"OK."

"The problem we have here, Jay, is that you are a 'sit on the fence' type guy and I'm not a 'sit on the fence' type girl. You're lovely but you don't have strong opinions on anything and your objective is just to get through life by keeping a low profile and trying to keep everyone you cross paths with happy. That doesn't work long-term, Jay. All that happens is that over a long period of time, everyone just sees that you are sitting on that fence and it just begins to piss everyone off.

Amy died and I get that losing your partner is the most tragic thing that could happen to anyone. On the back of that tragedy you have made what, on the surface, looks like a strong minded decision to respect her memory by stating that you are never having another relationship with anyone else for the rest of your life even though the rest of your life could be twice as long as the time you spent with Amy. The reason you made that decision though is because that's what she wanted, not what you wanted, but what Amy wanted. You aren't doing this to please yourself but to please someone else, someone who is oblivious to your sacrifice.

So you've gone along with Amy's request but then I came along. We like each other, we get on famously, we're both single people and if you hadn't been given an instruction ten or twelve years ago from your wife to stay single, we'd be dating now, probably dating at a slow pace because of your bereavement, but still dating.

What's happened instead though is you've tried to reach a compromise position, a compromise where we have this non-physical relationship but we still see each other a lot. I'm fine with it for now, I'll probably be fine with it in twelve months' time but I don't know if it will work long-term. I know I've said before the physical stuff doesn't matter that much and it doesn't but my bum is starting to get uncomfortable sitting on this fence with you. I'm an all action woman and to be totally frank, I can't promise you that I won't just decide enough is enough. Where we're at isn't ideal for me, you or even Amy if she's looking down at us from heaven which we both strongly believe isn't the case anyway."

Jay didn't say anything at all at first. He just continued the process of making the tea. He uses a teapot which I find quaint. I just throw a teabag into the mug, give it a stir and a squeeze. I haven't got the patience to be faffing around with a teapot. Jay is different though, he is an easy going, slow, methodical type person. I wished he would hurry up. I was impatient to hear his thoughts.

"So are you not going to say anything in response?"

"Mary, if I answered straight away I'd probably say the wrong thing, I'm not impulsive like you, just give me a bit of time to process what you've just said."

"OK, do you mean like a few minutes or do you mean you want to sleep on it?"

"No, just a few minutes."

Jay was right, I am impulsive. I don't like waiting for anything. I'd have been one of those kids, when tested, who would have taken one biscuit now rather than sit patiently for three minutes to get two. I found the few minutes waiting for Jay tough. I had to wait whilst he went through the process of making the tea and laying out the biscuits on a large plate of china with two individual plates also placed on the kitchen table. I felt like yelling 'Just get on with it!' at the top of my voice but I kept my calm and eventually Jay spoke.

"OK. I pretty much agree with everything you've just said. It's very easy when you've been left with no-one in your life romantically to think it'll always stay that way as long as you don't go searching for love. Love has a strange way of creeping up on you though. I wasn't expecting to meet you the day I was giving Alice a lift home from Erika's but then some random heartless lady mowed down a family of ducks and everything changed.

It would be very easy for me to say it's now the right time to move on and that I will throw myself wholeheartedly into this relationship with you but saying it and doing it are very different. Amy, even in death, still has a magnetic pull on me and I can feel an invisible force pulling me away from you every time we get close. I don't mean like Amy's spirit, as I don't believe in all that, I just mean once Amy died, it didn't just mean my love for her died too."

"I understand that."

"I know you do. You've been great. You haven't pressurised me into moving on or said it's all or nothing with you. In fact, all you've just said now is that you can't promise me forever like this, which I totally understand. You are one of the two most beautiful women I've ever met in my life, Mary. My problem is that I don't think I will ever shake off the ghost of the other one and I don't think I will ever want to either."

"So where do we go from here?"

"That's down to you. I'm happy with the way things are. I do think you're beautiful so I do worry I will have weak, drunken moments like tonight when I might fuck things up which I know confuses things for us both. So it's up to you whether you think we can just carry on as we are and, if possible, avoid crossing that romantic line."

"I don't know, Jay, it just seems unnecessary. Can we not just hold hands, take a chance and jump across that romantic line together?"

"It wouldn't work, Mary."

"Alright, let's just carry on as we are then. We've both been happier recently than we have been for a long time. Tonight was just a drunken mishap. Let's just go to bed, put it behind us, wake up tomorrow morning and pretend it never happened."

Jay put his head in his hands.

"Stop! I can't do this to you, Mary. It's not right. You deserve more than this. You're right, I do sit on the fence but if I can't give you the relationship you want then I need to let you go."

This didn't sound right. It sounded like some sort of corny speech in a romantic drama that my Mum would have watched back in the nineties. I wasn't even sure if he was joking.

"Are you being serious?"

"Yes, I can't ruin your lovelife just because I don't want to restart mine. You deserve more than that."

Jay was starting to irritate me. He probably didn't mean to, but he sounded patronising.

"Stop telling me what I deserve, Jay. I am perfectly capable of deciding that for myself. What you're saying doesn't make any sense, it just sounds stupid. I'm really happy, you're really happy and anyway you can't finish with me as there's nothing to finish."

"There is. Our friendship, I want to finish our friendship."

"I don't think you mean that."

"I do. I'm sorry, Mary."

"Why end our friendship? That's ridiculous."

"No, it's not. You've got a better chance of meeting someone else without me lingering in the background confusing things. We need to stop meeting up."

"Can we not just sleep on this and talk about it in the morning?"

"I think you'd be better going now."

By this stage annoyance had been replaced by upset and anger.

"I can't fucking go now, Jay! I've been drinking."

"I'll give you the money for a taxi."

"I don't want your money. I'll pay for it myself. Great birthday this is turning out to be."

"I'm so sorry, Mary."

I was tearful by this stage if I'd have been sober I'm sure I would have handled the whole bizarre conversation with a lot more decorum. Sober I'd consider myself to be pretty cool, drunk I'm somebody else. I let hidden emotions reveal themselves.

"Jay, I love you. I really, really love you."

Jay can take his drink better than me. He reacted to this big revelation with very little emotion.

"I love you too, Mary but we can't stay friends long term. I'll call you that taxi."

"What about my car? I can't just leave that here," I said sniffing as my nose was running, alcohol and tears removing any sign of elegance. I'd looked hot earlier too.

"I'm insured to drive any car. I'll drive it back to yours tomorrow and post the keys through the letterbox."

CHAPTER SIXTY FOUR

HUNTER

My bedroom is at the front of the house. I had been remotely playing on X-box for most of the night with Dominic, on Fortnite, but I was knackered so I told him I was packing in and going to bed. I was playing shit too and there're only so many times you can throw your remote control against the wall.

I had climbed out of my bed to switch the light off when I heard a taxi pull up outside. I went to the window to investigate. There was a fit girl who lived about three doors down and sometimes her and some of her dolled up mates would get a taxi. It was always worth thirty seconds watching those hotties with their long legs, short skirts and cute arses heading out. Turned out the driver had pulled up outside ours though. I thought at first he just might not have been able to see the numbers on the houses but then I heard our front door open. Mary and Dad exchanged a few brief words and then I watched Mary tottering along on her high heels. She was a hottie too, God knows why she was hanging around with my Dad. It struck me as odd she was leaving though as she was supposed to have been stopping over and the farewell wasn't exactly a rowdy drunken one. It was a muttered goodbye. I switched my light off and started trying to get to sleep but after a few minutes, I was still wondering what was going on, so I got myself up and went downstairs to check on my Dad.

When I went into the lounge, Dad was pouring himself a Gin from his drinks cabinet. There seemed to be a lot of Gin going into that drink followed by not very much tonic. He had the look of a man who didn't need that next drink. He looked drawn, pale and red eyed.

"Shit Dad, you look rough!"

"Good evening to you too, Hunter," Dad said in a voice that confirmed that he was definitely hammered.

"Do you know you've ripped a whole in your jeans?"

This seemed to confuse Dad, he went searching for it.

"Where?"

"On the knee, you're bleeding too."

"Doesn't matter, I've got other jeans."

"I thought Mary was stopping over?"

"Change of plan."

"How come?"

"We've decided our friendship was probably not a good thing."

"Have you had a row?"

"No."

"One of you get ideas above your station?"

By which I meant Dad. I could see, like anyone with half a brain could see, how he looked at her. He looked at her like some ancient Goddess had been teleported from another era into his life and he couldn't believe his luck. It was pretty much the same look he used to give Mum.

"What do you mean?" Dad asked.

"I mean did you do something that gave away how much you fancy her and she's run a mile now she's got wind of it?"

"No, as a matter of fact," Dad was saying as his Gin & Tonic wobbled around in his glass like a wave, "quite the opposite. It was Mary that wanted the relationship with me and I didn't think it was a good idea."

"Fuck off!"

There was no way I was falling for that one.

"No, honestly that's pretty much what's happened."

"Yeh and Kim Kardashian just climbed up the drainpipe, managed to get her big bum through my window and offered to shag me but I told her to go back to Kanye because I was too tired."

"Don't believe me then."

"Dad, tell me that hasn't just happened! You have not turned Mary down."

"I have."

"Why would you do that?" I said almost shouting at him.

"Because of your Mum."

Bless him, he looked so sad when he said that.

"Mum's dead, Dad."

"Thanks for that valuable piece of information, Hunter and there was me thinking she'd just nipped up to Aldi."

"You know what I meant. Mum isn't a reason for you not to move forward with your life."

"Yes she is."

"Why is she?"

"Just because she's dead doesn't mean I've stopped having feelings for her."

"My Mum meant the world to me, Dad. The day she died was the worst day of my life and will always be the worst day of my life. Every single day since, at some point, I have felt in pain because she's gone but I won't deliberately do things to make that pain worse like you're doing. I don't get it."

My Dad tried to give me a serious look but because he was drunk he didn't quite pull it off.

"Would it not bother you if I was with Mary?"

"Dad, I already thought you might have been. I thought you might have struck incredibly lucky and then logic got the better of me and I realised there was no way you'd pull someone that hot. It's not even as if she's hot and horrible either. She's a lovely person too. I'd say she's a lovely person inside and out but I won't because I fucking hate it when girls say that. It's up there with 'All Lives Matter' and 'New Zealand have dealt with Corona much better than we have' in the phrases that piss me off."

"I think you've lost me," Dad said.

"Sorry. Point is Mary's out of your league and you should have grabbed her quick before she came to her senses."

"Your Mum didn't want me to meet anyone else."

"When did she say that ?"

"On holiday, years ago."

"Had she been drinking?"

"She might have had a glass of wine."

"Mum used to say some bat shit crazy stuff when she'd had a drink."

"No, she didn't."

"She did. One Christmas when she'd been on the Cava, she gave you five free passes to shag film stars as a present! Who did you pick again?"

"Margot Robbie...Naomi Watts...can't remember the others...

oh Mila Kunis was one."

Dad looked like he was really concentrating hard to remember all five.

"Dad, it doesn't matter. Sometimes people say things they don't mean. Mum wouldn't have liked the thought of you with someone else but more importantly she would have hated, absolutely hated, the thought of you having a miserable existence. You've lost one woman you've really loved and there was nothing you could have done about that but this time you can do something, so stop being such a stubborn dickhead and go and tell her how much she means to you."

"What would I say?"

"Tell her you've been a bit of a tit and you've realised she's well worth shagging."

"I might not word it quite like that, Hunter......So you don't blame me for Mum's death.?"

"Of course not."

"You said I didn't spot the signs when she started coughing."

"Like I said, we sometimes say things we don't mean just to get a reaction."

"It might be too late with Mary now. I might have already blown it."

"Just go and speak to her."

"OK," Dad said, starting to get all flustered and moving around in circles, "where's my car key? Oh shit, no, I'll need to get a taxi."

"Are you not best going in the morning when you're not pissed?"

"No, I need to go now before it's too late. I need my phone and my wallet, where the hell have I put them?"

I left Dad flapping around and started to head towards the stairs. Before I made it, Dad grabbed me, gave me a drunken bear hug and kissed my forehead.

"I love you, Hunter."

"Love you too, Dad."

"You don't know where my guitar is, do you?"

"Yes, in the cupboard under the stairs. You're not going to take it with you, are you?"

"Yes."

"Poor Mary!"

CHAPTER SIXTY FIVE

JAY

As it turned out, Munib, the taxi driver who picked me up had taken Mary back to her house as his previous fare so he was a bit confused that I was going there too. He managed to put two and two together.

"I was going to ask if there was a party at this house but the lady seemed very upset so I guess you are going there to put things right. Am I correct?"

"Hopefully," I answered.

"You play the guitar?" he asked, which given I had my acoustic guitar on my lap wasn't that impressive an observation.

"I used to, a little. I'm not very good but I'm going to give it another go."

Munib was a friendly guy and we chatted through the journey with me trying, but probably failing, to give the impression I hadn't been drinking copious amounts of alcohol. When we arrived at Mary's, I paid Munib the fare but gave him an extra tenner to wait ten minutes. I thought if I fell flat on my face, the last thing I wanted to do was to hang around awkwardly waiting for another taxi.

Drunkenly, probably because I'd seen too many romantic comedies in the last thirty years, I headed to a spot below Mary's bedroom window and armed with my acoustic guitar started playing the song that had come into my head half an hour earlier, 'Mary' by 'The Four Of Us'. I'm not a proper guitarist, I just decided to have lessons for twelve months about five years ago from a bloke in Gregson Lane, but it wasn't the trickiest song to strum along to. I think I made a decent fist of it but Mary's light didn't go on so I made my way around to the front door. On my way there, I heard Munib's electric window go down.

"It's normally the cats that are wailing at this time of night!" he shouted over laughing.

"Was it that bad?"

"No, I'm only messing with you. It was actually quite good."

"Cheers."

I pressed the doorbell. No lights came on so I pressed it again. As I was drunk, I might have pressed it a few more times or I may even have just left my finger pressed in until I noticed a response but whatever I did it worked, eventually the lights went on and Mary came to the door in her nightie looking more than a little pissed off.

"Bloody hell, Jay! Could you make any more of a racket? Tilly's asleep."

"Oh shit, yeh, I forgot about Tilly. Sorry. What's a young kid like that doing asleep at this time of night though?"

"It's gone midnight, Jay."

"Exactly. Did you not hear me singing?"

"Singing? I thought it was a stray cat."

"Munib said that."

I pointed at Munib and he waved out his window at Mary, she waved back.

"He brought me back," Mary said looking a bit embarrassed, "he must think I'm crazy. What are you doing here, Jay?"

I noticed she was standing at the doorway with her arms

folded.

"We need to talk."

"Why do we need to talk? If my memory serves me right, it was only an hour ago you said you never wanted to see me again."

Mary seemed to have sobered up in that hour. I hadn't. If anything I was probably worse. I shouldn't have poured myself that G&T.

"That's not quite what I said," I argued without really being able to recall if it was literally what I'd said.

"You wanted our friendship to end and you never wanted to see me again was pretty much the message I got."

I leaned in impulsively to try to kiss her but I was drunk and it was clumsy so she took a step back and turned her face away.

"No, Jay that's not how this works. You can't play with my emotions like this. You can't tell me our friendships over and then turn up an hour later singing songs at my window and try to snog my face off."

"Did you like the song?" I said with a cheeky smile on my face in an attempt to get her to lighten up a little.

"Did you write it?"

"Write it? No, did I bollocks. It's by an Irish band called 'The Four Of Us'."

"How many of them were there?"

"Five, I think."

Mary smiled.

"It was nice, Jay. You did a good job."

"Thank you…. I was scared, Mary."

"About singing?"

"No, I don't mean that. I mean before. It was scaring me how strong my feelings for you were becoming. It felt really great to kiss you but it also felt really wrong. I spoke to Hunter about it, well not about the kiss but about you and me. He made me see things more clearly."

Mary looked shocked.

"Hunter made you see things more clearly? That's a turn up."

"He really likes you, Mary."

"Well, he's growing on me too. He can be a bit of an arse but I think he'll turn out alright."

"I do too. I wasn't so sure there for a while, but I am now."

"What do you want from me, Jay? At this very moment, I am still very confused about what you want from me."

"I want us to be best friends, like we've been, but if the moment takes us and we feel like kissing or hugging or whatever else given time, then I want us to run with it."

"How do I know this is what you really want though? You say this now, smashed off your head but you could wake up in the morning and change your mind yet again."

"Hunter said something which summed everything up perfectly. He said I'd lost one woman I really loved and there was nothing I could have done about that but I didn't want to lose another one through being an idiot."

"Fair point. I'm impressed with him. Given Hunter thought a period drama was something to do with tampons that's quite profound. I'm less impressed with you though, Jay. You can't just tell me you want to end the friendship and then turn back up and tell me you've changed your mind and you want the whole shebang with bells and whistles and just expect me to go along with it. You've really upset me tonight, Jay. It's my bloody birthday too!"

"I'm sorry, Mary. You did say you wanted me to be more forthright!"

"You aren't being forthright though, instead of sitting on the fence you're now swinging from one extreme to the other."

"Can I give you a hug to say sorry?"

"Not yet, Jay. Let's see how we both feel in the morning."

This was the first thing Mary had said that made me realise I was going to be forgiven. The adrenalin really stared to pump at this point.

"Does that mean I can send the taxi driver home?"

"No, it means you can phone me in the morning."

"Oh," I said with disappointment, "what if you get anxious in the night?"

"Tilly's here."

"What if there's a burglar?"

"I'll ring the police."

"What if he cuts the wires?"

"It's not 1975, Jay! I'd use my mobile."

"Please!" I said cupping my hands in begging fashion.

"Oh for goodness sake, Jay! Go on, just send him home!"

"Great. How's your back by the way?"

"Sore. Really sore. I've had to deal with a pain in the arse tonight too."

"Very funny. I still think a hug would do it the power of good."

"Go and tell your taxi driver first that he won't be needed. You're a bloody pest, Jay Cassidy!"

"But you love me."

"You'll need to do a lot more crawling before I'm saying that again."

"But you'll say it eventually?"

"I might. Go on, go and tell that taxi driver to go to his next fare."

"OK, hold this," I said passing Mary my acoustic guitar.

I ran towards the taxi, impulsively picked up pace and half-way along the drive did a perfect handstand and then gave Munib the thumbs up.

"Thanks Munib. It's all sorted. Well, sort of. Cheers for waiting!"

"No problem, mate. See you around."

Munib's taxi sped off into the night. I turned and jogged towards Mary.

"I so wanted you to fall flat on your face then!" she said with a reluctant smile.

"You've got a bit of a nasty streak, haven't you?" I joked.

"Look who's talking!"

"But you love me?" I prompted again.

"Do you know what, despite everything, I think I might."

I smiled a huge, drunken, face filling smile.

"I love you too, Mary Hewitt."

"Oi, don't be getting too pleased with yourself, I only said I might. Come inside and let me get you a glass of water. You look so pissed. I'm still gutted you managed that handstand...."

[B1]

BOOKS BY THIS AUTHOR

Forever Is Over

"Forever Is Over" is a story of love, laughter and loss. It is set in Ormskirk, Lancashire from the 1980s to the present days and is the story of the life of Richie Billingham. In the opening Chapter, we find Richie terminally ill, but the story is then told by several characters, as his life and loves are pieced together.

The book was written to appeal to both males and females. Fictional lives are mixed with real life events as football, gambling, sex, violence, relationships and growing up, all form part of the plot.

"From crying (which I did a lot of reading this - well not crying exactly but proper sobbing) to laughing out loud this book has it all. The characters are compelling... and...if you were brought up in the 70's/80's you will relate even more to this book! A definite must read and a book you will not be able to put down - brilliant! "**

**one of the book's 5* reviews from Rachel Goodwin,

The novel was initially inspired by the song "Sunny Road" by Emiliana Torrini.

Kiss My Name

On the eve of Simon Strong's wedding day, a young woman, Flo, armed with a double barrelled shotgun, arrives at his front door. She is there to avenge the mistreatment of her best friend, Zara. Simon begs for mercy, claiming he has no knowledge of anyone called Zara. What has happened to Zara to create such an extreme reaction from her best friend?

Kiss My Name follows the lives of several characters from childhood in the 1980s to adult life in the twenty first century. As several of them gather in Blackpool, for a Stag Do and a Hen Do, mayhem ensues. Has Simon cheated on his wife to be and will he make it to the church at all?

Waiting For The Bee Stings

Mia Maher is nearing forty. She arrives at the funeral of an old friend, Chrissie, who has died suddenly. Happily married, with two school age children, Mia is unaware that this will be the day that changes everything and her life will switch on to an entirely new path.

'Waiting For The Bee Stings' is a story about the lives of four friends who met at Newcastle University in the mid-1990s. It is a tale of love, friendship, passion and betrayal.

This is the third fictional novel by Calvin Wade, following his debut, 'Forever Is Over' which rose to Amazon's Top20 ebooks in the United Kingdom and the critically acclaimed second novel, 'Kiss My Name'.

Living On A Rainbow

'Living On A Rainbow' is a story about mental health, bullying, growing up, battling against adversity but most of all it is a story about love. The love between a man and a woman. The love between a boy and his best friend. The love between a mother and her son and the love between a boy and his father.

Harry 'H' McCoy is not an ordinary boy and his life is not an ordinary life.

Another Saturday & Sweet Fa

In the summer of 2013, Calvin Wade, a man with football in his blood and very little in his wallet, decided to embark upon an F.A Cup adventure that he and his father had discussed for over thirty years. The idea was to head to a game in the Extra Preliminary Round of the F.A Cup and then follow the winners of each game, up and down the country, through every round, until eventually reaching the bright lights of Wembley and the F.A Cup Final.

This is not only an autobiographical account of a nine month journey through the 2013-14 footballing season, especially the F.A Cup, but it is also a story about family, friendship, financial struggle and a footballing past. It is about tales new and old with English Peles, a man known as 'The Casual Hopper' and football fans of all ages throughout the British Isles.

With a foreword by former F.A Cup winning manager, Joe Royle, 'Another Saturday & Sweet F.A' seeks to show that Bill Shankly was right after all and sometimes football can be more important than life and death.

* Fifty pence from the sale of the paperback and Kindle versions of this book will be donated to The Christie Charity. The charity raises money to fund projects at The Christie Hospital, Manchester, which are outside the scope of the NHS.

Brutal Giants & The Village King

Having completed every round of the FA Cup in 2013-14, groundhopper and Charity fundraiser, Alan Oliver and his footballing friend, Calvin Wade decided for the 2014-15 season they would move on to the FA Trophy. They would pick a tie in the Preliminary Round and follow the winners of each game thereafter on to the following round, irrespective of where in the country it would take them.

Both men were unsure whether the FA Trophy would hit the same emotional highs as the FA Cup. The FA Trophy did not attract the same crowds as the FA Cup, nor grab anywhere near the same media attention. No non-League club would be lucky enough to draw a Premier League club and the financial rewards were far more limited. The competition did, however, provide a rare opportunity for non-League clubs to play at England's national stadium, Wembley.

What happened during Alan and Calvin's ten round adventure proved all their doubts were unfounded. In a land of Premier League football that is beamed all around the world, sometimes the stories of the smaller clubs go untold. As Alan and Calvin travelled thousands of miles, up and down the country, their love and passion for the non-League game grew and grew. They witnessed managerial outbursts, an abandoned game, an excellent female referee, a man who made his debut twice and this was all before in the Third Qualifying Round they crossed paths with a special football club, situated in a village of less than 4000 people, called North Ferriby United.

Alan and Calvin would be taken on a journey by the players, officials and supporters of North Ferriby United, that would seem far fetched if it was witnessed in a Hollywood movie. It is a tale of a team whose spirit, determination and resilience seemed to know no bounds. Could this side, that looked at first glance like an unspectacular bunch of part-timers, upset the odds and create unforgettable memories for everyone involved with the club? Sometimes truth is stranger than fiction.

** 50p from the sale of every copy of this book/ebook will be donated to Alan Oliver's fundraising campaign for 'The Christie' (a specialist cancer hospital in Manchester). **

The Unbreakable Vase

'The Casual Hopper' (Alan Oliver) is one of the big characters in the Non-League groundhopping world. Having been to every round of the FA Cup in 2013-14 and the FA Trophy 2014-15, in 2015-16 he aimed to do every round of FA Vase and the FA Sunday Cup. He has raised over £17,000 for 'The Christie' Hospital in Manchester throughout this journey and has taken his unique, Mancunian charm to the four corners of Britain.

There is a lot more to 'The Unbreakable Vase' than simply a footballing journey. It is about the footballing bond Alan has made with fellow football fanatics, Calvin Wade and Gordon Johnson, giving an insight into their lives over a twelve month period when unexpectedly they faced some terrible lows as well as footballing highs.

'The Unbreakable Vase' has the FA Vase as its central focus but it is also about characters they meet on the pitch and at the side of it. There are even a few chance meetings with some of the biggest names in English and even world football along the way. Furthermore, it tells the story of the blossoming football careers of younger members of their families as they battle for football scholarships. 'The Unbreakable Vase' is very different to the previous two parts of this footballing trilogy but hopefully just as interesting for any football fan.

* 'The Unbreakable Vase' is dedicated to the memory of Steve Garcia and 50p from every full-priced sale (25p on promotional sales) will be passed to his widow, Angela Garcia, to donate to the British Heart Foundation.

Printed in Great Britain
by Amazon